A MEETING OF MINDS

On a cold November morning, Detective Superintendent Mike Yeadings and his team are called to a pub car park in Henley-on-Thames where a woman's body has been found. Detective Sergeant Rosemary Zycynski is horrified to realise that the dead woman is her next door neighbour, Sheila Winter, the owner of a local garden centre. Sheila lived with her ageing mother and didn't appear to have much in her life outside her work, so the discovery of her body, naked and wrapped only in a black fur coat, is a shock. Could one of Zycynski's new neighbours at Ashbourne House hold the key to the mystery? Or the garden centre manager, Barry Childe, who has just served time for a brutal attack on a young woman?

CLARE CURZON

A MEETING
OF MINDS

Complete and Unabridged

ULVERSCROFT
Leicester

First published in Great Britain in 2003 by
Allison & Busby Limited, London

First Large Print Edition
published 2004
by arrangement with
Allison & Busby Limited, London

The moral right of the author has been asserted

British Library CIP Data

Curzon, Clare
    A meeting of minds.—Large print ed.—
    Ulverscroft large print series: mystery
    1. Yeadings, Mike (Fictitious character)—Fiction
    2. Police—England—Thames Valley—Fiction
    3. Detective and mystery stories 4. Large type books
    I. Title
    823.9′14 [F]

    ISBN 1–84395–440–0

X000 000 012 6997

Published by
F. A. Thorpe (Publishing)
Anstey, Leicestershire

Set by Words & Graphics Ltd.
Anstey, Leicestershire
Printed and bound in Great Britain by
T. J. International Ltd., Padstow, Cornwall

This book is printed on acid-free paper

1

The boy in the frayed straw hat reeled in, detached the flapping fish from his hook and inspected the prize. It wasn't unlike one of those displayed last night at the restaurant at Los Abrigos. But smaller, of course. Anyway a catch.

He threw it behind him on to seaweed where it continued its desperate contortions. Sickened, he reached back and struck it with a rock. It lay instantly still, spoilt now. The boy grimaced. He lifted it by the tail and threw it back in the waves.

Hunched, he sat brooding over the sea's reflected glare. His lips tasted of salt, his shoulders were beginning to peel. He'd forgotten the barrier cream.

He un-stoppered a plastic bottle of water, warm to his hand, and drank, then let the liquid trickle down his face, splash on to his naked chest. God, it was hot. Why must Marty pick on August to dump him on the Canaries?

Although he hadn't so much picked as

been picked. It was for a job, and jobs meant bread. They kept him and in circumstances to which he'd always intended to become accustomed. Marty went where he had to go, but chose when the opposition was most vulnerable. He, Neil, was the little woman left behind, this time having to pretend, for other eyes, that a stomach upset had prevented his sailing too.

It was six days since *Tourmaline* had puttered single-handed out of Puerto Colon on its Volvo pentas, ostensibly on a tour of the islands, to fetch up at Lanzarote. The weather had stayed calm. By now Marty would have reached Agadir, trekked inland towards Marrakesh and located the isolated Moroccan farm.

That was the point where things could go bottom-up. If they did he'd never learn how it happened, or why. There'd be an unendurable wait, then notification from the harbourmaster at Agadir of an abandoned twenty-seven-footer registered to a marine hire firm in Tenerife. By then Neil Raynes would have scarpered to the UK and a new address. And an unfaceable future.

Damn him, why couldn't Marty do a nine-to-five job like anybody else — sell expensive cars like he pretended to, or get his highs on some trading floor in the City? If he must chase risks, why sail single-handed, refuse back-up?

The boy — twenty, but looking like a young Tom Sawyer in the frayed trousers and battered straw hat — collected his fishing things, slung the empty water bottle in the sea and picked his way, barefoot, back over the rocks. A golf buggy wheezed past as he climbed over the barrier to the cinder path. He slid his sandals on to trudge uphill towards the hired apartment in the row of villas that faced the tenth hole.

Cinders pricked between his toes. When he was little they used to scatter the stuff to stop him sliding on ice. Here it was the natural surface of the south end of this volcanic island, coming in all sorts of weird shapes and chemical colours. Walking on it was like crunching over a vast furnace floor. Except, of course, for the cactus flowers and butterflies.

He dumped his line, box of bait and empty creel on the doorstep and continued up towards the clubhouse for the mail, stopping off at the mini-market for more bananas and coffee. Pointless stocking up until Marty got back. It was too hot to cook, or to eat.

The dark little shop, stinking of overripe pineapples and melons, was full of ghastly English parents being pestered by kids for

3

ices. He shouldered his way through to pick up a hand of green bananas. He'd learnt already that if you bought them yellow they'd be black next day. There was a banana tree in their diminutive garden but it hadn't picked up the idea of fruiting. Wrong sex, he supposed: the sort of balls-up that could happen to anyone.

He tucked a packet of ground coffee under one arm and doled out the despised euros. Then he padded into the clubhouse and peered into their mailbox.

There was a thick, official-looking envelope with Isle of Man stamps. His heart lurched as he recognised the name of Marty's solicitor printed on the reverse. But the letter was addressed to himself.

God, what now? Was this the final pay-off? Had something really dire happened this time? Marty taken a risk too many?

He carried it unopened back to the apartment, stood shakily on the cool tiles of the kitchen floor and steeled himself to face the worst.

Unbelievable! Nothing of any importance. A few clippings from estate agents' catalogues, and a covering letter informing him that owing to a withdrawn offer it was now possible to acquire the desired first floor apartment at Ashbourne House, near

Mardham, South Bucks. Would Mr Neil Raynes, as representative for Mr Martin Chisholm, authorise a bid for the said property up to the value previously agreed?

Better than that, Neil decided. He should have a firm commitment faxed from the hotel in Los Cristianos where the young duty manager was open to financial persuasion. The signature would appear to be Marty's, admirably forged after long and meticulous practice (as also by previous agreement.)

He was glad of the chance for positive action, however minor. His part in the project to date had been totally negative: not stepping out of line; not getting drunk or stoned, not laid locally or depressed. That last was the really dodgy bit, and would be until news came through.

★ ★ ★

Ten days later there was a fax waiting for him at the clubhouse: 'A great journey. See you soon. Hope you're feeling fitter.'

The message started with *A*, which was code for Albufeira in the Algarve. So Marty had pulled it off, got away unscathed, and was anchored off the south coast of Portugal. (Omit the indefinite article, and *Great journey* would have meant Gibraltar. V

5

— 'Very good crossing' — was to indicate Valencia. The simplest codes are the safest.)

Now Neil had to phone a number in England, advise that the flight tickets to Faro were the ones to use. Marty would meet the client there, hand over the goods and be free to sail back.

Relief flooded Neil. A day or two more, then he could pick up where they'd left off. He unlocked the apartment safe and removed the spare photograph of a heavily bearded Marty, as shown in his fake Egyptian passport.

Over the kitchen sink he set light to the photograph and watched it curl to fall in ashes, which he swilled away.

Another venture accomplished. By the weekend *Tourmaline* would have eased back into its mooring at Puerto Colon with Marty on board, clean-shaven and once more a British subject. With a satisfyingly swelled bank balance waiting for him back home.

2

Four weeks earlier

Plump, sixtyish and cheerfully flaunting garishly hennaed curls, Beattie Weyman was riding cloud nine. She had never bought anything so enormous, so enrapturing, in her life. Never had the money to do it, of course.

The other house, three-storeyed and wedged into a modest Victorian terrace, was constructed round a windowless stairwell which amplified sounds and smells from her lodgers' illicit fry-ups and after-hours partying. Buying the property on retirement seven years back had celebrated her lump-sum pension pay-out. That purchase had been in recognition of achievement. This new project was thanks only to a twist of fate.

It meant going upmarket; and she'd reached the time of life when acting out of character, being frankly eccentric, pepped one up with an illusion of youthful dash. The fun of *planning* crowned it: it was heady, looking forward when you'd grown accustomed to looking back and thinking, 'life's not been all that bad, but if only . . . '

So however often the builder — chummily she called him Bob — said, 'Leave it all to me, hinny. I know what I'm doing,' she'd had to be in there with him, encouraging, suggesting, checking, commenting, at every stage of the conversion into seven flats.

At an early point on a glorious Tuesday in July, observing Ashbourne House from the gravel driveway, their interest had switched from the near completion of its interior to centre on the elegant front balcony.

'With separate apartments,' 'Bob' reminded her, 'you gotta consider privacy. So I'll hafta put a screen between the owners' walkways out there.'

'I'm not daft,' she told him. 'Course there 'as to be a screen. But your plan 'as it plonked dead centre.'

'For balance,' he explained, weighing a weathered, upturned palm to either side of his shirt's straining buttons. 'This here house is Regency, symmetrical. So the partition goes right over the front entrance. I'll see it's not obtrusive.'

'But you know we've made those front-facing upstairs flats different. That one — ' and a plump index finger stabbed towards the left — 'extends over part of the 'all. Think of its size. The way you've shown it, 'er right-hand window could be overlooked from

8

'er neighbours' balcony.'

'Bob' (real name Frank Perrin) considered. 'See what you mean, hinny. But if I shift the divider along it'd look cockeyed from out here. Spoil the front elevation, like.'

'Nuh. The folks I'm selling to aren't going to spend all their time out 'ere looking up. They'll be inside, *living* it up. 'Ow's she to 'ave any privacy if the new people can walk past and peer in any time it suits them?'

Beattie had made her point. They then agreed on a wrought-iron arabesque screen because solid walls belonged to the tower-block tenements of their separate child-hoods, which both had firmly shucked off.

'Come in 'n 'ave a cuppa,' Beattie invited, to celebrate her fresh victory.

Frank grinned at the cheery little body topped with a fuzz of hair which a Japanese Koi carp might have been colour-matched to. She caught the direction of his eyes and patted it proudly. 'All me own, and nacheral too,' she boasted. 'The curls, anyways.' She chuckled, her heaving shoulders bouncing ample breasts in a way that raised his hopes of loose-sewn buttons.

Munching his lunchtime cheese and pickle sandwich in his pick-up cab later, Frank Perrin considered what Beattie had let slip. Jobwise he'd known the old girl for quite a number of years, and they'd gossiped enough for him to guess that they'd had much the same kind of early life, she born into London's war-shattered East End; he from a part of Tyneside which slum-clearance had relegated to history in the seventies. Both had risen through hard work and a refusal to be put down. Frank, having relocated south to catch the boom-years' redevelopment, now ran his own reputable firm with fifteen skilled workers to call on. Beattie, starting out as assistant dresser to the showgirls of the old Windmill Theatre, had scraped to save for a college course and qualified as a beauty consultant. Ability and a bouncy personality had finally found her managing the toning and cosmetic department of an Oxford Street store.

All the same, Frank knew, however successful a career, it didn't account for setting her sights on Ashbourne House. That had to be thanks to her recently deceased, childless sister who had emigrated to South Africa, twice married money there and twice been blessedly widowed.

With the sceptical outlook of a confirmed bachelor, Frank guessed that, for all the implied luxury, that too might have involved the poor cow in a lifetime of hard labour. He'd worked enough for the rich, had an eyeful of life behind the scenes. Nobody, he knew, got anything for nothing.

What tickled his curiosity now was Beattie's use of the word 'she' as purchaser of the larger flat; still just two bedrooms, but easily the most roomy of the seven apartments. It hadn't been 'they', which you might expect. And the other upstairs front apartment, although with a less spacious reception area, was to have multiple residents. 'They' mustn't be allowed to peer through 'her' windows. Which reminded him to reach across for the copy of his plans and pencil in the alteration to the balcony partition, three of the long French windows being 'hers'; two for the 'new people'. He sketched in the exterior detail to match the interior conversion.

The apartment Beattie had retained for herself was on the ground floor, a compact unit of three medium-sized, square rooms plus kitchen and bathroom, towards the rear on the east side. 'I don't want it fancy, but I must 'ave the sunrise to shoot me out of bed ev'ry morning,' she'd explained. Having a fondness for the old girl, he'd taken care to ensure that everything built into that unit was of the best quality obtainable.

The west side had a corresponding set of rooms, and the ground floor front contained

11

two smaller apartments, one to either side of the house's original hall. The seventh flat ran across the rear upstairs. While the two front ones used the hall's grand staircase, No. 7 had access by the back door and the onetime servants' stairs.

★ ★ ★

Two days later the 'new people' for the front-east upstairs flat arrived to view progress while Frank was on site. They slid noiselessly up in a silver Alfa Romeo; two well-built, fleshy blondes, obviously mother and daughter, Mrs and Miss Winter. The older, shorter one was a right royal Queen Mum; the daughter handsome and pleasant enough but, to Frank's mind, somewhat subdued.

The plasterer was just finishing inside, so they discussed colour schemes. Mother hankered after lilacs and pinks with brocade-patterned wallpaper. The daughter preferred ivory shades and vinyl matt paint. 'Still, you'll be spending more time at home than I shall, Mother,' she conceded, 'so choose what you like, except for my bedroom and office.'

Assured of that crucial concession Mother waved away consideration of the balcony. She viewed the newly fixed screen with little

12

interest. Her suggestion was offhand: 'You could grow a vine or something up it. That fancy clematis you go in for.'

'Right.' But Daughter already knew what she wanted. 'Fit a mirror on our side,' she commanded Frank, as she saw her mother into the car. 'Get good quality hardened glass, and I'll add a *trompe l'oeil* archway. The reflection will extend the effect of the verandah.' She paused. 'And I'll need to know what weight it can take. For plant tubs and so on.'

'Right,' he said, stolidly, in his turn. So much for frontal symmetry. It seemed this lot was aiming for a Chelsea Flower Show. He wondered what 'she' on the far side of the mirror would do to retaliate. Be a bit of a joke if he put in a two-way mirror like they had down the cop-shop for identity parades. Nice idea, but Beattie wouldn't be on for it, and he couldn't risk upsetting a good customer.

He'd had bother enough from the single chap in the ground floor rear apartment on the west side. With a Fort Knox fixation about security, this Mr Paul Wormsley had ordered Spanish wrought-iron grilles fitted over lockable casements which opened inwards. Beattie had agreed, since those windows weren't visible from the road, and such extras would be at Wormsley's expense.

13

He'd also ordered electronic surveillance covering the rear. Less a home than a fortress, in Frank's opinion.

Central to the ground floor was the huge, two-storied entrance hall, with its galleried grand staircase, behind which a modern laundry and utility room was now discreetly housed, replacing the original domestic offices. All apartments had separately-fired gas central heating.

Frank had yet to meet most purchasers. Which reminded him: he'd need a list of all their names from Beattie before Charlie, his electrics man, completed the phone-entry and doorbell system. He waved a hand at the ladies leaving.

Pulling away, Sheila Winter had clipped on her seat-belt, checked the rear-view mirror, switched on and put the car into gear. It would have to be the van next time. There'd be stuff to bring back: plants for the balcony and something easy-care for Mother's room.

Mother, she thought, and a shadow stirred in her mind. How long must it last, her zigzag, but inevitable, slide into premature senility? She was only just over menopause.

Her mood changes were painful to endure. Sheila was aware, in theory, of the clinical symptoms of dementia, but unsure each time whether she recognised the stages in real life.

One moment it seemed certain, but Vanessa was such an actress. The gushes of enthusiasm and the plunging despair might not actually be her, but some leftover memory of roles she'd once played. At times her mind drifted off entirely. Then, next moment, she came out with some shrewdness that made you wonder just how disturbed her sense of reality was. Of course her drinking didn't help. If only there were some reliable way of controlling her intake.

Sheila resented being forced into spying and recording, but for safety's sake someone must remain wary. It fell to her because there was nobody else: a frightful responsibility here at home when at work the new project was just taking off and needed her full-time attention.

Hang on a little longer, she told herself (or telepathically commanded her mother). At some later stage — but when exactly? — she would have to advertise for a full-time carer. A clinical gaoler.

At least out here Mother would be less a prey to danger. She'd never cared for the country, so was more likely to stay indoors and play at housekeeping with the new apartment. Thank God they'd managed to off-load that great house in Putney. Its removal had cut down the chaos and, she hoped, brought Mother closer under control.

Chaos: her mind nudged her with the word. Yes, there was that at work too, but only of the manageable, practical sort. She switched into business mode and settled more firmly in her seat, preparing to deal with the CCTV people about the garden centre's security system.

In a rear seat Vanessa (or April, as she sometimes liked to call herself) complained, 'That's a very common old woman we've bought the place from. I hope you've checked that there's nothing dubious about the purchase.'

'I had our solicitor look into her, Mother. She bought the house with money inherited from family.' She watched in the rear-view mirror how Vanessa appeared either not to hear, or chose to ignore, her words.

She sighed. It was as well Mother had made that remark because for a moment she'd almost forgotten she had her there in the back seat. She'd heard that sometimes when you live with one you can get to be the same. If she didn't pull herself together people might wonder which of them it was whose mind was adrift.

3

With the entry-phone requirements in mind, Frank Perrin gulped the last of his coffee, stowed thermos and mug under the pick-up's passenger seat, wiped his mouth with the back of a horny hand and set off for the 'old house' where he knew Beattie would be busily making preparations to move out.

Rosemary Zyczynski was in the kitchen shelling peas on her free day and looked up as Frank was ushered in. So this was Beattie's wonder-worker, kept under wraps until now. On a tall, gangling frame his rounded head with its weather-beaten features sparsely topped with coarse, wispy hair of much the same ruddy brown, gave the impression of a large and shaggy coconut.

She rose to leave them together. 'When Max arrives would you send him up?' she asked Beattie, halting in the doorway.

'Right, ducks,' she was assured. 'Get 'im to bring down your stuff for the charity shop then, will yer? It'll save us time later.'

'That's my Rosemary,' Beattie explained fondly as the door closed behind her. 'She's coming with me. Gonna 'ave the upstairs front.'

In her bed-sitter Detective Sergeant Rose-mary Zyczynski rested her elbows on the gritty windowsill and sniffed in the familiar scents of the outer neighbourhood. The ceaseless sound of traffic from the main road was a constant drone. Even in the early hours there was always movement out there, bringing sounds like the sea with waves approaching, receding, washing up again. Out at Ashbourne House she would find country silence. At most the cry of a fox or hunting owls.

Someone nearby was frying onions, and above the dusty bitterness of town-bred evergreens there crept the pervasive odour of cat. Today something new: not far off a road surface was being re-tarred. Appreciatively she drew in the hot metal scent of the burner. This was her feet-on-the-ground world.

She was going to miss this place, cramped as it had become now that Max expected occasionally to spend the odd night here. It was the sleeping part of sleeping together that was the trouble: the rest was wonderful. But Max had the cat-nap habit, and would get up at odd hours to boil a kettle for drinks, then boot up the computer to knock out a few paragraphs of mint-fresh ideas; climb back into bed to read for twenty minutes; sigh, set a leather marker in his book; extinguish his bed-lamp; and be asleep within seconds.

Z, by contrast, required her log-like eight hours, and he invariably disturbed her however mouse-like his intentions. She would lie awake, unmoving, pretending to be asleep until, long after his performance, wearily, she was.

In her new flat, offered by Beattie at a suspiciously low price — 'You might as well 'ave it now as wait until I'm gorn, girl!' — she and Max could do the sleeping part in separate rooms, as they did when she stayed over at his house in Pimlico.

*　*　*

Downstairs, Frank Perrin was grinning. So Miss Weyman had a daughter she hadn't admitted to. A nice-looker, and no wedding ring; living at home with Mum although she'd be well into her twenties. And Beattie could still go on playing mother hen, with young Rosemary given a sweetener of the bigger upstairs apartment at the new place, which had ample room for a live-in lover.

Cunning old Mum: keeping her kid close by giving her a generous rein.

'I've dropped in for the residents' names,' he announced. 'So's we can get on with the entry-phone list. Just the surnames'll do for now. They can make any fancy changes to the cards later.'

'Right. Wormsley you know, 'im downstairs across from me. And I'm Weyman. The other folks upstairs, front, are called Winter. All of us starting with a W. You'da thought I'd chose them for it, only I didn't. And the upstairs rear lot are 'Ubbles. Nice little fam'ly. A Mum, Dad and a kiddy about four.'

'Hubble, like the telescope, right? And then your Rosemary, upstairs front. We'll need to put her initial R on the bell card, to keep your — er, *callers* apart.' He'd been going to say 'mail', but remembered in time that there was to be a communal letterbox; all post to be sorted indoors and left on the hall table. A bit too matey for some folks, that. Beattie might be compelled to rethink that one.

At first Beattie didn't get the gist about the initial, thinking he somehow knew how jealously Rosemary guarded her privacy. That was her one condition on taking the flat. If anyone asked what her job was, no mention of police. Beattie was to say civil servant.

Then it clicked, that Bob-the-Builder took

the girl for a Weyman too. Which made Beattie feel quite warm inside for a moment. Undeservedly, though. Not that she was gonna correct him and give him the girl's real name; not without Rosemary's say-so. Anyway, leave it the way it was.

'Then downstairs front, in the one-bedroom flats, it's a Miss Barnes, who's a schoolteacher. She's on the east side, and Major Phillips on the west.'

Beattie watched him make a note, slide his carpenter's pencil back above his ear and close his notebook. 'You'll stop for a bite of lunch, won't you?' she invited. 'There'll be just the two of us. The young folks are going out.'

That was the first time Z set eyes on Frank Perrin, later to be encountered often enough in Beattie's kitchen at the new house. After he'd left, the old lady had made quite a show of wiping down the draining-board after washing-up. 'Nice feller, ain't he?' she demanded over-casually. 'Got very good taste.'

'He must have. So watch yourself, Beattie. Unless he's a widower or a respectable bachelor.'

The corners of the old lady's mouth puckered. 'Ain't that one of them fancy things you told me about? 'Respectable bachelor'?'

'Oxymoron?' Z laughed. 'You're getting cynical, Beattie.'

★   ★   ★

They took up residence on the first Saturday in August, sharing a self-drive van for the few items of furniture they intended keeping. Max Harris and an off-duty constable from the local nick came along to handle their heavy stuff.

On the Sunday Paul Wormsley took possession of the ground-floor flat opposite Beattie's, his belongings arriving in a plain white van and delivered by a trio of large, uncommunicative men in brown overalls. Wormsley himself remained seated in his sand-coloured, three-year-old Peugeot with all windows lowered, and declined Beattie's offer of refreshments. When the move was completed he sidled in, blinking through round, heavy-framed lenses which, together with his thick, centre-parted hair, gave the impression of a slightly bewildered barn owl.

The Winters were due the following morning, Monday being when Greenvale Garden Centre remained closed to the public for restocking, after the locust invasion of horticultural enthusiasts over the weekend. A Pickfords' van was only the second vehicle to

22

follow them in, sandwiched between the electrician and gas-fitter.

The purchasers of the two downstairs front flats arrived later in the same week. Miss Marjorie Barnes, who was the plump Deputy Headmistress of the local girls' secondary school, arrived in a self-drive van and shared all the humping and lumping of modern black ash, chrome and smoked-glass furniture with a large, simple-seeming man who wore a butcher's apron.

Major Phillips, tall, thin and silver-haired, with a weathered face that resembled grainy teak, was driven by a smaller and slightly younger, straight-backed individual whom he addressed as 'corporal'. Their transport was an ancient Triumph convertible, bright yellow. They too declined Beattie's offer of refreshments, set up camp in the empty rooms and drank milky tea prepared on a camper's stove until the removals van appeared, closely followed by the electrician.

Both new people promptly disappeared into their respective domains after dismissing their assistants, the corporal leaving, with a smart salute, on a Vespa which had materialised from inside the pantechnicon. The following day a garage delivered Miss Barnes's freshly valeted green Rover.

There was the expected delay in connecting everyone's telephones, but by Friday of the following week things had settled to surface normality. Only one of the seven apartments remained empty: that of the upper floor rear.

'Them 'Ubbles 'ave gorn and let me down,' Beattie declared. 'Sumpthink about their own buyers pulling out. Well, I'm sorry, but I can't afford to 'ang about. Gotta bridging loan from the bank as it is, and don't that manager jest know 'ow to shovel the interest on.'

'So what will you do?' Rosemary Zyczynski asked.

'Sell to the next lot. My agent said all along 'e'd keep a waiting list. 'E's jest rung up to say first one on it is a Mr Chisholm. Gotta younger live-in partner, it seems. If she's a nice girl you might be pleased to 'ave someone of your own age next-door, ducks.'

Maybe not, Z thought. And her doubt was confirmed when correspondence proved the 'younger partner' to be male.

Beattie, mildly surprised at this, wasn't displeased. 'Poofters' she announced with total disregard for political correctness. 'Metta lotta them sort in the beauty business. Easy to get on with, I always found.'

For the present that remained to be seen, because Martin Chisholm and Neil Raynes

24

were conducting all arrangements via the agent from a hotel in the Canaries. Negotiations weren't hung up by any need for a mortgage, but it still wasn't until early September that they returned to England.

Over the first few weeks at Ashbourne House Z saw little of the other residents. Few alien sounds reached her; perhaps an occasional voice under her open windows and the departure and arrival of cars between driveway and lock-up garages in the converted stables behind the house.

She saw less of Beattie than in the hugger-mugger conditions of their former home, yet was aware of her unseen on the periphery, lurking like some watchful spider at the web's edge, keen for the rewards of her intricate creation. Not that the residents were to be prey, bound and sucked dry of their substance, but she certainly expected something of them, prepared to allow time before they provided her with it.

Not until her characters were all assembled did she make any move to draw them in and activate the drama.

Or would it be comedy? Zyczynski wondered. When the engraved invitation card arrived she went down to sound her out.

'How will you manage?' she asked, surveying the old lady's well-equipped but relatively modest-sized dining-room and kitchen.

'I'm 'aving caterers in,' Beattie declared. 'They'll bring it all in a refrigerated van, set up the table in the main 'all; do the 'ole lot. I want a real 'ouse-warming and get-together.'

Then it became clear why she'd taken such care over furnishing the house's neutral ground. What had until then been no-man's land, visited only to pick up the mail, was to function as the pulsing heart of a community, a mixture of hotel foyer and club lounge. Beattie was seriously into social engineering.

Perhaps, Rosemary thought, she should offer to design a community flag to run up the virgin flagpole which projected from her balcony above the front entrance.

Whatever immediate reactions followed the invitations, acceptances duly arrived for Beattie from all six other apartments. The chosen date was a Friday; the intended hour 7.45 for 8p.m. Rosemary, amused and intrigued — since Beattie had given no hint of her detailed arrangements — was almost late home, delayed by paperwork arising from drugs thefts from pharmacies throughout Thames Valley.

The others were about to take their places at table. She made her excuses — 'kept late at the office' — and found her name card

26

between Martin Chisholm and his partner Neil Raynes.

They were, she decided after a rapid survey of the entire company, the most promising there, her dear Max excepted. The young man on her left looked no more than eighteen or nineteen, while Chisholm was in his mid forties. Neither was high camp but their relationship required a frequent exchange of glances across her as she tried to make conversation. It struck her that they'd agreed in advance a permissible menu of topics, and presumably edited their CVs. She managed to imply that her own work was clerical, and no it wasn't particularly interesting: pretty dull really. Which was why she relied on a more lively social life.

'Now *that* I can more readily accept,' Chisholm purred, 'than your choice of work. I should have guessed you were involved in a much more dashing occupation.'

'Such as?' she invited.

'Travel courier; something rather intellectually challenging in medical research; a barrister; a marketing manager for cosmetics; even a rally driver.'

'You're having me on,' she accused him. 'Actually, at the last deadly party I went to I claimed to be a brain surgeon, but at least two other people had got there before me. So

I changed to a Member of Parliament. Now, what do you do?'

It emerged that he sold expensive cars in London's West End. (Con-man, she translated this.) His appearance bore him out. It was a strange face, suave, dark-skinned, economically fleshed over a strong framework of bone, with wide-slanting cheek-bones, angular jaw, cleft chin. He had the added sleek maturity of silvered temples, although at the back his nape-long hair was almost black. There was something about him she found elusive, but compelling. His ears — she was still avoiding the cold, slaty eyes — his ears were flat, precisely sculpted; the nose large, slightly hooked and dominant. Which for her meant sexy.

He made her slightly uneasy. This was a man who counted. Counted: her choice of the word was Freudian. She guessed he counted in the transitive sense too: counted costs, counted gains, reduced people to statistics.

For a while neither had spoken. She was aware of him watching her, and wondered how much he saw. Simply his own impact? Or had he curiosity enough to penetrate her surface? How much in this short moment of encounter had she given away?

Deliberately she turned back to the young

man on her left. 'Are you a student?'

'Nah!'

She sensed a stiffening in the other man and knew he'd sent a silent warning over her head.

'Was once. But I chucked it in. I'm a hospital porter.'

So he'd accepted the hint to be polite, but there was something about his voice that wasn't quite right. It was as though the adolescent surliness was put on, and his natural way of talking could be more refined. She guessed he had been expensively educated, but preferred to be thought a rough-neck. Now that was interesting. Unless, of course, interesting was what he set out to be.

She picked up her spoon and applied herself to the starter, which was excellent: ripe avocado, its scooped-out contents mixed with shredded Bramley apple and onion, the whole topped with Cheddar cheese and gently grilled. However many calories?

'This is good,' said Max with enthusiasm from his seat almost opposite. Beattie had found that nine placings left the table unbalanced, so Max, as occasional resident, had been invited too.

Chisholm leaned across and clicked his fingers. 'I knew I should have recognised you. You're *that* Max Harris: the columnist. Not that the cartoon portrait they give you is exactly flattering.'

'I like to think mine is a unique kind of beauty,' Max claimed solemnly, then swiftly turned interest on the other. 'Do tell me; as a specialist, what kind of car do you choose for yourself?'

She should have known that he'd been listening. Max didn't miss much. Many a dinner party such as this had provided copy for his mocking pen. She listened now to find what raw material he'd be drawing out of the self-confident Mr Chisholm; but it was mainly technical talk, magnetos and bearings and zero-to-sixty in n seconds. It was as bad as a night out with a rookie from Traffic branch.

She grinned at her other neighbour. 'Working in a hospital do you ever feel you'd like to take up nursing?'

He stared at her as if she were some weird kind of insect. 'Nah,' he said again. 'Less I see of all that the better. I don't mind chatting up the old biddies that get parked on trolleys. It's true what the papers say. They're left in corridors for hours some days, no matter how scared or ill. Makes them fret. Still, the men can be worse.'

With that scornful observation his flow of conversation dried up. He reached for the little tasselled white card that was their menu, read out, '*Médailles d'agneau, Artichauts Farcis, Pommes Frites*,' in acceptable French and declared, 'So long as there's *pommes* bloody *frites*, I guess that'll do.'

Max grinned across at her and started refilling her wineglass. 'Beattie's really gone to town on this.' He nodded uptable to where their hostess was conversing animatedly with the younger Winter woman.

Between them the owlish Wormsley sat with his elbows nipped in and his napkin tucked between the second and third buttons on his dark jacket, which he'd not thought to undo. He seemed totally switched off except that she caught his eyes flitting between the others as they fenced with the business of enforced socialising. She guessed from his unnatural solemnity that he was secretly laughing at everyone.

'What does Mr Wormsley do?' she asked Chisholm, who had broken off his sales talk to savour the scents of the plate of lamb just deposited in front of him.

'Not a lot, I should imagine,' he said lightly. 'I'm told he'd very little luggage.'

Unlike yourself, Z silently commented. Beattie hadn't missed logging his computer and work station, wide-screen television, exercise bike, music centre, surfboard and skis. Doubtless he was making good use of the loft space above his apartment.

Beyond Chisholm the middle-aged schoolteacher, Miss Barnes, was deeply in conversation with Major Phillips, his narrow, silver head inclined to catch her low voice. Z, watching them, wondered if Beattie had been matchmaking there when she accepted them on interview. There had been no shortage of local people eager to buy into the property.

Max succeeded in getting Mrs Winter alive. She had sat there like a gift-wrapped sack of potatoes until he hit on the sesame words that opened her up. Now she was becoming increasingly animated, waving her claret glass as though leading the *Student Prince* drinking chorus. Z strained her ears to catch what she was saying. And yes, it was operetta, but actually *The Desert Song*.

As a child Z had been taken by Auntie to various amateur productions and remembered a particularly hilarious presentation of *Rose Marie* when the corpulent local postmaster had taken the lead. The Mountie's tight uniform had accentuated his unfortunate pot belly, and for weeks afterwards Z had waddled about in the privacy of her bedroom, singing 'When I'm calling *moo-oo-oo-oo-oo-oo-oo*!'

It wasn't easy to guess Mrs Winter's age. A lot of money had gone into her preservation, but she could hardly go back as far as the original shows. The stage successes she was archly recounting to a transfixed Max Harris were probably at amateur level.

Distanced from her by Max, her daughter was casting anxious glances in her direction, while Beattie still persistently invited more details of the management scene at Greenvale Garden Centre.

By the time the dessert arrived everyone else appeared relaxed and comfortable. Z had expected Beattie to order one of her favourite steamed suet puddings and was agreeably surprised at the caramelised pears in lemon syrup, sprinkled with toasted almonds.

The wine had done its work. When they left the table for coffee there reigned a sense of real camaraderie. Sheila Winter had offered to keep the house's public rooms — mainly the hall — in fresh-cut flowers (at an equally cut price) and complained of recent difficulties at the garden centre over break-ins and thefts. She had been advised on several monitoring systems and was having CCTV installed to deal with this.

Martin Chisholm was dryly recounting his farcical adventures at an international car dealers' convention in Toronto, and Vanessa

Winter was waltzing with majestic uncertainty with Max to Strauss and Lehar from a CD player she'd insisted he should bring down from her apartment for the purpose. The party looked as if it could go on all night.

Beattie came across to the sofa where Z was sitting and laid a hand on her knee. 'Seems to 'ave gorn off all right,' she said as a question.

'It's been perfect, Beattie. Thank you.'

Neil Raynes, stretched out on his back on a bearskin rug at their feet, suddenly sat up, clasping his hands about his knees, and demanded thickly, but in his natural, cultivated voice, 'Why can't everyone be civilised like this all the time?' There were tears in his eyes.

'Neil, old son, time for bed,' said Chisholm, breaking off in mid-anecdote and rising to his feet. He smiled at Z, watching the youngster weave towards Beattie to thank her before leaving. 'I'm afraid wine mixes badly with his medication.'

The move signalled their break-up. Vanessa Winter performed her final staggering swirl, gave a last wave of her floating chiffon scarf and permitted Max to see her upstairs to her door. Miss Barnes and Major Phillips wished everyone goodnight and let themselves into

34

their own apartments. Paul Wormsley, grinning fatuously, followed Beattie out to the nether quarters, leaving Rosemary Zyczynski and Sheila Winter to gaze around at the desolation of dishes and cutlery which the caterers had abandoned.

'She should have booked the still-room staff from my restaurant,' Sheila said. 'They'd have cleared it all overnight.'

Z saw to the lights and followed her upstairs. They parted on the gallery.

'Good food,' Max said affably as she entered her bedroom. He was throwing off his clothes and expecting her to follow suit.

'And food for thought,' she said after a slight pause. 'Did you get the feeling there's more going on under this roof than readily meets the eye?'

4

Nine weeks later: November 10

It was the sort of grim morning when you half-wake to realise that it's Sunday, shiver, burrow deeper into the mattress, pull the duvet up over your ears and experience a rush of gratitude for the invention of the Christian Sabbath. It was plainly November.

Freshly tanned after a family week spent in Madeira, Detective Superintendent Mike Yeadings accepted he was totally out of practice with cold; especially the greasy, raw, damp, throat-catching kind that now clung to his windows. Fog, he decided, he did not do.

So the ringing phone was intolerable just as he was again sliding over the edge of sleep. 'Shop,' Nan announced with hurtful brightness, passing the instrument across the bed. And today seniority permitted no escape, because the team was still short of a DI, Angus Mott's transfer to Kosovo having suddenly come through before the top brass had named a replacement.

While a brace of detective sergeants attending a possible suicide should normally

36

be more than enough, Yeadings wasn't happy to leave it to them. Any other two perhaps; even Beaumont and Rosemary Zyczynski at any other time; but at present there was too much tension between them, each over-conscious of an acting-inspectorship hanging above like a shared Damoclean — though welcome — sword.

Both had done well in the promotion exam. By length of service it should be Beaumont to receive the accolade, but he hadn't Z's dependability: a regrettable case of a quirk too far. Maybe, Yeadings thought, it should be decided on the outcome of today's call-out. Best perhaps if he was on hand there to watch both respond.

So, as pitch dark yielded to phlegmy grey, his intended rest day found him wrapped as for an Alaskan winter and driving down from the rolling, silver Chilterns into ever more densely swirling mist in the river valley. Ahead and below spread a thick sea of white from which the tops of trees jutted black like the broken masts of stranded ships. Even inside the heated car the air had a reedy tang to it. He could already taste the wintry Thames on his tongue.

Arrived in Henley he was waved on by flashlight to the site. It was a pub yard. As yet there had been no enthusiastic turnout; just a pair of uniformed PCs in their jam-sandwich patrol car, plus a sickly-looking civilian who'd discovered the body, and an unfamiliar young medico identified only by the stethoscope hung round the upturned collar of his British Warm. His car, a red Jaguar, was parked at a respectful distance across the car park from the deceased's, so one might hope he would co-operate in preserving the scene.

As Yeadings stepped out into the dank chill, his breath coiling to hang in minute, visible globules, a police van from Traffic drove up and began to unload screens, bollards and rolls of plastic tape to secure the site.

A pub yard. The information relayed from the nick at second-hand had given no details beyond Henley-on-Thames, query female suicide, down near the bridge. So Yeadings had been expecting the riverbank, with a drowned corpse hauled in on a boatman's pike.

Nostalgically his memory retrieved a day in high summer — Henley Regatta: jostling boats; bright college blazers with white slacks; ladies lazing in float silks; local girls grilling themselves lobster-red in tank tops and hot pants; a cheery, beery crowd of spectators hanging over the water.

But today that was all gone: there were no corporate hospitality marquees dispensing champagne and strawberries with cream for the would-be toffs. This was a quite different scenario.

At least the river wasn't involved. He wasn't required to gaze on the waxen bloating of long submersion, and the obscene ravages of fish. But it would be bad enough. He would never grow accustomed to the sight of life suddenly and violently destroyed. Each new body was that of someone's son or daughter.

On first sight this one in the black Vauxhall Vectra appeared decent: well-preserved, female, thirties, fleshy but not obese, fully — and rather stylishly — wrapped in a black fur coat. She was seated in the driving seat, fallen half-sideways, her face partly hidden in the deep collar, the fingers of both hands splayed across the fabric of the passenger seat.

Could it yet be a natural death, or something else? Whatever had been implied in calling him out, he had experience enough to wait for the doctor to climb out from the far side, straighten and smooth down his hair.

'Death confirmed at 08.13,' he offered. 'I guess that's all that's expected of me. I'm Sam Newbury, by the way. I've disturbed the body as little as I could. Anything further needed?' His accent wasn't native; perhaps Australian or New Zealand.

Yeadings identified himself. 'Air and anal temperature readings?' he suggested mildly. 'Professor Littlejohn will be here in his own good time, which, given the fog, may not be all that good. He'll want to view her in situ, but he'd appreciate some statistics from square one.'

'Then I'll see what I can do.' Newbury came round to the driving side, blocking off the doorway with a powerful pair of shoulders. Yeadings waited, leaving him space. A few minutes later, the young doctor emerged again, grim-faced. He offered no cause of death and Yeadings demanded none. Nevertheless the young man quizzed the detective: 'Are you expecting suspicious circumstances?'

'You think I should?' Yeadings's furry-caterpillar eyebrows rose as he watched him snap the latex gloves fastidiously off his fingers. 'I'd certainly consider the set-up needs a little explaining: why here? why now? why her?'

The police surgeon grunted. 'That's your business. I've finished mine, so — happily — back to bed, which someone quite gorgeous is keeping warm for me.' He grinned cockily, but Yeadings wasn't deceived. The lad was covering up distaste at a still unfamiliar job. A local practice might not

40

offer him much violent death, beyond the occasional drunken brawl that went a tad too far.

Uniformed men were erecting a plastic tent to screen off the car, and not before time, because lights were beginning to show in windows all around and at any moment someone might come out of the pub and demand to know what was going on.

While Dr Newbury was occupied a blue Ford Escort had drawn up in the road opposite, and now DS Zyczynski got out, wrapping a silver-grey sheepskin coat tightly round her. She hurried across to Yeadings. Her head was bare, and almost immediately little beads of moisture started to collect and glint on her cap of brown curls. 'Morning, Boss. What've we got?'

From the corner of his eye the superintendent saw DS Beaumont struggling to climb out of her front passenger seat, still buttoning his coat. Z followed his gaze. 'I picked him up,' she said quickly, dispelling any inference that they were cohabiting. Which never would have entered Yeadings's mind. He knew the car-sharing wasn't to conserve fuel. Either Beaumont's own wouldn't start on this damp and cheerless morning or he was still fragile from last night, compelling him to beg a

41

favour, however it might show up as a bum card in his hand.

'Just as well to have you both together,' he said comfortably. 'Let's hope it won't keep us here for long. From where I'm standing it's still possibly an accident, though the doctor's manner implies otherwise. I leave it to you.'

Zyczynski had sense enough not to dive in, but stood alongside, hands deep in her coat pockets. Since the subject was certified dead they could wait for the photographer to finish before touching the body.

He caught the question in her eyes and pointed. 'Half-eaten ham sandwich near its plastic wrapper on the passenger seat. Plus a hip flask that's leaked on to the floor. It could be she choked on her picnic. But ours not to reason why, nor even how, at least until Littlejohn's taken a look. SOCO team's on its way.'

Beaumont had joined them in time to get the final sentence. He grunted, looking the worse for wear, slumped whey-faced in a dark waxed jacket. He was saved from any effort at conversation by arrival of the Scenes-of-Crime van and the simultaneous emergence of the landlord of the White Swan in dressing-gown and slippers. Yeadings moved away and left it to the others to make the regulation police noises.

42

From a nearby stanchion at the car park's entrance the civilian witness rose groggily to his feet and moved off towards the pub, until Yeadings challenged him.

'I take it you discovered the body?'

The man, small, weasel-like and unshaven, shook his head in confusion, but apparently meaning yes. 'Can't believe it. Give me a real turn, it did. Never expected to find anyone in the car. There's often one or two left over from a Sat'dy night. Their pals takes their keys off of them if they're too tanked up to drive, see. I jes' went across to have a shufti in the window, make sure there wasn't no valuables left inside. So then I sees this bird. Thought it was a tart'd spent the night in some punter's car, didn't I. Only then I opened the door and tried to shake 'er awake. Cold as charity she was. Worse, she was a right slabba marble.'

Now that he'd started to talk he seemed unable to stop. Yeadings was familiar enough with the symptoms of shock, but he had one question more before the man slunk off indoors. 'Why were you up and about so early?'

'Gotta clean the public rooms, 'aven't I? Sunday's a big day. Roas' beef and three veg, winters. Barbecue in summer. Getta lotta people turn up midday.'

'So we'll be as quick as we can, letting you get on with it.' Yeadings signalled to Beaumont to come and take over. 'Get him inside,' he ordered. 'Check the driver's door really was unlocked. Find out how much he disarranged the body. And have a word with mine host about last night. It's all a little unusual, so give it a good shake out. I'm off home now. You can ring me there when you're through.'

He made it back before Sunday breakfast was cleared. Nan promptly produced her cholesterol-reduced version of the fry-up he felt the weather owed him, and he was half-way through it before the phone rang.

It was Zyczynski. Her voice was sombre. 'Photography's done. Prof L's arrived and we're still waiting to hear what he's found. But why I'm phoning — I've got a name for her, sir. She's my neighbour at Beattie's: Sheila Winter. Owns that big garden centre, *Greenvale*, out on the Caversham Road.'

He observed her use of the present tense. She'd known the woman; was momentarily shaken. 'Get back home now,' he ordered. 'Beaumont's fit enough to see this through.'

'I'd like to stay on, sir. We'll clear it more quickly together.' She hesitated. 'I'd have guessed at once who it was if she'd been in her own car. This is a new one on me. I didn't

44

see her face until Prof Littlejohn straightened her out. Sir, do you want me to break it to her mother? She'll be needed to identify her later.'

'That would probably be best eventually, but don't push yourself. It comes hard when it's someone you know. And leave SOCO to wind it up there. It's no weather to stand around in. It wouldn't help to have both my sergeants down with bronchitis.'

A thought struck him. 'Will you be at home later, Z, say twelvish?'

'Apart from seeing Mrs Winter, I'd not intended going out.'

'Good. You can leave it until I arrive.' He made an attempt to lighten his tone. 'You know how I like my coffee.'

'Sir.'

He nodded and replaced the receiver. It was Z he would recommend to stand in for the missing Angus Mott. She'd finally satisfied him on the main count this morning; plus the possible bonus that she'd some slight knowledge of the dead woman.

It was several months ago that Z's landlady had launched out to buy Ashbourne House, had it converted into flats and given the girl first refusal of the best apartment. It was a distinctly upmarket move, which Z had described as Beattie's attempt to script, cast

45

and direct a real-life soap of her own. She'd complained that those currently on TV were getting drably predictable and failing on the family front. Yeadings, amused, had a mental image of the old lady as a motherly ewe nosing round the lambing field for orphaned or cast-off subjects to foster.

Beattie Weyman, irrepressibly good-natured cockney and retired beautician, no longer had any family of her own, and the more modest house she'd owned before was haunted by the bloody ghost of her dead sister propped up at the table in her basement kitchen. She'd ridden the shock waves of that murder like a Trojan wife, but she didn't need to face another sudden death; certainly not one connected with the new house. It was as much to check on the old lady as to hear any developments from Z that he'd invited himself round for coffee. Meanwhile a long soak in the tub should be next on his Sunday agenda.

He was barely — in both senses — immersed when his mobile phone, just out of reach, bleated. He resisted the temptation to slide under the water and ignore it. As he stepped out, the dank November fog seemed suddenly to seep through the steamed window and clasp him in an intimate embrace.

'Yeadings,' he snapped.

46

It was Beaumont. 'Thought you'd like to know who the car belongs to.' He sounded smug.

'Surprise me, then.' Did he expect a commendation because the National Police Computer had accessed the information for him?

'Barry Childe.'

For a brief instant it meant nothing, then Yeadings recalled canteen black humour at the name. There had been little that was childlike about the man, pulled in some years back for a particularly brutal case of GBH. He'd been lucky to escape a murder charge. The young prostitute he'd attacked had lingered in coma for over a month. Childe must have served half of his seven year stretch and been released on parole.

'So what are you waiting for?'

'He's moved from the last-known address in Reading. I've been round there but no joy. The local nick says he's reported in on time but not informed his parole officer of any move. I guess we'll have to wait for Monday to get anything more. Meanwhile, the Prof's willing to do the post mortem this afternoon at 3.30 since his weekend's ruined anyway.'

Yeadings, shivering despite the central heating, considered this. He guessed there were two reasons for Littlejohn's eagerness to tackle the job at once. One was that the body interested him; the other, that he disliked working on half-frozen and rethawed flesh. 'So he found something unusual?'

'That depends on what you take for normal these days. It certainly wasn't natural causes or suicide. Even from where I was standing I could recognise multiple stabbing. And the black mink coat isn't going to be of much use to the charity shops. It's pretty sliced up. That, incidentally, was all she had on.'

Back in the bath foam, with a liberal addition of hot water, Yeadings lay thoughtfully regarding the hump of his own belly. Nan was right: his muscles needed toning. But that, like tracing Childe, was for another day.

The present observation exercising his mind was that not only was Littlejohn being economical with information, but his sergeants were also waging a two-man war of non-intercommunication.

5

'So that welcome dinner of Beattie's was your first real meeting with Sheila Winter,' said Yeadings. They were side by side on her kitchen window-seat, drinking the promised coffee. Behind them the November sky loured felty grey. The midday sun was making a blurred effort to penetrate the fog, which by now had lifted enough to be recognisably low cloud.

'I didn't gather much about Sheila as a person,' Z considered. 'She seemed total business-woman. Even at the dinner she talked about nothing but her precious Greenvale garden centre. Her thank-you to Beattie for the dinner party was an offer of cut-price houseplants over a period. Apart from that nothing really struck me, except that she did seem anxious about her mother, who went on a drinking spree and was flirting outrageously with Max.'

'Who naturally took it in his stride,' Yeadings guessed. 'That was over six weeks ago. What about after that?'

'As Beattie intended when she launched the social thing, it took off. The hall is ideal

49

for get-togethers. Sheila Winter gave a drinks party there a week or so later for her workers at the Centre and various suppliers. We residents were automatically included. I stayed on for about fifteen minutes on my way indoors. Upstairs front people have to come and go by the main entrance, you see. Owners of the three rear flats have a back door, and they can reach the hall through the communal utility room. I don't know who else of our residents turned up. Beattie told me later that she hadn't gone.

'While I was there Sheila was busy acting hostess and seemed quite normal. I didn't notice her spending more time with any one person than another.

'Then, about ten days ago, the Winters gave a small dinner party in their own flat. It was just for what she called 'us upstairs people'. Max was away so, ostensibly to even up numbers, she'd invited her new assistant manager from the Centre. Actually I'd noticed him circulating at the earlier drinks party. I decided she'd really meant the dinner to welcome him, with me thrown in as the handy extra.'

'And her demeanour then?'

'What you'd expect of a boss permitting a limited sight of her home life. Her mother stayed subdued throughout and was only poured mineral water. I wondered at the time if she'd taken a mild sedative. The conversation was general chatter, tabloid front-page stuff: favourite television shows; speculation on private lives of people famous for being famous, and on how many years the Diana factor would make heavy demands for cut flowers at her funeral anniversaries. I felt Sheila was talking down in a way, for the man's benefit, but she wasn't patronising.

'I asked how they found the CCTV, and got the usual answer: that a run-through of the tapes later revealed a number of thefts, but losses were definitely down. They had the same moan as everyone else: that there weren't enough staff on busy days to have someone sit watching the monitors.

'Sheila seemed competently in control of the conversation and quite impersonal. I didn't learn anything more about her than at Beattie's dinner-party.

'Which had been almost negative too.' He sounded regretful.

'Yes.' And yet. She caught his glance and knew that he'd picked up on her hesitation.

'I had the impression afterwards . . . '

'Yes?'

' . . . that I'd missed out on something.'

'But its source wasn't Sheila Winter?'

'No-o-o.' She closed her eyes, switched

51

back to that first occasion and saw them again seated round the table: Beattie's flushed pleasure; the homosexual couple's silent communication punctuating exchanges with herself. No, there was nothing in that to cause special unease. Nothing, that was, beyond the sudden personal attraction she'd felt for Martin Chisholm. Which she certainly preferred to keep private.

Leaving whom as the disturbing factor? Had it been Vanessa, with her instinctive actress's need to upstage, leaving Max and herself half entertained, a quarter sceptical, and a quarter watchful — but not watchful enough, it now seemed? Or young Neil Raynes, unexpectedly hostile at first, and later sentimental, almost weepy? Then there was Paul Wormsley, the dimly smiling barn owl, giving nothing away. Was he covertly laughing at everyone? — enjoying some private joke at their expense? Did that make him an enigma? A Mystery Man?

While she pondered, Yeadings appeared to have moved on. 'We'd better see Mrs Winter now and break the sad news to her. Come along as a concerned neighbour, to introduce me. There's no need yet for anyone here, apart from Beattie, to know that we're connected professionally.'

'Right, sir. The Winters' door is at the far

end of the gallery, opposite mine. So far as I know, she's at home.'

★   ★   ★

That misty Sunday had begun miserably for Vanessa Winter. On waking late she'd stumbled to open the curtains and looked out on a shrouded countryside. It reinforced the confused sense of her personal world all awry. Resentful, she determined to milk it of every atom of agony.

Last night had been bloody; initially because of some upset at work that Sheila had brought home magnified. So they had quarrelled. Badly. God knows what about, but there was always something.

Yes, that had been last night. Or she thought it had been. Couldn't be sure because afterwards she'd rather mixed the drinks. Before going out, Sheila had hidden the bottles away, though in a place this size it didn't take long to unearth them.

Then, as she roamed the flat this morning, it was obvious that Sheila's bed hadn't been slept in. There'd been no warning, no apology, and she was left high and most appallingly dry. Which was even more bitchy of Sheila than usual.

Was she meant to worry over the stupid

girl; picture her grotesquely coupling with some quite unsuitable man all last night? Like that Childe person she had brought home last week. No culture, no conversation, so that they'd had to scrape the bottom of the barrel of tabloid gossip or they'd have been silent from terrine through to cheese-board. It wasn't enough that Sheila had only peasant ambitions, but she must have her bit of rough outside her career as well.

Disagreeable girl. And a bully!

She went on protesting silently, her insides churning. Why must you do this to me? I knew moving out here would never work out. Where is there to escape to?

There are no shops, no galleries, no beauticians, no hotels.

She slunk into the bathroom, put in the plug, turned on both taps.

I could slit my wrists, she thought self-indulgently, and lie in the warm water staring at the white ceiling; just slip away.

But she wasn't sure Sheila would grieve; and she knew it for a role she wouldn't take on. Not now. Perhaps never. Not the fragrant April Fenner.

But to be honest, if one must be, she was still Joan Winter. Such a bleak name, as though right from the start her puritanical parents had been determined she should have nothing that was pretty. So, marrying early, she'd exchanged Winter for Fenner, and for her burgeoning stage career she'd chosen to be April, all sunshine and showers — plenty of scope there for a young actress, turning on the charm and the tears. Admitting she was past juvenile romantics, she'd then matured into 'Vanessa'. She'd known the right people and achieved a handful of good roles, because, despite her harsh mother and the reclusive father, she'd turned out a beauty after all. So she'd had her successes: two decades of almost-fame.

No; ending it just wasn't on. Someone must be there to take the curtain calls.

She started to open the bathroom casement but slammed it shut as cold wisps of fog started to curl in. The real world was more chilling than past dreams.

Reality? — she wasn't sure what it amounted to any more. What was she reduced to, living here under Sheila's management? Going on going on, with nothing to look forward to? If you can't make plans any more, can't fill up the diary pages ahead, you're no longer alive. Not fully. When was it that she'd last been conscious of *living*? A vital dimension had simply vanished, like the surrounding fields into today's mist.

She shrugged off the silk robe and

un-stoppered the perfumed bath oil which Sheila complained was hard for the daily to clean off. She upturned the flask, watched the thick globules hang suspended a moment from its lip, then fall at arm's length, drop by calculated golden drop, into the water. She was Agrippina dispensing poison for her decrepit emperor husband. Clever, incestuous Agrippina, the greatest viper of them all — a better role for her than Cleopatra's immortal longings and her finale with the asp.

Agrippina, yes, she comforted herself as the warm, scented water slid over her shoulders. She could do that superbly. But she'd lost out on the TV part which had gone to Fiona Walker. And that had somewhat curdled her passion for Jakobi.

Central Casting seemed to lose interest in her at about that time. Which was when she'd started to accept second best, taken some singing parts, even done a few charity jobs, joined the amateurs. Ultimately — and this long years after her marriage too had fallen apart — well, ultimately *flopped*.

She mouthed the word wryly, turned over in the bath, flopped heavily on her breasts, throwing water out on the floor; became a sea lion, whiskery face dunked in the water. It seemed to soothe her pounding head a little.

Should she leave it there? Breathe in Lethe's calm?

Who would mind? Not Sheila, for sure.

★ ★ ★

The unwelcome visitors arrived at lunch-time; or what would have been lunch-time if she'd felt at all like eating. As it was, she still had a towel wrapped round her streaming hair and went to the door in her bathrobe with patches of damp showing through where she hadn't properly dried off.

It was the Rosemary girl, Beattie Weyman's by-blow, and a rather interesting-looking man in his forties, big — as she'd once liked them — and with strong character lines on his rugged face. He'd have made a Roman senator, not hawky enough for a Pilate.

She realised she'd been staring too long and missed what he'd said. 'Look, come in,' she invited. 'Have a drink. Sun must be over the yard-arm. Wherever that is.'

Yeadings held the door wider for Z and followed her in. Vanessa waved them through to the drawing-room, waited for them to be impressed by its splendour.

'Well, sit down,' she ordered, when neither spoke. She walked across to the drinks cabinet, shakily poured three generous scotches — less bother than asking them their preference, and anyway this was the last bottle she'd managed to unearth, hidden behind the kitchen disinfectant. Her head was pumping again. She wondered what they wanted, how long they'd take explaining.

The girl asked her to sit down. In her own apartment! Such impertinence.

She stayed standing, complained, 'Someone'll need to carry these across for me.' There should have been a tray, but she rather thought it had been left on her bed.

Rosemary brought her drink to her and then she did sit down. The others left their tumblers untouched.

'Mr Yeadings is a policeman,' Rosemary said. 'I'm afraid he's brought bad news.'

Bad? She was used to that. 'How bad?' she demanded, crossing her legs and sipping. She could see that she was making an impression. He couldn't take his eyes off her.

Then the big man told her.

She didn't believe him. No. Not Sheila. She wasn't the sort that — that things happened to. 'No,' she said almost firmly. And then, after an eternity, 'But how?'

He explained that her daughter had been attacked. He didn't know who was responsible, but they would find out. In the meantime was there anyone who could come and stay with her? A friend? Her husband?

'God, he'd be the last . . . '

'He will have to be informed, Mrs Winter. If Sheila was his daughter he needs to know. Do you have his address?'

It would be somewhere around. 'Sheila knows it.'

Rosemary stood up and walked across to a rosewood davenport. 'Is this her desk?'

'Yes, she leaves some personal stuff in it. The rest is in her office.' Vanessa seemed to have withdrawn. She nodded rigidly when the girl asked for permission to search.

Z came up with a blue leather address book and handed it to Yeadings. He inserted a thumbnail in the W index and read the names rapidly through. 'There's no Winter in this,' he said.

'Fenner,' Vanessa told him sharply. 'Winter's the maiden name I went back to after I left him. I had Sheila's changed at the same time. 'He's Dr Gabriel Fenner. His subject's Archaeology. He lives somewhere in Cambridge.'

Yeadings had another look. 'Fenner. Yes, the address is in here.'

'I'll get on to it,' Z offered.

Yeadings frowned. 'I'd rather you found Beattie first. She'll know what to do.'

'Right, sir.'

'*Sir?*' Vanessa echoed dully. The implied respect struck her as odd, but she didn't pick up on what it might signify. Rosemary left and the two of them sat staring at each other across the room.

'I am so very sorry,' Yeadings said.

If he was, why didn't he come across and take her in his arms? She needed comforting. Couldn't he see she was now utterly alone? Unconsciously she reached out a dimpled hand and hugged a cushion close, burying her face for minutes in its shiny softness.

To Yeadings it looked as if she had fallen asleep, her body was so relaxed. They stayed silent until Z came back, alone.

'Beattie not there?' Yeadings asked quickly.

'She's cooking. A sponge cake. It's just rising.'

He couldn't believe that she'd refused to help, but Z wouldn't admit in front of Vanessa that the news had struck Beattie like a slap in the face. It echoed too closely her sister's tragic end.

'Take over here,' he ordered Z, and went out on the misted balcony to use his mobile phone. As he came back there was a tap at the door.

Beattie let herself in and went straight across to Vanessa. She plumped herself down on the sofa and took the other woman in her arms. They began slowly rocking together, not a word spoken.

After a minute or so Vanessa's head lifted and she stared at Beattie almost blindly. 'Why don't you come downstairs with me?' Beattie asked gently.

Yeadings nodded. It would leave them space to have Sheila's room searched.

As if hypnotised, Vanessa let herself be led away. When Z went down later with a selection of clothes from her wardrobe she was seated on a kitchen chair beside the oven, blankly staring ahead. The flat was warm and filled with the cosy smells of baking.

As she watched, Vanessa put out a tremulous hand to Beattie and asked in a small voice, 'Can Joanie have a bikky?' Her face suffered a nervous tic. She seemed to cower away from an expected rebuff. '*Pretty please*,' she whispered.

Z nodded to Beattie. 'I found her doctor's phone number in the desk. He's on his way.'

Upstairs Yeadings had walked through to her bedroom, observing the disordered bed with a tray of used dishes on the floor nearby. There were croissant flakes on the rumpled under-sheet and spilt stains of red wine beside an overturned glass on the bedside table. Last night's clothes were abandoned on or around a Victorian nursing chair upholstered in rose satin. Two paperback novels had silk markers in their pages, one halfway through, the other at page twenty-seven. Vanessa's reading glasses were on the floor, their bridge bent as though she had walked on them.

He went through to the bathroom and, without touching, inspected the contents of the wall cabinet. There were various pain remedies, cures for indigestion and two bottles of prescribed drugs. Their labels were printed with Vanessa's name and the address of a High Street pharmacy. He would ask Dr Barlow about them when he arrived. Not that he hadn't already guessed at their usage.

There was nothing here with her daughter's name on. If the dead woman had used medication it was kept elsewhere.

There was, however, a little screw of plastic in the far corner of one shelf, and this he opened to reveal a green substance with a familiar odour. Definitely not prescribed, that one. Was this also the older woman's? He wondered if she got it from a dealer on the streets or relied on someone else to pick it up. Not that he felt any need, for the moment, to press her about it. For all he knew she might have some physical ailment that she believed it could ease.

Back in the lounge — he guessed she

would refer to it as her drawing-room: it was impressive rather than cosy — he picked up the address book again and used his mobile phone to try a second time for the Cambridge number.

'Fenner,' a languid voice answered him. He could imagine the book-lined study; the Sunday after-lunch torpor of a well-wined don.

'My name is Yeadings,' he said. 'I'm a Detective-Superintendent with Thames Valley Police.' He was loath to break the news without seeing the man's face; or knowing something of his relationship with the dead woman.

'Could you tell me, sir, when you last saw your daughter Sheila?'

There was a silence which his imagination failed to fill. Was the man occupied by doing something else; astonished; or working out a reply suitable for a policeman?

'No I can't.' Fenner said at length. It was cool, considered, utterly impersonal: an academic fact given for an intrusive question.

'An approximation would suffice,' Yeadings said stiffly.

'I saw her shortly after her eighteenth birthday. She would be thirty-seven by now. So roughly almost twenty years ago, I suppose. Is that of any use to you, Superintendent?'

'Thank you, sir. So would you say your relationship with her was not close?'

'If it concerned me sufficiently to remark upon, I would do so.'

'I ask,' Yeadings explained, 'because I have to tell you of your daughter's death.'

He went on as baldly as the other man had spoken. 'Last night she was the victim of a brutal murder and I am the Senior Investigating Officer for the case.'

'Dead?' There was genuine horror there, but then the voice became sardonic.

'Dead . . . and never deigned to call me father.'

'I believe you are separated from your wife, sir.'

'Both my wives.' His voice was brittle. 'The first, who was delicate, died some thirty years ago, and I was persuaded to 'make an honest woman' of my young daughter's mother. You follow the chronology, Superintendent?' His tone was becoming increasingly astringent. He was, after all, a lecturer, and probably one impatient with slow learners.

Yeadings sighed. With Vanessa an actress, they must have been at odds over who should hold the stage at any one moment, both accustomed to demanding the full attention of their audience. What kind of parents would they have been for the child?

'It was not . . . ' Fenner remarked bitterly, and for Yeadings superfluously, ' . . . an ideal match. April, as she had started to call herself then, was as little enchanted with her life of social bondage as was I. It was for the child's sake as much as anything, that I endured it for a tedious eight years, when a financial agreement was drawn up and my wife returned to her maiden name. I learned later that my daughter's name had also been altered by deed poll.'

'And on, or after, her eighteenth birthday you went to see her.'

'I was curious to meet the new adult. It was no more than that. I found she was unsuited to an academic career and had distinct preferences of her own. She was also independent enough to have set up a programme for training in practical horticulture.'

He paused. 'At least she had inherited my passion for digging. She made it clear to me that she didn't need my help, and went her own way. So you see, if you wish for information about the circumstances of her everyday life and contacts, I am not the person to help you.'

'Thank you, sir. Just a final question.

Although you didn't meet later, did you communicate in any way?'

There was another short silence; then, 'Congratulations, Superintendent. I had expected you to miss out on that one. Yes, we have kept in touch, once a year after that. On the occasion of her birthday she would always write to thank me for my gift and to give a concise but comprehensive account of her activities.'

'Indeed?' Yeadings hesitated to ask for access to those letters.

'So, you might say,' the man went on, 'that I hold a diary of sorts, which allowed me to form my own opinion of her character and interests. Even a distant father can take some pride in a child who makes her own way in the world. And is now gone.'

This last phrase was an admission of loss. The carapace was split momentarily, to reveal the soft flesh underneath.

'When would it be convenient,' Yeadings said slowly, 'for me to come and have a word with you in Cambridge?'

There was a moment's silence. 'I should prefer,' Fenner said heavily, 'to make the journey myself. Next Saturday, perhaps. I doubt the funeral will be before then, given the circumstances you mentioned.'

'Thank you, sir. I can be available from

9a.m. at Reading police station.' Yeadings waited a moment for some further reaction, and wasn't disappointed.

'Damn it!' the man exploded. 'There's nothing here of such importance that I can't arrange a substitute. I'll be with you tomorrow.' And with that he put down the phone.

6

Yeadings, far from satisfied with the interview with Vanessa, was pleased with the outcome of his ringing Sheila's father at his Cambridge college. He turned back as Z saw him to the door. 'Since you've already met Miss Winter's manager at Greenvale in your private capacity, I'll get Beaumont to interview him. What did you say his name was?'

She hadn't mentioned it. 'Childe,' she told him. 'Barry Childe.'

He stared at her, momentarily startled. 'You didn't . . . ? Of course, the name would mean nothing to you. It was before your time. But Beaumont does remember him.'

'Childe has a criminal record?'

'Given seven years for GBH, just short of manslaughter. He's out after half that time. What you also didn't know is that Beaumont has traced the black Vauxhall Vectra back to Childe.'

He frowned at her. 'See to it in future that you and Beaumont share all information immediately on receipt.'

'Sir, I wasn't to know that Childe was in anyway involved.'

Yeadings remained stiff-featured. 'Just as DS Beaumont wasn't to know that the dead woman was identified as Sheila Winter, the man's boss. I'll see you both at the post mortem; 3.30 sharp.'

★　★　★

Professor Littlejohn was talking on the telephone when Yeadings came in, shucked off his waxed jacket and dropped it in a corner on the scrupulously disinfected floor. After the outdoor gloom the brilliance of the overhead lights was dazzling. Mirror-backed globes were reflected in polished steel surfaces, white walls, glass vessels. Sounds in that harsh-surfaced area were equally brutal. The body lay covered by a coarse cotton sheet, only the feet exposed, one big toe tagged.

Yeadings observed that both his sergeants were present and deep in conversation together. That indicated an improvement. He walked across.

'When I met Sheila with her mother,' Z was explaining, 'there was tension between them. Sheila seemed anxious for her; afraid of what she might do, overstep some agreed mark. And, for all that Sheila was the practical one, Vanessa constantly upstaged her, having the more robust personality.

'Vanessa's so . . . ' Z paused, frowning as she searched for the right word.' . . . self-sufficient, extrovert, sometimes a bit over the top. She can make rather a fool of herself. If she does realise that, it doesn't appear to bother her.

'Sheila was the opposite, anxiously watchful. Even on her own she was tense, as though she didn't dare let herself go.'

'You get that sometimes between parents and children,' Yeadings remarked, having joined them. 'It's the fear of inherited genes — 'Dear God, don't let me turn out like Mother!' '

'Inherited jeans,' Beaumont offered wanly. 'It was my big brother's I got handed down. The tie-dye kind, baggy bum, spindly thighs.'

The other two ignored his misplaced attempt at humour. 'What we need is an opinion on Sheila from someone at her place of work, when she was away from her mother's influence,' Yeadings said.

'I'll get on to that after Littlejohn's finished with the body,' Beaumont intoned in a wounded voice. 'Now that the right info's to hand.' He darted a sour glance at Zyczynski.

'Sunday's usually the busiest day at those garden places. Childe should be on hand to oversee closing up at the end. Especially with

70

his boss gone missing.'

'Right!' Professor Littlejohn sang out, hurrying across. 'A *table, mes enfants.* Let us settle round the Sunday joint.'

Two of them in a mood of tasteless humour, Yeadings regretted. But the pathologist was less flippant than he'd appeared. The tune, when he started to hum over his work, was Pagliacci's lament.

He broke off to murmur into the mike pinned to his plastic apron. 'The body is female, aged approximately 35 to 40 years. Height — ' He looked over his half-lenses at his assistant who supplied the measurement and weight.

'Splendid,' said Littlejohn. 'Now let's see what we can find. Exterior first.'

He hadn't far to look to confirm that she had multiple stab wounds. 'Clothing?' he demanded.

'It's been bagged and sent to forensics lab,' Beaumont provided. 'You saw it on her. There was only the one item. A fur coat. Hobbs is working on it.'

'Well, I need it now,' Littlejohn insisted. He was far from gruntled, as Beaumont would say. 'We can't have slip-ups.'

Yeadings recognised it was his own ultimate responsibility as Senior Investigating Officer. But he'd left Beaumont in charge;

71

who had allowed SOCO to whisk it off. Only a few hours into the investigation, the absence of a controlling DI was already screwing up the works.

'I'll see that they report directly to you and return it.'

'Three distinct stab wounds,' Littlejohn continued without comment. 'And two slashes from a right-handed direction, assuming, as we must, that the attacker stood in front. I think we dare say that those two were preliminary. The killer can't have avoided being splashed by blood.'

He inserted a probe into the largest wound, under the left side of the ribcage, pulled the edges of the flesh apart like a snarling mouth, waited while his assistant washed them clean of blood with a concentrated jet of cold water, hummed a few bars of something unrecognisable, then consulted a steel rule. 'The weapon was a knife, single cutting-edge, at least six inches long, or 15.3 centimetres if you prefer. At its widest it measured 2.5 centimetres. The sort found in most kitchens, I imagine. Do we have the weapon?'

'It had been removed,' Beaumont said promptly.

'Not by us this time,' added Yeadings mildly, and was rewarded with a knowing look over Littlejohn's half-moons. He returned to an examination of the body. 'Recent scarring of the left knee. Four small abrasions, loose scabbing and the remains of wider bruising. Let's take a look at the left palm. Yes, more rapid healing here, but I would say she had a fall some twelve to fourteen days back. A trip, not a collapse. She flung out a hand in the direction of the fall. No marks on shins to indicate a tripwire; so some snag at ground level, possibly a rutted path or a tree root. There would have been gravel rash.

'Nothing very significant in that. So let's look elsewhere.' He plunged his hands into the woman's hair.

'Ah, now here's something more recent. Surface occiputal lump. She fell backwards.'

'At the time of the attack?'

'Most likely. Bruising has yet to show properly under the hairline. No serious damage, but she'd have been momentarily confused. Which could account for the absence of defence wounds on the hands and the angle of the stabbing. So much for the exterior.'

The onlookers endured the sneer of the electric saw as the pathologist went into the chest cavity. He started severing and lifting out organs, which his assistant weighed and secured in labelled containers.

'Contents of stomach,' Littlejohn began, then shook his head. 'Not a lot. The lady died peckish. There was, as I recall, a half-eaten ham sandwich in the car beside her. I think analysis will find that we have caught up with the missing portion. Its condition suggests that death occurred very shortly after ingestion. Not hours; minutes only.'

The post mortem continued, providing nothing that was at all startling. Sheila Winter's body had been in a very healthy state. She was not *virgo intacta*, but one should assume little from that. She had not recently been sexually active and was not pregnant. She had never been delivered of a child.

'How recent is 'recent'?' Beaumont demanded, before Z could ask the same.

'Hours, depending on her habits of hygiene. To state a bald fact, there was no semen present or natural lubrication.

'As for time of death, there are wide parameters because nothing's known about length of exposure to outside temperature or indoor heating. We need to know place of death and under what circumstances she was moved. Until you can give a lead on that I can get no closer than between seven pm yesterday and three this morning. Death almost certainly occurred elsewhere and she

74

was later placed upright in the driving seat of the car. Rigor had begun. Post mortem changes could account for her slumping. Alternatively that could have been caused when the body was disturbed by the potman when he opened her door.'

'Eight hours,' grumbled Beaumont under his breath and sucking his cheeks in.

'Cause of death,' Yeadings prompted, knowing that Littlejohn in his present prickly mood wouldn't volunteer the all-important item without some kind of supplication.

'Provided that chemical analysis later rules out a toxic substance in the blood-stream, we can accept that the deepest stab wound, made upwards under the left ribs and penetrating the right ventricle, was responsible. The lady was certainly alive when the wound was made. Undoubtedly dead when the knife was finally removed.'

'And place of death?'

'Your guess is as good as mine. We don't know how much blood soaked into the missing fur coat. If the knife was left in place for some period that could have accounted for the car being clean. However, stasis indicates that the body was moved after death, so I believe the killing took place elsewhere. But that's your puzzle, gentlemen and lady. Not mine.'

With that, Littlejohn detached the micro-phone, snapped off his latex gloves and binned the apron along with them. 'Well now, Mike' he said in an altogether more amiable voice, 'Where are you taking me for dinner? I think I deserve somewhere rather special after sacrificing my raunchy weekend, don't you?' His eyes were puckish under their shaggy, grey brows.

What about my lost Sunday with the family? Yeadings silently asked himself, then instantly relented. Kill two birds with one stone. 'You're coming back with me,' he told him. 'Nan hasn't set eyes on you for months, and she'll be delighted.'

And don't tell me that that's not 'somewhere special', his inner monitor warned.

Beaumont prepared to move off. 'You want to come along to interview Barry Childe?' he invited Zyczynski.

'There's a problem. Nobody at my new place knows what my job is. I'd rather keep it under wraps for as long as possible. They'll give more away then. I met Childe as a fellow-guest of Sheila Winter's; nothing more.'

'But when you broke the news to her mother you had to declare yourself.'

'The Boss was there. Mrs Winter barely

76

noticed my presence. Accepted me as a sympathetic female neighbour. She's of a generation that assumes men are the only ones that count.'

'So how did she take it?'

Z shook her head. 'God only knows. Dumb at first. Incredulous. Then she started groping for sympathy, appealing to the Boss. She used to be an actress, you know. Still pretty heavy on the histrionics. And plays up the helpless little woman role. Even in shock she was doing that. I suppose that in her profession it's almost second nature to project a forceful reaction.'

'Made a meal of it? Probably a tough old boot under the feminine vapours.'

'A robust ego, certainly; but I'm not sure how she'll cope later. She must be in her late fifties, and it's doubly traumatic when your child dies before you. There's survival guilt to get through.'

'And this one didn't just die. How did Mrs W react to the idea of murder?'

'The Boss was careful; led gently up to it. I think we left her believing it was a mugging that went too far. She wasn't able to take in where it happened or the circumstances. Didn't enquire. She wasn't fully dressed when we called, and this was about 12.30. I'll drop in this evening and see how she is.

Beattie Weyman took her downstairs. She's had experience with stage-folk and she's more than capable of handling her.'

They had been walking from the morgue to the hospital car park. Now Beaumont glanced at his wristwatch. 'Better shove off it I want to catch Barry Childe. It'll be interesting to see what tale he spun to get himself a job like that. I'll get a lift off a patrol car, then pick up my own. If it'll start.'

Fog had crept up again and slid into the blue Ford Escort along with Zyczynski. She sat a while with the engine running while the car warmed up. She hadn't told the Boss everything she knew. Or, rather, guessed. There was that later occasion she had preferred to ignore.

It had been only five days back, on Tuesday afternoon. When she came home she'd had her arms full of shopping and so hadn't picked up her mail from the hall. Upstairs she packed away her groceries, switched on the kettle and went down again to fetch the letters. The day's mail was still in the wire box on the back of the entrance door, unsorted. She was busy over that and never turned to see who came out of the utility room and went upstairs behind her back.

There were several letters for Beattie and she decided to take them through, but the old lady was out, so she left them on the floor outside the ground-floor flat, propped against the door jamb. To save Mrs Winter negotiating the stairs, she collected the mail for her apartment too, tucking her own letters under one arm. Half way up she heard her kettle click off, went into her kitchen and poured boiling water on a tea bag. It was after it had cooled enough for the milk to be added that she remembered the Winters' mail.

Along the gallery the door at the far end from her own stood unlatched. A gleam of light showed in a vertical line. She knocked gently but there was no answer. Rather than disturb the woman she went in to leave the letters and a small package on the antique settle in the hall.

An olive green silk scarf lay on the floor, and just beyond it a snaky-patterned silk dress she'd seen Sheila wearing the previous week. She reached to pick them up and heard laboured breathing. Someone in the throes of an asthma attack? Or angina?

The drawing-room door stood ajar. She pushed it further open as the sounds became little cries accompanied with animal grunts.

But no serious medical condition. She saw the white ankles linked above the man's shoulders, and his naked buttocks thrusting and mounting as he drove into her.

They were too involved to see or hear anyone. She crept out, picked up the mail again and left the apartment, closing the outer door on a reassuring click. Nobody need learn that there'd been an audience. At least she'd spared Sheila that.

As for the man, whoever he was — she made no claim as a connoisseur of buttocks — at the time he remained anonymous.

Now it could be vital to identify him.

It was early for Sheila to have come home that afternoon. Had she brought someone with her, specifically to make love? Or arranged to meet someone from inside the house? That could have been the person she heard come from the utility room and go quietly upstairs while she sorted the letters.

If he'd come in by the front door she would have seen him. From the house's rear, three apartments had access through the utility room: Beattie's and Wormsley's on the ground floor, and that of Chisholm and Raynes via the former service-staircase.

So, as Sheila's lover couldn't be Beattie, that offered a choice of three from among the residents. Of whom two were supposedly gay. Or perhaps bi-sexual? Z would have to get to know them better.

7

Sundays might normally be the busiest time of the week, but the weather had slowed things down at Greenvale Garden Centre. This evening there were few people wandering the dank, outdoor aisles, and in the covered part the only interest being shown was in an early display of Christmas glitter. Even then the numbers loitering under the gilded cherubs and illuminated star-bursts didn't account for the tightly-packed car park.

Beaumont wandered over to the bulb bins, helped himself to two paper bags and filled one with hyacinths, the other with tulips. At the checkout he asked for Ms Winter, was told she hadn't been in today, but would the manager do?

'Guess he'll have to. Where'll I find him?'

He was pointed towards the office, where a brisk young woman redirected him to the restaurant. That, he discovered, was the honeycomb of the hive, swarming with three generations of enthusiasts for pizzas, omelettes and homemade soups, chocolate cheesecake, apple pie and dollops of whipped cream. He queued for a cappuccino and carried it with his paper bags on a tray to the corner table just vacated. Immediately a waitress whizzed up, collected the used crockery, sprayed and wiped the melamine surface for him; actually smiled.

It seemed that Ms Winter had access to a superior kind of staff. Why, then, pick on the unalluring Barry Childe?

Staring around, Beaumont recognised him three tables away. He had put on weight since being sent down, and grown his sideburns into mutton-chop whiskers, which made him look Victorian and substantial. His mid-grey suit, however badly cut, was a distinct improvement on the string vest, hairy armpits and flashy medallion of his previous persona. He was looking mildly pleased with himself. To change that, Beaumont lifted his tray and carried it across. The glance he got was wary, as if expecting a customer complaint.

'You don't remember me,' Beaumont told Childe, 'but then I was in uniform when we last met. You'd come across so many coppers by that point that you never noticed their faces.'

It didn't shake the man. 'It's a face I do remember, though,' he admitted. 'Anybody would.'

Beaumont grinned. He would enjoy cutting

this one down to size. 'Fallen on your feet, have you?' He produced his warrant card and repeated the name.

'I've been very fortunate, Mr Beaumont.'

'Is Ms Winter, though? It makes one wonder.'

'She's had no cause for regrets. She took me on trust, recommended by the governor.'

'Your dad or Wormwood Scrubs's gaffer?' he goaded.

Childe ignored him. 'The only digs that interest me nowadays are in the soil. I'm in my final year horticulture, get my external degree next summer. That's good enough for her. If you went to Chelsea Flower Show or Hampton Court instead of to the dogs, you'd know that the lags do a nice line in competitive gardening these days.'

'Reflected glory from the Leyhill lot? You're not telling me you actually showed her your genuine CV?'

Childe didn't have to answer. His smirk told all. 'I'm a different person, Mr Beaumont. Born again, Sally Army, teetotal.'

'They've got you banging a tambourine? How come you work Sundays then?'

'Every day's the Sabbath, Mr Beaumont, when you've got the faith.'

The DS was tiring of this vaunted

respectability and his own name monoto-nously repeated. It was time to introduce the business in hand. 'So what do you make of your lady boss?'

'That's what she is. A real lady. Not that she's a softie. Runs a tight little ship, as the expression is. Expects me to jump on any slackness. And if you'll excuse me, I don't care to overrun my tea-break. Perhaps we can continue this in my office. If there's anything worth continuing, that is.'

'Oh, believe me, there is.' He watched the other for a flicker of reaction, but Childe turned on him wide, round eyes the colour of brown Windsor soup, and waited for him to explain.

'I just want to know why you killed her,' he said simply, pushing back his chair.

★ ★ ★

He carried away with him a brilliant image of the man's amazement, horror, incredulity. Never had he seen a jaw drop so literally. It was as if the screw was right out of the hinge and only skin held the lower face together. It had to be genuine; or else Childe had also achieved miracles in dramatic art while he trenched and sowed and pruned in the prison gardens.

They had gone to his office, and there the man asked all the right, concerned, innocent questions of how and when and where. He knew enough about the lengthy and convoluted ways of police work not to demand, 'Whodunnit?' The nearest he approached was to ask, 'Have you got him?'

Beaumont stared back. 'The body was only found early this morning. It could have happened sometime after eleven last night.'

'Somebody saw her at that time?'

'That's when the pub closed. Give another half-hour for the car park to clear. Hers was the only car left there. Only, of course, it wasn't hers, was it? It was yours.'

He watched realisation dawn. 'No!' Childe shouted. 'No, you're not going to stitch me up! She borrowed the Vectra yesterday. We did a swap. I drove her Alfa to get the bumper fixed where she'd backed into a tree. I was going to pick it up later and run it home for her, only the garage hadn't a replacement part.'

'Of course, you knew where she lived, having gone there for dinner sometime before. Convenient. Very friendly, your boss; close. Almost intimate, you might say. Did I mention she was short of some clothes when we found her?'

The man's face had taken on a sickly

pallor. 'For God's sake! It wasn't like that.'

'Like what? You were sent away for GBH. On a woman. That's what this was, only this time it went just too far. But, understandably, it had to. If she didn't die, your boss could name and shame you, then we'd have you for attempted murder. End of a promising earthy career; end of your newfound liberty.'

He pointed a finger. 'You couldn't afford to let her live. So you finished her off.'

Childe rose out of his seat, pushed the desk bodily away from between them and loomed over the shorter man, fists bunched, face now flaming. 'You ain't gonna get away with this!'

'Ain't I?' — goading him to violence: possibly assault on a police officer. Just let him try!

Childe made a supreme effort to contain his anger. 'You're fishing. You haven't got anything on me or there'd be two of you here. You'd have to read me my rights.'

The trouble was, Beaumont brooded, that nowadays the villains swotted up on PACE better than the coppers themselves. They used the Police and Criminal Evidence Act to shackle the legitimate guardians of the peace. In this unfair world law-makers and law-breakers played a screwy kind of ball-game together; but the police were hobbled, reduced to pig-in-the-middle.

'Perhaps not today,' he mocked, 'but I'll be back. You can bet on it. So have a better story ready. Meanwhile try to remember, if you can, exactly where you were yesterday evening.'

'I went out clubbing,' snarled Childe. 'And before you ask me, yes, I was alone. I don't have an alibi because I bloody well don't need one!'

★   ★   ★

Belting himself into his car Beaumont reflected ruefully that he hadn't got anything on Childe, apart from a probable lie about going teetotal. But that was no reason why he couldn't enjoy taking a rise out of the vermin. It hadn't gone too badly for a start. With luck Childe would go haring around to set up an alibi for too narrow a period.

Sheila Winter's body had been 'cold as a slabba marble', to quote the unfortunate potman who'd found her this morning. Littlejohn had yet to work it out exactly from heat loss and rigor, but the clientèle of the Bat and Ball wouldn't have ignored a fur-coated doll sitting alone in her car. She was certainly dumped there after closing time, but the killing had taken place earlier and elsewhere, with the pub car park a random choice for disposal, to divert suspicion from the actual murder scene.

He called Control with a message for Superintendent Yeadings who would have left for home.

'What's wrong with your radio?' the duty sergeant asked sourly. 'Try switching it on sometimes. We've been calling you for near on an hour. Mr Yeadings wants all you lot in his office in seven minutes. You'll need to be near to make it on time.'

So something urgent had come up to curtail the Boss's wining and dining of Littlejohn. As he drove, Beaumont sorted his report for a debriefing. They'd need a warrant to search the garden centre. There was CCTV at the entrance, in the car park and at several points inside the complex, although not in the office. That last might have struck clerical staff as a bit too much of the Big Brother treatment. Even without it, there could be a comprehensive record of who came closest to the dead woman at work, and with luck it might throw up some very personal contacts.

He wanted to commandeer those films before Childe beat him to them. And the sooner the Fraud experts went over the last quarter's accounts, the sooner he could start to take Barry Childe apart and make him sweat some more. Not that he was a medal-winner in the brains department, so scarcely likely to start up as a swindler. By nature Childe was more of a vicious thug, but there was no guessing what other courses than agriculture he'd been taking in the Institute of Felonry.

The Boss might need some persuading that they had enough on the man to justify a search warrant, but ownership of the Vectra and his connection with the dead woman's business could be reason enough for some magistrates he knew. They wouldn't hesitate to produce the necessary paper work.

He flicked a glance at his wrist on the steering wheel. Four minutes to go, and he'd be late if he took note of speed cameras on the way. Better assume they were empty of film than risk the Boss's sarcasm. If he was picked up for burning rubber he could plead an emergency. Keeping his nose clean at this critical point in his career certainly qualified as that.

The others were already assembled as he slid in. He slung his Barbour over a nearby chair and eased his tight collar. He kept his head down. Running the last fifty yards had given him a flushed face and he was conscious of the others' eyes turned on him.

Z made a grimace, nodding towards his

feet. One of the brown paper bags had burst from his Barbour pocket and half a dozen Delft Blue hyacinth bulbs were smoothly rolling over the floor like giant marbles thrown under a police horse at a demo. They were dry, casting crinkly purple skins which crackled as he tried to shepherd them together with the toe of one shoe.

'When DS Beaumont has concluded his soccer practice, I should like to introduce DI Walter Salmon,' Yeadings announced. 'From tomorrow morning he will take over everyday running of the present case, and all reports should be passed to him.'

That was all. The bottom fell out of Beaumont's world. He caught Z's wintry smile and knew she was feeling much the same.

Yeadings nodded and the newcomer stepped forward to address them. At least they hadn't brought in that sour, coffin-faced Jenner from Bicester, but this one didn't look reassuring. He was big, built like a brick loo, as the saying was. The width of his shoulders and the short car coat made a cube of him. The head on top was of much the same shape, with fairish hair close-cropped like a Victorian convict's. His large, knobbly features were all squashed into the lower three-eighths of his face, and the coarse-lipped mouth stretched almost the full width of his heavy jaw.

Not a pretty sight, Beaumont warned himself, but the man didn't appear to concur with that opinion. He had, in fact, a mighty conceit of himself.

Salmon. The DS ran the name through his mind, and recalled hearing it in canteen gossip. He was ex-Met, from West End Central. A recent newcomer to Thames Valley, he'd been tried out in Reading and created a shindig with a Paki which caused him a reprimand, but not down-ranking or public scandal. So maybe the Brass in their godlike wisdom now thought it safer to let him loose on the natives of rural Bucks.

Beaumont switched his eyes to Yeadings but could read nothing on the superintendent's face. Had he been a party to selecting the man, or had his wishes been overridden?

Beaumont sighed audibly. It looked as though his own chances, dammit, (and Z's) had been flushed down the pan and far out to sea on this one.

'OK.' Salmon addressed the two DSs as though they were a reinforced posse. 'Tomorrow we meet at eight sharp in my office. Have your reports on today's interviews typed up and submitted to me by

7.30a.m. A full briefing in the Analysis Room for all Area CID, together with uniform sergeants and above, at 8.15.' He stared at them as though they might retaliate or protest.

'Understood,' said Beaumont with forced amiability.

'Understood, *sir*,' Salmon prompted sternly.

Beaumont considered this. 'Sir,' he conceded. Anything but call him Guv. That title had been Angus Mott's.

Now *Sir* was turning his attention to Z. 'I'll be there, sir,' she assured him, cool almost to the point of indifference.

'Time we were all away home,' Yeadings remarked conversationally. 'I left Littlejohn and Nan capping each other's gruesome anecdotes. God knows what excesses of necrophilia they'll have reached by now.'

He caught the uneasy glance Salmon shot at him. He smiled back. 'My wife was a theatre sister,' he explained.

'So,' Beaumont said heavily as he and Zyczynski headed for the mist-shrouded car park, 'after that little scene do we get drunk, laid, or go for early retirement?'

'Retirement certainly.' She grimaced at her watch. 'And it's not all that early. Why not go straight home? You may find some scrumptious uglies waiting for you.'

It was a thought. Since his wife had taken up baking for a freelance catering firm there were consolations in having her back. It was three years now since Cathy had flounced out to 'get herself a life' and made a right hash of it. He and their teenage son Stuart (more intent on self-discovery than high exam grades at present) had enjoyed their period of freedom and bachelor fry-ups. Then without warning she was back, disillusioned and embittered. He had ungraciously granted her a made-up bed in the box-room on condition she respected his equal right to independence.

Since then all three had endured a state of cold war until the miracle advent of a white refrigerated van in their driveway, and a breezy young woman caterer whose enterprise was expanding into banquets and sophisticated dinners. Since the one thing Cathy had been good at was fancy cooking, he had walked in one night to ambrosial fragrances, oven-flushed faces and a wife's excited announcement of a new home-based career.

Since then all less than perfect products were for family consumption and had even led to occasional contact between converted box-room and ex-marital chamber.

Beaumont wished Z goodnight and set his

car firmly on the road for home, hopeful of profiteroles or pecan pie.

★ ★ ★

On Monday morning Superintendent Yeadings had no intention of taking life easily simply because the upper echelons at Kidlington had whipped a new DI out of their conjuror's hat. If Salmon expected the others in by 7.30 at the local nick the superintendent would be there himself half an hour before.

This morning the fog was, if anything, thicker and more throat-searing than on the previous day. It was as though time had gone into reverse and they were back in the pea-soup era of Jekyll and Hyde.

'Still a bit grey,' Sally had said, peering past him as he opened her Pocahontas curtains.

'It's more than a bit.' But maybe he was making too much of it, still spoilt by the azure skies of Madeira. This was Thames Valley, autumn moving into winter. Get real, man.

'I miss the flowers,' she said, as if reading his mood.

'I tell you what,' he promised. 'Next Saturday, if you're a good girl, we'll all go to lunch at a garden centre which I've just heard of. How's that?'

94

But Sally looked unsure. 'How good must I be? More good than ever before?'

He gave her a bear hug. 'No, just ordinary good will do, sweetheart.'

The car seemed sluggish starting but he soon found that the fog was patchy. The radio, reporting on travel conditions, said it was clearing in the western Home Counties, but there were tailbacks in both directions after a multiple pile-up on the M40.

There could be delays too on Fenner's route from Cambridge. He'd most likely come by way of Luton, then M1, M25 and M40; unlikely to arrive before ten at the earliest. He'd sounded the laid-back type. An academic after all: scarcely Action Man.

★　★　★

Dr Fenner was in fact already on the road, having made arrangements the previous evening for his Monday lectures and seminars to be farmed out among the department's tutors. This morning he had made better progress than expected and, finding himself with time in hand, looked for a convenient place offering breakfast to long-distance lorry drivers.

The pull-in he chose, just after Chalfont St Peter, served up a generous plate of scrambled eggs, back bacon rashers, baked beans and Cumberland sausages, all washed down by two large mugs of very strong tea. He felt, at its end, that he had missed out on not taking an HGV licence and following a less intellectually demanding career.

'OK, mate?' The man who, uninvited, was unloading a piled tray at his table struck him as typical of his kind; large, heavy-shouldered, beer-bellied, lumbering, perhaps not very bright. The don watched him demolish his gargantuan meal and settle back to read a newspaper produced from inside his leather jacket. It was a little startling to discover it was the *Times* and that the Neanderthal had already half-completed the crossword puzzle.

It was still only 08.23 and Fenner had time to spare. 'Have you driven far this morning?' he asked.

''Eathrow,' the other said simply. 'Mondays it's 'Eathrow to Bucks and Berks. Western International, 'olesale veg and plants. That's where they're flown in to, see? From 'Olland mostly.'

'Oh really. I imagined it all went to Nine Elms.'

'Most does. But big dealers get it direct from us. Like my next stop. They stock up Mondays after the weekend trade. Gotta lotta exotics on board. 'Ot'ouse stuff.' He rose to go, leaving the *Times* on their shared table.

'Don't you want that?' Fenner asked hopefully. His own copy hadn't arrived before he left.

'You 'ave it. I only get it for the crossword. It's got me beat today. I get all me news from the *Express*.'

The academic thanked him.

''Ave a good day, mate,' the other replied. Fenner doubted he would.

For the first time that morning he faced up to what must be done: find out just what had happened to his daughter; identify her body at the morgue. That gruesome task should have fallen to Sheila's mother, as being more familiar with her recent appearance, but Yeadings had thought it inadvisable due to her state of shock.

His breakfast lay heavy on his stomach. He wasn't sure now that he should have come. There would be Vanessa to confront. Or, more precisely, she would confront him.

It was grim enough, without her histrionics. Somewhere in the paper under his hand there would be a headline about a woman's murder. And perhaps two or three paragraphs on an inner page. That's what his only child's life was reduced to.

★   ★   ★

97

DI Salmon had covered the briefing competently enough, steely-eyed and untrusting of his audience. Yeadings doubted that any of those present who were used to Mott's painstaking precision and openness to others' ideas, would warm to the present treatment.

'I'm expecting a visit from the dead woman's father,' he told the DI as they broke up. 'Would you care to be in on it?'

'I've read what the mother said about him. They've been estranged for nearly thirty years. He'll have nothing relevant to offer.'

'A civil gesture,' Yeadings murmured.

'Just as you like,' meaning the opposite.

Clearly the new man would expect his SIO to deal with the niceties while keeping his hands off the active operation.

Beaumont, overhearing the exchange, grinned fiercely inside. The Boss's mildness wouldn't fool anyone who knew him. He'd put money on him giving Salmon enough rope to tie them all in knots, and then come along with his Houdini fingers to sort it good and proper. It would be quite some entertainment to watch.

'Can I sit in on the interview?' he asked innocently.

'Don't forget I need you on hand when Childe's warrant turns up,' Salmon answered, overriding Yeadings.

'You heard what the DI said,' the Boss cautioned. Not by a flicker of an eyelash would he give cause to think he undermined the new man's authority.

The espresso machine in the superintendent's office had just begun its burble when a PC knocked at the door and asked leave to usher in their visitor. 'A timely arrival, sir,' Yeadings greeted him.

He introduced himself and his DS. 'Have a seat. Do you take cream and sugar?'

8

Dr Gabriel Fenner was tall and spare of flesh, his gaunt features grey under a bare, domed forehead. The deep-set eyes were shadowed by bushy brows, and harshly etched lines double-bracketed a beaky nose above an unruly, grizzled beard. He was dressed slackly, like a gentleman farmer who has seen more prosperous days. A craggy man in shaggy tweeds was how Yeadings mentally filed his physical appearance.

He folded himself on to the chair indicated, and even then there was still a lot of him left protruding. He must, Beaumont reckoned, be six feet four in height. If, as it seemed, with brains as well, then Nature had been generous indeed.

Yeadings had already expressed condolences over the phone, and the visitor expected now to get down to action. Yet he still hoped for a let-out. 'Is there no chance of mistaken identity, superintendent?'

'I'm afraid not, sir. One of my sergeants recognised Miss Winter. Over several weeks they've been near neighbours. But we still need you for the official identification.'

Fenner nodded. 'I should like to speak with him afterwards.' He looked questioningly at Beaumont.

'It's DS Rosemary Zyczynski you need then. She's elsewhere at present, working on the case. I'm sure she will value any information you can offer her concerning your daughter, sir.'

'Ah, a woman. But I'd been thinking of what information she could give *me*. I knew little enough of Sheila: only what she chose to tell me in her annual letters, and now the opportunity is — has passed.' He moved stiffly in his chair. 'Superintendent, I should prefer to get this business at the mortuary over as soon as possible.'

'Of course, sir. I'll take you there myself.'

A phone rang. DI Salmon announced that the search warrant had been procured, so Beaumont should proceed to the garden centre and serve it on Barry Childe. Reluctantly the DS detached himself.

In the car park, as Yeadings advanced on his Rover to activate the door lock, Dr Fenner admitted flatly, 'I couldn't locate a visitors' area. Will my car be all right where I left it?' He indicated an ancient but well-kept Riley saloon.

Despite the vacant spaces for lesser mortals, Yeadings observed that he had chosen to take the place clearly reserved for an Assistant Chief Constable. 'Perfectly,' he told him, hiding a smile. It seemed the visitor had no false modesty.

On arriving at the hospital Fenner made no move to leave the car, although previously impatient to have the distasteful business over. Yeadings, acutely aware of how he too would feel in the circumstances, allowed him time. Eventually the man reached for the door handle and got out.

Warned ahead by phone, the hospital chaplain was waiting for them inside. Fenner darted a sharp glance at the man's dog collar but bit off the remark that it almost provoked. The clergyman saw this and stepped back into anonymity.

The chapel itself was interdenominational. A simple beech cross on one wall was balanced on the one opposite by an illuminated crescent. Yeadings wondered if behind the blue velvet curtain there might lurk a Buddha, or Shiva, or Ganesh the Hindu elephant god. Inclusiveness was today's ruling political virtue.

There was no need to pull back any sheet. Sheila Winter's body lay on its back under an embroidered coverlet that reached to the base of her throat. There were no visible injuries. Her blond hair was tidily dressed over the flat pillow, her face calm. She might have been asleep in bed. Yeadings walked away and left Fenner alone with her. His nod and the tight-voiced 'yes' had indicated all the superintendent needed to know.

Fenner emerged into the grey morning light some ten minutes later and crossed to where Yeadings waited in the car. 'Now what else do you want of me?' he asked harshly.

Yeadings made no answer, turned the car towards the Caversham road and made for Ashbourne House. Dr Fenner sat forward as they came up the drive with the house in clear view against a background of misted trees. 'Yes,' he said. 'Sheila mentioned last year that she intended to sell the London place. She needed to be nearer her work, and believed it would be safer.'

'Safer?' Yeadings was alerted by the word. Had she been conscious of impending danger?

'Safer for her mother.' He didn't elaborate on this.

'It's a beautiful house,' Yeadings said to fill the gap. 'I remember when it was a family home. Later it was turned into a private school, but that closed down after six or seven years. It was briefly a nursing home. Since then it's been quite sensitively converted, into four single-bedroom flats downstairs and three larger ones on the first floor. Your daughter's is up there, facing south and east: front and right side as we look at it.'

Fenner nodded. 'Is she still here — Vanessa?'

'With a neighbour downstairs. I have a key if you would like to go in and see your daughter's rooms. My men will have finished there.'

'Later, I think. I want first to visit the garden centre. It was so much her special creation. She wrote to me in detail about her plans for it.'

Yeadings had no idea how far the intended search at Greenvale had progressed, but he called up Control and was told that Beaumont's men were there and the management co-operating.

'I've never been there,' he said, 'but I'll be glad to take you.'

They found the place closed down, with tubular steel barriers padlocked across the entrance. In the car park several lorries and vans had been allowed so far and their further access blocked. Among the drivers wrangling with a security officer, Fenner recognised the man who had shared his table at breakfast.

'Are your men halting deliveries?' he demanded.

'The centre's own security men, it seems.'

Yeadings called Beaumont on his mobile phone. 'We're out front. Meet us inside the checkouts.'

As Yeadings showed his ID the barrier was opened. Behind them a surge of protesting delivery men with a sprinkling of reporters was waved back by the man on duty.

'Their stuff is perishable and they need to make further deliveries,' Fenner reasoned. 'Why can't they dump it all in a cleared space and get back on the road?'

'Why not indeed? We'll have a word with the manager.' He turned to Beaumont who appeared from beyond the checkouts. 'Is Barry Childe here?'

The DS was smouldering. 'No. He left straight after my earlier visit and he's not been back. It could be that he's removed files from the office. I'm trying to get sense out of his secretary.'

'So who's in charge?'

'Supposedly I am, but there's nobody to represent the business side.'

'As family,' Fenner said slowly, 'I'm willing to authorise acceptance of the deliveries, under surveillance. Can you get somebody trusty here to oversee movements and check invoices? If the superintendent has no objection, that is.'

'None, provided that nothing is removed,'

Yeadings allowed. He left Beaumont to organise it and led Fenner through a vast glasshouse full of gardening merchandise. An arrow pointed towards the Greenvale office. Inside they found a plump young woman whose flushed face witnessed to the tussle she had just had with the DS.

'Can I help you?' she demanded in a challenging tone.

Yeadings explained who they were and that Dr Fenner wished to see round his daughter's garden centre.

Immediately she softened. 'Well, her private office is through there. And can I say how very sorry I am. We all are. I can't think what it must be like for you. Here we're just knocked all of a heap.'

Fenner thanked her and declined her offer of coffee. He grasped the doorknob to his daughter's office, then released it. 'Someone's been at the lock.' He pointed to the splintered woodwork. 'When did this happen?'

The girl's face coloured afresh. 'About three quarters of an hour ago. Mr Childe needed some papers and he didn't have a key. Apart from the cleaners', Miss Winter's was the only one to her private office.'

'So he broke in?'

'I'm afraid so.'

'And did he find what he was after?'

106

Yeadings asked mildly.

'I couldn't say, sir. I wasn't here at the time.'

'Why was that?'

'I went for Mr Childe's cappuccino.'

'You went or were sent?'

'Mr Childe said he needed it early because he had to go off and see a local grower. But he must have been in a terrible hurry, because he didn't stay to drink it. It's still where I left it, on Miss Winter's desk. I told all this to the sergeant.'

'Are we to understand that you didn't see Mr Childe leave?'

'No. I mean yes, you are to understand. No, I didn't.'

'Thank you . . . ' Yeadings glanced at the name-tag on her lapel. ' . . . Miss Dunster,' he added as Beaumont reappeared in the doorway. 'That's all. Can you find something to do, across where the deliveries are being made? Invoices to collect, and so on. We need to check that everything is as it should be in here.'

Fenner uneasily watched the girl leave. 'Don't you need her to go through the files and see what's missing? The man obviously was up to something in here on his own.'

'I don't think he bothered with the files. He didn't need to,' Yeadings said. Hands in pockets, he was peering at the surface of the polished teak desk. In its centre stood a vase with an arrangement of small, star-shaped dahlias. A light dusting of pollen from them was smeared as if some object had been dragged forward beside it, leaving a clear rectangle where the wood was bare.

'I think Miss Winter had a laptop computer. Did she write to you with a pen, in type or print, sir?'

'Always in printed form,' he said. 'That's how my students turn their work in to me now. I use one of the things myself for my lectures.'

'Yes, it's almost universal. Let's hope your daughter used a password and that Childe wasn't a party to it. Beaumont, try opening up the company computer in the outer office. I doubt if Miss Dunster had time this morning to fiddle with denying access.'

They all went back to the outer office where they found the screen-saver blinking away with shooting stars.

'What do I go for?' Beaumont asked. He seated himself and a single click brought back a list of accounts for garden furniture and barbecue equipment.

'Hit Save and bring up Personnel,' Yeadings ordered. 'I want Childe's present address; not the phoney one his parole officer's got.'

Beaumont flicked at the keyboard and they all leaned forward as the cursor started running down the alphabetical list of employees. 'Here we are. Childe, Barry, entry dated three months back. Address — 11 Montague Lane, Marlow. D'you want me to pick him up, sir?'

'Him and whatever he's got that he shouldn't have,' said Yeadings grimly. 'Put him in an interview room. He can cool his heels until I get back to base. Dr Fenner and I will stay on for a little while longer. There could be quite a lot that's of interest here.'

They walked back to where Miss Dunster was watching the unloading at Goods Inwards. There was everything from winter pansy plugs, for potting up, to full-grown ornamental trees; plastic tunnels; reels of hosing; cultivators and motor-driven hedge-trimmers. 'There's a lot of capital expenditure here,' Yeadings remarked. 'Was your daughter a wealthy woman?'

'Comfortable, I'd say, though she never discussed figures. She worked strictly to season, avoiding overstocking, which meant being slightly ahead of the market and clearing goods by deadlines which she set up herself. She had a good brain for business.'

'So whose will all this be now?'

'There's bank involvement, of course. It's a

limited liability company and she held twelve per cent of the shares. I have forty. That dates from way back when she needed help to get off the ground. Originally there was a small-holding here which produced vegetables and cut flowers. She waited to buy that out until she'd already taken over the adjacent timber yard when the owner went broke. There was some opposition from his family when they realised how she meant to develop the land, but she got permission to build and expand.'

'You know a lot about someone you haven't seen for nearly twenty years.'

'I told you. She wrote about her plans in detail. She needed a sounding-board and maybe it helped that in a way I was a stranger, yet trustworthy. We neither of us went in for cosy relationships.'

'I was wondering about that. She never married. Do you know if there was anyone special in her life?'

'Nobody close that I know of. But she wasn't celibate, superintendent. Any more than I am.'

'Thank you. Did she confide whether she had ever made a will?'

'It wasn't a subject that came up; but knowing how she was, I'm sure she wouldn't overlook precautions to protect her world. In

110

her life this project took the place of a child, you see. An only, and very cherished, firstborn.'

They had walked right through the covered part of the centre and now stood looking over gently sloping terraces set out in squares, with paths between long benches of potted plants and tubs of greenery. Along the right-hand side was a large heated glasshouse with vivid, exotic blooms on show. An arrow indicated that through this was the entrance to the restaurant, closed today except for the vending machines with the staff's hot drinks and sandwiches.

'In summer,' Fenner said, 'the terrace beyond there is opened for meals too, with a view of the trial fields below where they grow things like roses, delphiniums and carnations. It's very popular for parties and weddings.'

He stood, hands deep in jacket pockets, staring gloomily. 'Everything is so like she described it. I feel as though I've been here before.'

'Are you sure, sir, you weren't?'

He turned to meet the superintendent's eyes and his own were cavernous. 'No,' he said simply. 'That wasn't the way we were.'

But perhaps, Yeadings thought, he wishes now that they'd done things differently.

'I think I'm ready to see where she lived,'

said Fenner, forcing himself to a new briskness. 'It should be possible, since you say Vanessa's away in a neighbour's apartment. I've one thing to ask you first, though. Sheila must have been caught at some time on these security cameras. Perhaps, when you've examined the films, you would save me a photograph of her.'

$$\star \quad \star \quad \star$$

Montague Lane, Marlow, was little more than a mud track. It trickled gently downhill, with scrub land towards the riverside, and a short row of Victorian cottages on the other. Number eleven was the last before the lane petered out into a rutted field. A Yamaha motorbike was leaning against the front wall of yellow brick.

Beaumont reversed his Toyota and left it blocking the escape route. When he could see nobody through the poky front window he applied himself to the bell. And kept his finger there. After a short wait the door was snatched open and Childe's belligerent face scowled down at him.

'Bloody hell!' he was greeted.

'Yes, me again. Can I come in?'

The man wavered, then past Beaumont's shoulder glimpsed a uniformed officer inside the Toyota. He drew back and allowed Beaumont to squeeze past, heading for the rear quarters. There was a light on in the poky kitchen. A laptop computer was open on the table beside a plate of congealing beans on toast.

'Brought your work home with you, then,' Beaumont remarked amiably.

'Little chance of getting any done, if your lot were coming to swarm over everything.'

'A pity, though. It left nobody in charge at the centre. There were decisions to be made, questions answered.' Hands in pockets, Beaumont leaned over the computer screen. 'You don't seem to have got very far with it. Perhaps that's because you don't have Ms Winter's password. It is her personal laptop, I imagine?'

Childe looked uncomfortable, hesitated, then opted for bluff. 'Of course it is. I need to take over where she left off. It's all up in the air without someone to direct the business. How otherwise will suppliers' accounts get paid or orders flow?'

'You weren't in total control then? What exactly was your function as manager?'

'I had charge of landscaping contracts. Once the garden plan was agreed with the customer I costed it; made out the order for stonework, decking, building materials, plants, trees, water features; collected the stuff; arranged for the labour and transport; then oversaw the work. Then there was all the jobbing our gardeners do for private customers. You know: lawn trimming, pruning, planting, tree-lopping. And there's council work we've taken on besides, now that everything's going out to private tender.'

'Very impressive. I suppose all of that is on the computer I saw Miss Dunster using when I arrived?'

'Most of it, but . . . '

'You were saying?'

'I didn't cover the ordering or opening contracts. You saw what chaos it was this morning, with all that stuff coming in and her not there.'

'You mean Ms Winter? She kept the money-handling side of the business in her own hands?'

'All the paperwork for it, and the correspondence, yes.'

Beaumont's wooden puppet-face took on a look of innocent wonder. 'D'you know, I find all this fascinating. Perhaps you'd like to show me how you would tackle it. I've often thought I ought to do a course in computer skills.'

'I can't.' Childe tried to conceal his frustration. 'I need the right password to access the programme.'

114

'Which only Ms Winter would have known? I see.' Beaumont allowed enlightenment to spread across his features. 'So her being dead is a bit of a nuisance. But she'll have told it to someone, for safety's sake. Who at Greenvale, do you think, would have had that confided to them? Miss Dunster? No? Well, who was the unfortunate lady closest to?'

Childe scowled. 'Nobody. She wasn't one to have close friends.'

Beaumont was regarding him with the baffling insouciance of the host of a million-pound quiz programme asking, 'Do you want to ask the audience?'

He let a silence build between them, then, 'I just happen to know a computer expert,' he said at last. 'A policeman. Which is lucky. We'll take the laptop to him. And as I said, there are questions to be answered.'

He closed the computer and tucked it under his arm. 'I can give you a lift to the nick. Your motorbike will be quite safe here, if we leave the constable to look after things.'

It seemed for a moment that Childe would object as the uniformed man climbed out of the car and at a nod from Beaumont strolled in through the open front door.

'All right, Mr Childe?' Beaumont invited perkily.

He had no choice.

115

9

At Ashbourne House the Winters' flat had been left open. As Yeadings and Fenner reached the upstairs gallery DS Zyczynski appeared, framed in the doorway. 'I was just going to close up. Can I leave the keys with you, sir?'

'Yes, but don't go. Dr Fenner would like a word with you. Sir, this is another of my sergeants, Rosemary Zyczynski, your daughter's neighbour. Let's go inside.'

Z led the two men into a large, square room furnished as a lounge in peach, pale green and white. The sofas and chairs were covered in soft, ivory leather, their voluptuous lines exaggerated by the addition of shiny satin cushions — square, round and cylindrical with gold-tasselled bolster ends. At the two long windows on the front wall and a third on the adjacent one, swags of peach-coloured taffeta dipped with heavy, corded fringes. The matching curtains were looped back by thick, silk ropes.

Fenner stood under a crystal chandelier, his lanky frame just clearing its lowest cut-glass drops. 'Vanessa's empress style,' he commented with a little twist to the lips. 'Some things never change.'

Which included his austerity, Yeadings guessed. But at some point there must have been a break in it, or he'd never have become involved with Vanessa. The man obviously regretted that lapse now, perhaps was ashamed of the brief weakness. Yet could a little of the original tenderness remain? Perhaps there would be a chance to find out.

He went across to look out at the verandah and nodded, taking in the stone bench, the tubs with twin miniature cypresses, bay, lavender, hebes and pungent-leafed dwarf chrysanthemums. 'This was Sheila's part,' he said. 'And where is the looking-glass?'

Yeadings looked blank.

'There's a mirror at the end,' Rosemary explained, unlocking the window and stepping through. 'There, before my balcony starts. Sheila had it fitted to the dividing screen, to double the garden effect.'

He paced both ways, examining the pots and creepers, then peering over to get a glimpse of the arched pediment above the central front entrance, faintly smiling as if he recognised objects he was familiar with.

'This is her writing-desk,' Z told him when he came in and locked the window behind him. He went across to open the lid. 'Tidy, of course.'

'We tried to put everything back as it was. But we've kept her address book.'

'Yes, I suppose you would need to go through things. Did you find anything that could account for what happened?'

Z glanced across at the superintendent. 'Disappointingly little,' he admitted. 'But then we are hoping that any personal information will be kept in her laptop computer. Z, did you ever notice Miss Winter carrying one in from the car, or out to it again?'

'Yes, she usually had one with her. It was as much part of her as the business suit.'

'She was a power-dresser?' Fenner asked, faintly smiling, but Yeadings was frowning over Z's answer.

'If she nearly always had it with her, why was it left at the garden centre when she came home that last evening?'

'Possibly because she intended going out. She knew she'd have no time to work. And anyway on Sunday she'd be back in the office. That was the centre's busiest time of the week.'

'That seems a safe assumption,' he said, nodding at the girl. 'Now you have only to find out where she went. And with whom.'

'Would you like to see the rest of the flat?' Rosemary asked. 'There are two bedrooms and a third which Sheila turned into her study, plus the kitchen and bathroom. Our experts have finished looking around here.'

'Just her bedroom and study.'

Both rooms were quite severe, which hadn't surprised Zyczynski. She remembered Sheila at Beattie's dinner party talking of little but her work; and again when she entertained Childe here, bringing the conversation down to levels he might be more comfortable with. She hadn't seemed a complicated person and, although brusque, not unkind. It couldn't have been easy still to be tied to her mother, particularly since the older woman was more than a little dotty. Or was that a harsh assumption, and she was perhaps just eccentric?

As if to illustrate her question, there came a sudden, theatrical interruption.

'*Why*, may I ask, this *invasion* of my *home*?' And Vanessa was there in the doorway, rigidly outraged, her voice rising in scale and passion to the tragically broken final syllable.

'Joan,' Fenner greeted her laconically, 'how are you? But perhaps I don't need to enquire.'

For a brief instant she was deflated by use of the despised name but she rallied magnificently. '*You*! I should have known you would come to — to *mock* me in my grief. *I — have — lost — my — daughter!*'

He was looking at her with a kind of distanced pity. 'I too.'

Yeadings made a little throat-clearing noise and moved between them. 'Why don't we sit down and talk? It must be some time since you both met. Mrs Winter, would you like Miss Zyczynski to make you some tea?'

Vanessa swung her head to take in the two spectators. Her mouth tightened like a drawstring purse. She closed her eyes. 'Coffee,' she said faintly but firmly. Then she swept across her drawing-room, sank on a sofa and lay back among the cushions.

'Everything all right?' demanded an abrupt voice from the corridor as the two men were finding seats. Beattie stomped in to stand there, hands on hips, staring at the other woman. 'You went off without a word. I wasn't sure you'd make it upstairs on your own after downing all that gin.'

'Rosemary's gone to make us all coffee,' Yeadings said to cover Vanessa's recoil.

Beattie picked up the hint. 'Right, love. I'll take over in the kitchen and send her back in.' While Vanessa moaned gently Beattie and the DS exchanged places. Then silence fell.

When eventually the tray arrived with a

large cafetière and cups for them all, Vanessa sat upright and waved a gracious hand at Zyczynski. 'You pour, Rosemary.'

She turned on Fenner. 'You see what I am reduced to.' Her arm swept widely to include the room and the world outside. 'I am utterly alone, with my lovely home sold to strangers. I am abandoned here in the country among aliens who cannot care whether I live or die. And, indeed, by now neither do I.'

'Sugar and cream?' demanded Beattie looming over her with a second silver tray, smaller than the other.

'Both.'

'Give it to her black,' Fenner advised. 'Now that I'm here we need to talk. Properly. Not drivel.'

Vanessa gave a sob and glanced helplessly at Yeadings as if to say, *you see how he behaves to me!*

'So,' her husband said, leaning towards her, 'what was Sheila up to, that someone had to kill her?'

It had the intended shocking effect. Vanessa ceased acting and shook her head. 'How should I know? She never confided in me. And there is no call to be so crude. If you had fulfilled your part in her life and been there for her as a father, we might have been a normal, fond family. And I should not have

121

lost my two darling children.'

He stayed impassive. 'We needn't waste time on all that again. You know we are both impossible to live with. Sheila was the only good thing to come from our misalliance. And now she's gone.'

He remained silent a moment then addressed her squarely. 'I am determined to find out exactly what happened, and I expect you to do all you can to help.'

'Well, if you are asking for my *help* . . . '

Fenner didn't reply. 'We're all asking,' Z said gently. 'Nobody must be allowed to get away with brutality like that.'

Vanessa looked genuinely crushed, then her mouth took on a petulant twist. 'How can anything I say be of any use? I had no idea where she went or who she was with. She could have had a dozen lovers and she'd never have said a word about it to me. I only know that she left me alone here all day, every day, and sometimes of an evening too. I have to use taxis to go shopping or to a film or the hairdressers. And it isn't like London where we could always find something interesting going on, and amusing people to be with.'

She turned violently on Fenner. 'I shan't stay!' She almost screamed it at him, as though he was forcing it on her.

An embarrassed silence was broken by

Yeadings clearing his throat. 'It must have been quiet for you,' he offered, 'but your daughter did invite people here. Was there anyone you got to know quite well?'

She stared back at him, affronted. 'They were all people from *work*. I had nothing in common with them.'

Fenner was regarding her sardonically, suppressing the temptation to remind her that the stage too was a workplace and she'd deigned to grace that in her more active days. But he said nothing.

Yeadings caught Z's eye and gave an almost imperceptible nod. She picked up on it. 'Mrs Winter, Vanessa, would you tell us how Sheila was the last time you saw her. What time of day would it have been?'

Vanessa looked startled. 'Well, evening, of course. It was just the same as usual. She would come home after work, have a meal . . . '

'You would eat together?'

'In the dining-room, yes. Mostly she would bring something in, which one of her chefs had prepared. She seldom bothered cooking since it was just for her and me.'

'But that last evening — Saturday — was there any difference? What did you eat?'

Vanessa put a hand to her head. 'I don't remember. How can you expect it of me?

Some meat or fish, and salad, I expect. She was always bringing back salad. Or vegetables.'

'There was some leftover pineapple gâteau in the fridge,' Beattie said. 'Did you both have some of that?'

'I suppose so. Yes, I remember the pineapple.' But she sounded uncertain, almost fearful.

She shook her head. 'Look, I'm not sure now that Sheila ate anything. I had mine in my bedroom.'

Yeadings took up the questioning again. 'We need to know what your daughter was wearing when she left here Saturday night.'

Vanessa looked stricken, turning her head away and covering her eyes with a trembling hand. Her attempt to control herself appeared genuine. She fought for words. 'All this — has been a terrible shock. I'm not up to being pestered. Can't it wait until tomorrow? I need to rest. Not that I'm likely to sleep at all.'

Fenner stood up. 'Superintendent?'

They filed out, with Zyczynski at the rear, murmuring their goodbyes. Only Beattie remained beside the woman, who lay back with closed eyes. 'I'll fetch your nightie and a glass of water. Then you can take one of those capsules the doctor left with me.'

124

'No!' Vanessa shouted, starting up. 'You can't *all* leave me alone. I need somebody here. Run after my husband. He can have Sheila's room tonight. He doesn't have to go back to Cambridge right away.'

Beattie had her doubts, but went after the others to speak to him. When she returned to report that, unsurprisingly, he declined the offer, she found Vanessa nestling up to her mobile phone. She frowned as Beattie gave her the message. 'It doesn't matter. I think I shall be better on my own after all. Just leave the sleeping pills. I'll take some later. Goodnight, Mrs . . . er, Mrs . . . '

'Weyman,' Beattie said firmly. 'I'm Beattie Weyman, as you well know. And I'll leave just one, like I said.'

★   ★   ★

Beaumont was taking Barry Childe into the nick at Henley-on-Thames, and with every mile was able to appreciate in his driving mirror how the man's unease took firmer grip. Once arrived there he arranged for an interview room to be made free and left him to stew under the observation of a uniformed constable.

He helped himself to an unidentifiable hot drink from the vending machine and required a personable young WPC in Control to contact the man he'd left at the Marlow house. 'Anything of interest?' he asked hopefully when they were connected.

'Not so far as I've seen so far. There's not much furniture here: the minimum for getting by. I've looked around downstairs; just started on his bedroom and it's pretty bare, like you'd expect for someone recently out on parole.'

'What about the other upstairs rooms?'

'Second bedroom's stripped, except for some DIY equipment and a load of electrical junk.'

'What kind of electrical?'

'Several convector heaters, cables, ducting, lights and so on. Funny thing is — '

'Go on. I'm ready to laugh.'

'Well, there are eight separate double sockets. Looks like they're new. And there's a smell. Sort of disinfectant. Everything's very clean.'

'There's a loft, isn't there?'

'Yes. It's got a hinged panel. There are black marks where it's been prodded shut. I'll see where the pole is for opening up.'

The DS waited while further thumps announced that PC Dennis was investigating the small hot cupboard on the landing. Eventually a cry of success and the metallic slithering of an aluminium ladder descending; then the scrape of constabulary boots on bouncing rungs.

'Gawd,' came the reverential voice at last. 'It's like Santa's grotto up here. Never seen insulation like it. Everything's covered in shiny aluminium foil; the walls, the roof, everything. And the space is huge; goes over the whole of the house.'

'What about the floor?'

'Bare boards, fresh-scrubbed. Hang on, though. It looks as if — '

There came the sound of a heavy object being dragged across wooden planks, then an excited, 'Yeah, I thought so. There's a loose one here. I'll get it up and see what's underneath.'

Beaumont waited, continuing to sip the anonymous brown liquid. Then the constable came on again, his glee barely disguised. 'There's a space about eighteen inches deep, with a sort of guttering fitted. And there's all sorts of junk down there besides. I'm going after a large cardboard box. Nearly got it. Wait a mo.'

There followed muffled thumps and slidings, then a ripping noise as the treasure was broken open. Silence, followed by a disappointed, 'Thought we'd really got something there. It's just more rolls of

127

kitchen foil. Rolls and rolls of the stuff. With these he could roast enough turkeys for a whole town. What you laughing at, sarge?'

'Not poultry, you wally. His line's horticulture. Only he hasn't got the project up and running yet. We're a tad too early. Think man: a well-heated loft in a cottage out in the sticks, the walls and roof insulated with foil, and no doubt a sprinkler system ready to be fitted. Heat, light, moisture and secrecy: everything needed to produce a good crop.'

Light at last broke on Constable Dennis. 'Gawd. You mean cannabis? He's set it up to grow his own grass indoors!'

'Wouldn't be the first time. But not just for himself. He must have access to wholesale seed supply. And who's in a better position to find a market for the finished product? Keep your hands in your pockets from now on. I'll send the fingerprint lads out to you. I want dabs off everything, with it all photographed as found.'

Beaumont made the necessary arrangements and decided he'd need to play it canny from now on. More particularly so since there was a new gaffer aboard in the person of DI Salmon, who could seize on the discovery as his own. A call now to the Boss wouldn't come amiss. He'd report progress in the shape of a request for advice on present handling of the suspect.

First he used his mobile to call Salmon and managed a couple of sentences before running his fingers along the teeth of his pocket comb and complaining in staccato bursts of interrupted speech that contact was breaking up. He left the DI alerted to action but uninformed on any detail.

Next he called Yeadings who, having passed Dr Fenner on to DI Salmon, was about to clear his desk and make for home. Beaumont succinctly explained his actions regarding Sheila Winter's manager and the discoveries at the man's home address.

'Thought I'd keep him here overnight for questioning,' he said, and waited for the superintendent's comment.

'With what charge in mind?'

'There's always theft of the dead woman's laptop computer.'

'Yes,' Yeadings agreed. 'That should do for a start. If you do decide to charge him clear it with your DI.'

Yeadings made a note of the call in his daybook and reached for his coat. He wasn't dissatisfied with the way things were going, but it seemed he wasn't finished with dead bodies for the day. Cruising past Chesham Bois his fog lights picked out an ominous shape huddled in mid-road. Sighing aloud, he pulled up, got out and went forward, torch in hand.

It was a young deer, male, dead, but still warm to the hand. The throat showed bloody lacerations where some vehicle had struck it. He stowed the torch in a capacious pocket, took the beast by its back legs and gently dragged it to the grass verge. Then he pulled out his mobile phone and settled to advising the appropriate authority.

The local nick informed him that since he'd already removed it from the highway they were exonerated: the responsibility now lay with the District Council. A sleepy voice there offered to connect him with Environmental Health; who in turn passed him to Waste Disposal.

Poor little creature, sweetly pretty, even in death. What a way to end. He'd have done better to drop it off at some wayside pub with outbuildings, where it could hang for a couple of weeks, then feature as venison on the menu. That way someone could have pleasure of it.

A souring end to an otherwise encouraging day. Now the fog, which had thickened again, seemed to creep inside the collar of his waxed jacket, extending cold fingers down his spine.

He switched on the car radio. A forecaster was predicting that misty conditions would continue for another two days, with the addition of ground frost overnight. He climbed back into the warmth of the car, and sighed.

In the open-air pool back in Madeira, he could still have been swimming.

10

Neil Raynes zapped down the TV's volume, padded to the door and listened. The car had purred past. From the landing window he caught only stabs of its headlights between the trees screening the row of lock-up garages. All six made the same indistinguishable clang on closing. Impossible to know whose it was.

He went to sit on the third stair down, waiting, ready to vanish when he recognised the top of Marty's head. A lingering smell of roast pork reached him from one of the downstairs apartments. He guessed that would have been Beattie Weyman going the whole hog with parmesan parsnips and baked potatoes. She never did anything by halves, and now she'd taken on Samaritan duties for Milady Winter.

Seconds went by, then a key in the lock and the back door opening. It wasn't Marty. Just that owl Wormsley, glancing up with his crooked grin to catch him watching. Neil grunted, stood and retreated upstairs.

He roamed the apartment, uneasy. Sign

132

after sign had suggested Marty was considering a new commission. It was like recognising
a fatal disease where each dreaded symptom
emerged one after another to create a dead
certainty. There had been suspicious phone
calls, with the door firmly closed between the
two of them; sealed packages in the safe;
spare reading-specs left permanently by the
computer work-station. (Marty despised
surfing the net unless it was to wise up for
some specific job.) Everything indicated he
could be away again in a matter of days. Neil
knew it was too soon: he wasn't ready.

Marty had been late returning from
London for three nights now, with an extra
576 miles on the car's clock since four days
back. Neil scorned to divide by six to make
guesses where he'd been heading. In any case,
over that period he might have made only two
return trips, suggesting a venue just some
hundred and forty odd miles distant. Which
could mean anywhere in North Wales,
Lancashire or Humberside.

Not that it mattered where the jobs
originated. The shit bit was where he would
be sent. Seven times out of ten it was the
fucking Middle East, or Pakistan, even once
Indochina. With hellholes like that, if the
opposition got wind of him, Marty could end
down a well shaft or with a knife between his

133

shoulder blades; simply disappear, or be clapped in some fetid prison without trial; and the fucking Foreign Office not bothered because he wasn't officially there and they took him for some useless bum meddling in things he didn't understand.

The US or Europe, Neil thought, wasn't so bad. There, if Marty went overdue, he might at least be traceable.

Whatever happened, he, Neil, was expected to stay stumm, instantly switch to the discipline phase, stick it out alone. This time he wasn't sure he could make it. Marty being on hand allowed him to be himself, go wild a bit. Nearby, as safety net, Marty was Batman to his own quirky Robin. If things went right off the rails Marty would always see him right.

But, alone too long, having to act the hero that he wasn't, he got this shitty fear that the past might catch up and swallow him. Marty had to be close in case that happened.

This new place, being among strangers and with a job of his own, had made him relax, so maybe he'd gone over the top a bit. Now he might have to face any outcome. And there'd been mistakes at work: all those drugs around, and locks that wouldn't challenge a two-month old. So he'd joined the others to horse about. No real harm done yet, but it left him exposed. Play the *idiot savant* and they'd expect him to go further, just when he needed to cut his losses and clam up.

And now a further hazard: this house was crawling with police because of the Sheila Winter thing. He was already paranoid, feeling that the residents had begun to regard him sideways. Beattie Weyman — little, bright-eyed, red squirrel — was no dozer, and her girl, Rosemary, had an amused way of glancing at you as though a guy was transparent. He'd told Marty that, as a sort of joke, and he'd laughed. He'd accused him of hot flushes because she was a doll and he lusted after her. Maybe he did too, in a way.

Whatever, it was another complication he didn't need right now. Added to all the rest, it made it no moment for Marty to walk out on him.

He turned from the window and made for the other's dressing-room, rolled open the wardrobe doors and ran his hands along the rails of hangers. There were no obvious additions or subtractions. The lightweight stuff was still there, but it didn't mean Marty hadn't bought more. He kicked at the stack of travel cases and they yielded with an empty feel. He would have checked inside the gun cabinet but he didn't know where the keys were hidden.

When Marty did, almost silently, materialise, Neil was still waiting. It was past 2a.m. and he was offered no apology.

The man unlaced his shoes on the stairs and carried them in. 'Still up? What shift are you on this week?'

'Earlies. But what's that to you?'

Chisholm gave him the one-eyebrow response, coolly detached.

The boy swallowed hard. 'You're setting something up.' It came out as accusation.

'As you said yourself, 'What's that to you?'. We're not married, Neil. Lighten up.' He walked almost wearily across to an armchair, dropping shoes and backpack at his feet as he sat. 'Remember we have to eat. So there's no choice, unless you want to become main breadwinner.'

'That's bloody cheap.' Neil knew he wouldn't have reminded him he was the charity boy if he hadn't been half-dead on his feet. He dug himself out of the nest he'd made and straightened. 'Had anything to eat?'

'I stopped off on the way for a hot dog and coffee made from fag ends. Is there any real food?'

'I did chicken suprêmes with char-grilled peppers and shallots. You want it reheated?'

'That would be good. A tray in bed? I'll

take a shower first.'

Neil stomped off to the kitchen. So he'd been right. It was out in the open now. Or as open as it ever got. The brush-off meant only one thing: a new job. That was the sum total of what he'd be told, unless there was a minor part in it for him back at base. It was a shitty way to be treated, but what else was on offer?

He fixed the meal, covered it and took it through; folded Marty's dropped under-clothes ready for the linen basket. The contents of his pockets were already laid out on the bedside table and gave no clue to where he'd been.

Sardonically Neil turned back the bed's duvet in a precise triangle. Might as well do the whole Abigail act. Then he went off to his own room and partly shut the door. Eventually he heard the shower cut off and the susurration of Marty's cord dressing-gown in the corridor outside. He had paused to knock but didn't come in. ' 'Night, Neil. Thanks. See you in the morning.'

It *was* bloody morning. The boy stayed silent, then relented sullenly. 'I'm asleep!' There was an answering laugh. 'Right, kiddo!' A door quietly closed.

Neil Raynes beat his pillow. So he sounded childish. Well, wasn't that how the universal hero always saw him? Shit, shit! Later he'd phone in sick, take the day off and get thoroughly pissed. Let Marty see how he wasn't ready to be left yet.

★ ★ ★

By the first light of Tuesday, Rosemary watched cars leaving under her front window. First came Wormsley's sand-coloured Peugeot, followed a few minutes later by Chisholm's blue Saab, each with a single occupant. Then the 'corporal' arrived on his Vespa, left it at the rear and collected Major Phillips in his yellow Triumph. Last, at 8.37 am, Miss Barnes drove off to school.

That left only young Raynes, Beattie, Vanessa Winter and herself in the house until the two cleaners turned up at nine, after off-loading their children at the village school. Her instructions were to extract what information on the dead woman she could while still appearing to be a neighbour with a free day off work. She'd few enough residents to work on.

When 8.50a.m brought a familiar pick-up truck with Frank Perrin's teaky elbow protruding from the driver's open window Z struck Beattie off the list for a couple of hours at least. Since Vanessa was no early riser, that left no choice but the Raynes boy. She looked around for something breakable to qualify her for a helpless-little-woman appeal.

Neil was in pyjamas when he opened the door to her ring. 'Sorry to visit so early,' she said, smiling, 'but I've really come on the scrounge.'

He took in her casual clothes and assumed that, like him, she was skiving. 'What do you need?' It sounded abrupt, which made him more conscious of his own unwashed, unshaven state.

'It's not urgent. Just something I'm not sure how to tackle. It takes a man, I guess.' Mentally she crossed her fingers behind her back, hoping he wouldn't pick up a false note.

He'd caught on to the implication and was flattered. 'I'll do what I can. Come in while I fling some gear on.'

'I could come back. As I said, there's no hurry.' She didn't offer to wait on her own ground for him. That would have prevented a good recce round the Chisholm flat. Fortunately for her he was being expansive, seeming almost grateful for her arrival. 'I'll put some coffee on, then you can slurp it while I take a shower, OK?'

'Sounds fine to me. Why don't you leave me to do the kitchen thing?'

He ran a hand through his tousled hair and

gave a boyish grin. 'Espresso machine's in full view. Likewise the grinder. Coffee beans — left upper cupboard. Choose whatever brand's to your taste.'

Very nice indeed, she thought. This is a set-up the Boss would appreciate: Belgian-roasted, Columbian or Italian. She opted for an opened package resealed with Sellotape and used the roaring of the grinder to cover her quick tour of the other rooms.

No comfort spared, she decided. Basically the flat was on a par with her own, but a lot more money had gone into the furnishing. Yet it wasn't over-decorative; quite masculine in fact. Or pleasantly androgynous — if you could describe material possessions so.

When Neil reappeared she was seated in an armchair in the lounge with a tray on the coffee table before her. The young man, shiny from steam and tangy after-shave, bounced into a matching chair opposite. Now, for the first time in daylight and at near view, she could take a really good look at him.

The survey was mutual. 'Will I do?' he demanded puckishly.

She made him wait for the answer, tilting her head and appearing to examine him minutely. He was really rather a poppet; not what she expected of a man exactly, but well on the way there. His hair, which had been

140

lank and sun-dried when he first arrived at the house, now sleekly capped a rounded head with neat ears, straight nose and fine eyebrows strictly at right angles to it. His mouth was neither tight nor loose, the centre line curving firmly to end in small, deeply cut brackets that made him appear to smile most of the time. But the eyes — she stared at them. They were large and set unusually far apart, which should have given an appearance of frankness. Instead, it made her think of a frog. Or perhaps Toad, the mad motorist and prison-escapee who whooped and boasted while Ratty, Mole and Badger routed the weasels from his riverside mansion.

The eyes themselves? — the eyes were *pretty*. And had no depth. She felt her gaze reflected in the periwinkle blue edged with starburst, curling lashes, black as the sleek, neat-edged cap of hair. Her own eyes edged away, seeking distraction.

'Quite presentable,' she told him.

'I suppose you think that deserves flattery in return.'

'I'm not bothered really.'

The tease was that she meant it. Perhaps it was age that gave her such confidence. Some seven or eight years older than himself, he guessed. And females matured more quickly. She could have tired already of easy compliments. All the same he wanted her to know he was attracted.

'Max not at home?' he asked, making a connection.

'He is, but his home's not here. He lives in Pimlico.'

'So sometimes he just stays over?'

'That sort of thing, yes. How about you? Have you been a long time with Martin?'

The directness shook him for an instant, then he grinned. 'Since he picked me out of the gutter, a squalling, unwanted babe.'

She leaned forward to pour coffee for him, then handed it across. 'But, seriously, *are* you adopted? Don't you have family of your own?'

'Do we need to be serious?'

'Not if you'd rather not, but I'm interested.'

He considered for a moment. It was no business of hers; of anyone's really. But he felt expansive. Intimacies bred intimacy, so why not go with the flow?

'My mother died when I was born. My dad made a hash of making up for it. We never got on, so he sent me away to school.'

He hadn't meant to give quite so much away, but the wide gaze of her warm brown eyes disarmed him. He was a believer in Fate, and she'd happened along so opportunely. He

142

sensed in her a strength he might find a use for, might sometime need; and by then the words had started of themselves, each half-revelation leading to the need to explain a little more. But he knew when to stop. He didn't want her pity.

'It wasn't so bad for a while, but I — I had health problems and was in hospital for a while. School gave up on me. I drifted around at home, thought I might try for Uni, messed that up, and that's when Marty happened along.'

Z nodded. He could be two or three years older than she'd supposed. There was something Peter Pan about him.

The boy's mouth screwed in a sort of twisted pleasure. 'He took me on as a remittance man — you know how the no-good son was proverbially pensioned off as a family embarrassment. Well, Marty is entrusted to hold my reins and purse-strings, *in loco parentis*.'

His voice had become bitter. Whatever their normal relationship, it seemed that Marty, as guardian-gaoler, was presently out of favour. Z decided to divert the boy's spleen. 'That makes your father sound a pretty lonely man.'

Neil made a grimace of distaste. 'That's how he wants it. He doesn't need people. He

143

has money, and the family paper mill that I wouldn't go into if they first chewed me to pulp.

'We can't talk; never could' He was silent a moment searching for the measure of their apartness. 'You see, all his big things are little things. He doesn't *do anything*; only ever rhubarbed on and on. With nobody listening.'

Z nodded sympathetically. She could imagine the set-up: inherited wealth and the successful family firm into which the son was to be automatically fed. And after the man's shock at his wife's death, his son's later breakdown; a pitiful inability to express whatever feelings he had.

She wondered what sort of illness Neil had suffered. That might be significant if she needed to follow up the boy's background. But there'd hardly be any connection between him and the dead Sheila Winter. Their paths had barely crossed.

When he seemed to have talked himself out they sat silent for a few minutes. He looked uneasy, as if already regretting his willingness to open up.

Smiling, she stood up and held out her hand. 'You know, I'm so glad there's someone else young in this building. That's cheered me up. I was feeling a bit forlorn. Especially now the damned boiler's gone dud on me. That's what I was hoping you could advise me on.'

He didn't take the proffered hand but he uncurled from his chair and stood staring, half-puzzled. Then the ends of his mobile mouth twitched upwards. She read his expression as one of relief. 'Sure,' he said. 'I get the feeling we're going to be buddies.'

He followed her down the back stairs, through the utility room and into the main hall. The wire basket affixed to the front door was crammed with letters. Z lifted them out and dumped them, unsorted, on Beattie's antique table. Then they took the grand staircase to the gallery. Z's apartment door stood wide open and she led him straight into the kitchen, waving an arm to offer the freedom of the wall-hung boiler. 'Gone dead on me,' she said.

'Um,' said the boy, inspecting its outside. 'This looks the same kind as ours.'

'Does that mean you're familiar with its workings?'

He looked doubtful. 'Well, I got the thing going when we first arrived, and it hasn't gone duff on us yet. OK if I take off the casing?'

'Help yourself,' She perched on the kitchen table as audience, while he knelt on the working surface to wrestle with the thing. It took him a few minutes of inspecting and

145

tapping, then he gave a little cluck of satisfaction. 'It's the electrickery. See?'

There followed a series of clicks and on one of them the gas jet briefly fired. He removed a small, squarish unit which he waved in her direction.

She looked bemused. 'Is it serious? I can't stand any more expense! This flat has about finished me.'

'The thing must still be under guarantee. Anyway, I can fix it. Just a bent pin in the relay. It hasn't burnt through, or anything drastic.'

It took him less time to have the pin straightened than she had spent twisting it. It didn't occur to him to speculate how the damage had come about. He replaced the casing and got down, grinning.

'That was so kind. I don't know how I'd have managed without you.' She grinned back, relishing the irony that Bob-the-Builder Perrin was in the house, calling on Beattie.

Neil sketched an extravagant, cavalier bow and slapped the wall beside them. 'Our kitchen must be just on the other side. Let's knock a hole through and cut out the journey by two stairways. What do you say?'

She was saved from answering by the warbling of her mobile in the next room. She went through hoping that if it was a work call she'd give nothing away, with the boy still in earshot.

She recognised Dr Fenner's dry voice. He was hoping to call and look through his daughter's papers. While he was in the area he'd need to contact Sheila's solicitor. Would it be a great imposition to ask her to let him in and stay throughout? 'A third person present could avoid — or minimise — any unpleasantness with my ex-wife.'

'I'd be glad to help in any way,' she offered. It was a slice of luck. If the chance presented itself she would also go with him to the solicitor's. Any hint of what the dead woman's will contained could prove important for the investigation.

'Ring my bell and I'll let you in,' she offered. 'It's the one marked R. Weyman: a mistake of the builder's, which I've never corrected.'

'In twenty minutes? Would that be convenient?'

'Perfectly. I'm free all day.'

As she cut the phone Neil sidled through the archway from the kitchen. 'Some lousy guy's stolen a march on me.'

'It looks that way. But it's Sheila Winter's father. I must do what I can.'

'A right little pair of do-gooders today, aren't we?'

'Afraid so, but I must let you see yourself home. I'll have to change into something less comfortable.'

Again she was treated to the elastic grin. 'I'll take my payment now, though.' He wrapped her in a bear hug and kissed her on both cheeks, then stayed there nuzzling her hair. 'I always had a taste for older women,' he said wickedly, winked and was gone.

When Z went down to let Dr Fenner in she saw that the mail had been neatly sorted into five piles, but Martin Chisholm's had not been removed.

11

Bear-like today in his heavy overcoat, Superintendent Mike Yeadings sat slumped in a corner of the briefing room as jabbering voices died away on DI Salmon's entrance. His head thumped and he was reconciled to the first real stinker of a cold for the season. It had been Nan's intention that Sally's half-term week spent in Madeira's sunshine should set them all up for the rigours of an English winter. In his case it seemed to have had the reverse effect, softening him up for the dank discomforts of their return.

Today the fog promised to lift by midday, thinning only to reveal a widespread silvering of frost on ground and rooftops. Cars left exposed outside had needed chipping out: which was another first for the season.

Some austere authority had decreed a turning down of the nick's thermostats at night, and the indoor atmosphere had yet to recover. DI Salmon looked more unprepossessing than ever in layers of dun-coloured sweaters and scarf, the down-turned corners of his mouth aptly fishlike. He slammed a file down on the desk and growled for attention.

149

His day had started badly when he found the Mondeo's battery flat. It hadn't helped that he'd left the sidelights on overnight. Then someone had moved the starter connections needed for him to power up off Cecily's Toyota. He'd wasted another seven minutes searching for the bloody things.

When eventually he arrived at the nick everyone's chatter had suddenly ceased as suspiciously blank faces were turned on him. He didn't cut an impressive figure, and today his insistence on punctuality had rebounded; but let them show by the flicker of an eyelash that they would make capital out of it and he'd hand out some ball-breaker tasking.

He glared at the whiteboard where a blown-up studio photograph of Sheila Winter was displayed. Underneath he had a trainee PC thumb-tack a dozen eight-by-ten shots of the pub car park at Henley; the Vauxhall Vectra; the dead body slumped in the driving seat; and close-ups of the main injuries. He reeled off a description of Sheila Winter's background, including the London address, the more recent one at Ashbourne House and her interest in the Greenvale Garden Centre. He followed this with a summary of post mortem findings simplified for the non-technical.

'What we must concentrate on now are her

movements on Saturday night. We need witnesses to confirm the swapping of her car with Barry Childe's, and any sightings of either car later. And yes, that name should ring a bell. I want anything further you can get on him, which hasn't already come up in court or on a charge sheet. It's no help that the only clear dabs found in the car were hers and his. He's bright enough to have engineered the exchange. We need to find out if her Alfa Romeo's defect was one he might have had a hand in.

'As you should all know by now, he was recently taken on as Ms Winter's general manager at the centre, given the post only three weeks after being released. He claims she knew of his criminal record. Especially we need to follow up his gardening chums in the slammer, especially any recently let out who could be continuing drugs-related interests. It seems he fancies becoming a local cannabis supplier. DS Beaumont will wise you up on details later. Find out who's likely to be supplying seed and covering distribution.'

'Couldn't both be the dead woman?' said a voice from the back. 'She'd have had the right contacts, and it looks suss, taking on an old lag.'

'Who's that?' Salmon demanded. 'Stick a hand up. Right, what's your name?'

'DC Silver, sir.'

'So that's your line to follow, Silver. Poke around at the centre, make friends in the canteen there. Tea ladies are never short of gossip.'

He scowled around at the others. 'Any more bright ideas? No? Then it's back to the hard slog. Sergeant Byng as allocator will draw up the teams and task them. Sergeant Maybury is office manager for the incident room. I'll be in charge of analysis.

'I don't want to catch anyone slacking on this, and I'll be close on your heels. Any information, however slight, is to be reported to me personally, instanter. I'll decide what goes on to NPC. Understand?'

He hadn't checked with Yeadings whether there was any other matter to raise, but the omission didn't trouble the superintendent unduly. He was there mainly to get the measure of the new man. From his corner he watched Salmon gather up the pages he'd spread from his file and prepare to leave, still studiously ignoring his presence. Clearly he regarded a Senior Investigating Officer as a drag or a numb-skull. Possibly both.

A more sinister aspect was that Salmon might clamp down on the extended team's initiative. Yeadings rose to his feet. 'There are some promising lads there,' he said comfortably, moving towards the door. 'You'll get to appreciate them before you're through.'

Salmon gave him an offended stare. 'I hope I'll not be here that long. It doesn't look a complicated case.'

So it seemed he'd already picked his suspect, and would be going all out to slap Barry Childe back in the slammer.

'The family angle,' Yeadings murmured, 'is being tackled at present by DS Zyczynski; which is why she didn't attend.'

'Who?' Salmon seemed genuinely not to remember the name. Then light dawned. 'Oh, the foreign girl made up to DS. She's dealing with the parents? Good. That should keep her from under our feet.'

She would have enjoyed hearing that, Yeadings thought; but it wouldn't do to pass on all his DI's idiocies to the underlings. Team loyalty, and so on. He sighed. 'She's British. Her grandfather was a wartime pilot with the Free Polish. Won a DFC, so I heard. Rosemary's inherited a lot of his gusto.'

'*Rosemary?*' Salmon's lip curled. The old boy was clearly soft on her.

'We don't call her that.' Yeadings instantly regretted letting it slip. 'In the job she's simply 'Z'. Nobody can manage the rest of her name without accessing Spell Check.'

He nodded casually and made to leave. It would be a day or two before he'd be sharing his good mocha with the man. Nobody could just slide into Angus Mott's vacated space. Even allowing for that, he felt he hadn't deserved a replacement with tunnel vision.

In the corridor, he turned back. 'Team Rule One:' he said mildly, but fixing Salmon with a hard stare. 'Of everything that comes your way, a copy will immediately be passed to me. With the time of receipt noted. And that is *your* responsibility.'

For a moment Salmon looked taken aback, opened his mouth to speak, then closed it and grunted. 'Right, Boss.'

Yeadings bowled off towards his office. And he needn't imagine I won't be checking, he promised himself. He peeled off his overcoat, refilled the percolator, sniffed twice at a decongestant inhaler.

On his desk-pad was a note: 'Please ring path lab.' He picked up a phone and asked to be connected to Littlejohn, who answered in person.

'Ah, Mike, I managed to retrieve the elusive fur coat belonging to your stabbed lady. An expensive item once, mink, female skins. It's not so valuable now, of course, with all those rips. Rewarding, though, to the suspicious eye.'

'You found something?'

'Had it put back on the body. No prizes for guessing why I like it so much.'

'The holes don't match up with the injuries?' Yeadings hazarded.

'Holed in one, as you might say. And the bloodstains in the lining told tales under the microscope. They were from her, but not present through natural seepage. More like applications, smeared on after the act. Your lady was almost certainly stabbed in the buff, then her coat slashed, daubed, and used to cover her in transit.

'You'll be getting the full report, with precise measurements, in due course, but I thought you'd like this direct from the horse's mouth.'

Yeadings thanked him, agreed that he sounded to be starting a cold, declined a luncheon invitation for Sunday owing to family commitments, and rang off. As he enjoyed his coffee he considered the new information.

As yet, no underclothes had been found, so it still seemed likely that Sheila Winter had either been with a lover or a would-be rapist, although no sexual activity had occurred. The separate slashing of the coat, and its replacing after her killing, might be a clumsy attempt to cast suspicion in a totally different direction

— on a mugger, or even animal rights activists.

In his brief tour of the garden centre with the dead woman's father he had noticed an arrow indicating an aquarium and pet shop. Staff there, or correspondence files, should give details of any threats, or accusations of cruelty to the animals.

This little tangent had a certain attraction for Yeadings, opening new possibilities. He determined to spread the enquiry as widely as resources permitted. His new DI might well be mistaken in expecting a straightforward case.

Another article missing was the dead woman's handbag, which should have contained some form of identification. Reports from the searchers at her flat had listed three, of different colours, all empty. So far, Sheila's mother had been unable to describe the one she would have taken with her. That meant that if and when it did turn up it might provide some clue leading directly to the killer.

He poured a second cup. The room was warming up, and he with it. The long radiator under the window gave a reassuring gurgle. As he sipped appreciatively it seemed that already his cold was clearing a little. Perhaps no more than a stuffy sinus after all.

At Ashbourne House Z had paved Dr Fenner's way, apologetically breaking in on Beattie's *tête-à-tête* with Frank Perrin and advising her of the state of play. Frank seized his cap to make a quick getaway.

Beattie was still in her pink, quilted dressing-gown and fluffy slippers. 'Sat up late,' she excused herself. 'Watching a late night film. Loada rubbish. Can't think why I did.'

'Less bother than going to bed?' Z suggested.

'Guess so. Not the only nightbird about, though. That Paul Wormsley wasn't back until after one, and another car came in long after that. Musta been Mr Chisholm's. Anyway, why aren't you off to work, then?'

'I'm to look after Dr Fenner this morning. As he's coming here, I hoped you might persuade Vanessa to leave the flat free for him to go through his daughter's things.'

'Didn't seem like he needed looking after. Bit of a cold fish, that one. Even made me feel a bit sorry for Vanessa.' She gave Z a straight look. 'And that takes some doing.'

'I'm sorry we dropped her on you; and now I'm having to ask again.'

'Seems like there's nobody else, don't it?

I'll just get me togs on.'

Beattie dressed quickly, dabbed on fresh lipstick and went up to hustle Vanessa off-scene with the promise of breakfast in her downstairs, cosy kitchen. Vanessa Winter, barely awake, was too muzzy to override the sudden rumbustious activity. She made little protest at being bundled into a kaftan and shepherded out, unaware of her front door being left unlocked behind them.

Z threw a coat over her shoulders and waited for the visitor outside, to prevent his driving round to the rear where he might be spotted from Beattie's kitchen windows. Dr Fenner arrived promptly. He looked tense, but his craggy features relaxed on learning that he would have the Winter apartment to himself. 'Except, of course, for me,' Z warned.

He gave her a searching look. 'As I requested. But today you're wearing your other hat, so to speak. Representing the police. Of what am I a suspect, sergeant?'

'Nothing,' she said promptly. 'Consider my presence a part of the service.'

For the first time she saw him smile and recognised that he wouldn't have been totally awesome to his students. Perhaps in other circumstances he could be stimulating company. He had the courtesy to enquire after his ex-wife, and was not surprised that last night she had demanded tranquillisers and was allowing others to make all decisions for her.

'In a little while,' he said, 'she'll be making specific demands. You must take care that the service you mentioned doesn't get over-loaded.' Again there was that strain of irony in his voice.

Z was sure he'd ample experience of Vanessa's need for attention. It was difficult to see how she would have fitted into academic Cambridge, distanced from her stage contacts and a captive audience. Perhaps the restrictions of being a don's wife had irritated her, or she felt herself a butt of his colleagues' waspish intellectualism. Had that been the reason for turning her back on him to throw herself into her acting? Or maybe it was simply that the sex wasn't right?

For whatever reason, the union hadn't lasted. Had one of them, or both, looked elsewhere for a more suitable partner?

There was something she'd said that Z couldn't account for: a mention of losing 'both my darling children'. Up until then Sheila had seemed to be her only child.

As Fenner seated himself at the davenport to go through its contents she put the question to him. 'No,' he said abruptly. 'Sheila was our only child. There was a boy

159

some years later, but he was nothing to do with me.'

'And what has happened to him?'

'Do you consider this is germane to your investigation, Miss Zyczynski?'

'I can't tell until I know more about it, sir.'

He laid down the papers he was scanning and sat in silence a moment. 'You are quite right, of course. But Gordon has no part in this. He was killed some ten years back when he was twelve, driving a stolen motor cycle over the quay at Bristol. He had been staying with school friends there. He died in hospital and the post mortem showed that he was high on heroin. Vanessa was in Venice at the time and flew back in a terrible state. She blamed me, madly claiming that if we had still been married the boy would never have been born.

'It was possibly at that time that she finally began to lose her grip on reality. Or else she chose to create that impression. It's difficult to tell just how unbalanced — or merely perverse — she actually is. You may have discovered that yourself.'

Staring past her, he seemed to wait for a reply. 'Sometimes,' Z offered, 'she can appear quite shrewd.'

'Shrewd, and shrewish, yes. I gave up on trying to make sense of it.'

He turned towards Z as though she might have some solution to offer. 'All the while Sheila was with her I could feel free of responsibility. But now — God knows what will have to be done. So far as my daughter knew, Vanessa has no permanent relationship with anyone.'

Z nodded. She noted the word 'permanent'. It implied that Vanessa had only casual acquaintances, or the sort of friends who didn't stay around long. That must have been an added burden for Sheila, unless she was a particularly dutiful and self-effacing daughter. Was that the reason she had never married or formed a lasting relationship herself?

Yesterday Vanessa, exasperated by police questions, had said that, for all she knew, Sheila could have entertained a dozen lovers that last night.

So the younger woman had managed to keep her private life to herself. That could make it difficult to arrive at a complete picture of her. It also limited the cast of obvious suspects — a line of enquiry which would have to be followed up.

'Ah!' Gabriel Fenner had extracted a letter from one of the desk's pigeonholes. 'We have her solicitor's address. Newham, Davenay and Partners in Mardham High Street. Are you at all familiar with them?'

'Yes. Alan Prothero is one of our duty briefs at Mardham nick. And I've met Miss Davenay in court. The practice is well respected.'

'Then, as I need to get back to Cambridge I shall leave matters in their hands. Can you direct me there now?'

He returned the papers to where he had found them, closed and locked the davenport and stood uncertain what to do with the key. 'Perhaps this should be left with you. The police may need to look into Sheila's affairs. I don't want Vanessa to remove anything they might find of interest.'

'Thank you, sir. And I'd be pleased to come with you.'

They left the outer door ajar as they had found it and went down to Fenner's car. A fifteen-minute drive took them into Mardham High Street, where Z pointed out the carriage gateway that led into a courtyard cobbled in stable setts. An outer iron staircase led up to a suite of offices furnished throughout in pale sycamore with olive tweed. A middle-aged blonde at reception looked up and smiled at Z in recognition.

'Dr Fenner,' the DS introduced him. 'He's come about — '

'Of course.' The woman stood and offered

her hand. 'You have our deepest sympathy, sir. Mr Newham will be relieved that you've come. We've been ringing your Cambridge number since yesterday. I'm afraid he's out at the moment, but I'm instructed to help you all I can. Do come through.'

Z took a vacant chair in reception, prepared for a long wait. Almost immediately the outer door opened again and Alan Prothero came through. 'Hi,' he said cheerfully. 'Have you come to fill me in?'

He was a rotund young man and to Z's eyes needed no further stuffing. 'Not exactly. Have you been picking up a case with us?'

'Was called in on behalf of one Barry Childe. Interviewed by DS Beaumont and the new wallah, whatsisname.'

'DI Salmon.'

'Bit of a change from Angus, what?'

Z avoided being led into personal comparisons. 'Has Childe been charged?'

'Yup. Conspiracy to procure and deal drugs. They'll never make it stick with what they've got so far. Not that your DI's bothered. He made dark hints about more serious charges to follow, so I guess he's got my client marked for the Winter woman's murder.'

He danced a little chassé and slammed his briefcase down on the reception desk. 'In which case, alas, it won't come my unworthy way. Newsworthy crime is Daddy Newham's prerogative.'

He treated her to what he considered his dazzling smile. 'When are you going to come out for a drink with me? I'd like to say a meal, but, as ever, I'm skint.'

'In which case,' she responded, 'I must admit I couldn't afford to.'

'Oh, *touché*, cruel woman. But I shall live in hopes. Anyway, what are you here for, if not for me?'

'Accompanying a client,' she said simply. She would rather have said nothing, but any attempt at noticeable discretion might dry up Prothero for future disclosures.

He seemed satisfied that this matter could not concern him, smiled his dazzler again and went off to his own quarters.

★   ★   ★

'I wasn't sure you wanted me to stay on,' Z told Dr Fenner when he emerged some twenty minutes later from the senior partner's office.

'I'm glad you did. I'd like to take you somewhere pleasant for lunch.'

When she seemed to hesitate he gave his rare smile and added, 'In case you feel that

164

that would waste valuable working time, we could always discuss your interest in the case.'

'I was actually wondering which restaurant you'd find most pleasant,' she lied. It had shocked her a little to hear him use the word 'case'. It sounded so impersonal, referring to his daughter's murder. She found such ingrained detachment quite formidable.

For the second time that morning she marvelled how separation could affect a father's relationship. With Neil the distancing had been a failure of communication. Sheila and her father had lost years through living apart, yet there had certainly been close understanding. Without her his life would be diminished now, but he would never allow it to show.

'Shall we try Amersham?' he suggested. 'There looked to be some reasonable places in the Old Town.'

They went to Gilbey's where Max sometimes took her, and although Fenner chose sparingly from the menu for himself, he seemed satisfied. His mind, she recognised, was more on dealing with present problems.

'From my knowledge of Sheila,' he said, as they waited for the main course, 'I find it difficult to imagine anyone being violently opposed to her. Some might have thought her hard because she was single-minded. But she was kind with it. I know she listened to others' views, because she had taken them into account in final decisions. What mattered most to her was her great project's success. Which makes me inclined to believe that in business she crossed someone more obdurate than herself.'

'That is something we shall need to look into.'

'You will want access to her bank accounts. I can arrange that as her sole executor.'

Z glanced swiftly at him

'Yes; curious, isn't it? — that she should expect me to outlive her. In case I should fail to, her solicitors were to take that on. But I was her first choice.' The realisation moved him, and he sat a while without speaking.

'As I recall it, her share of the business is in the neighbourhood of twelve per cent. Mine is forty, and the bank loan covers the rest. There had been a deal of initial outlay, but this year, for the first time, we are expecting a small profit. Without Sheila in control, I imagine the bank will be pressing to sell. As I am most loath to have that happen, it is essential to find someone reliable to take over the whole operation.'

'That won't be easy.'

'Especially as I am fully occupied in Cambridge. My programme is set up for the

166

next three years. I simply do not have the time. We really should be looking for two directors; one a horticultural specialist and the other a financial controller.'

'Perhaps you can persuade the bank to help with that.'

'Let us hope so. On the botanical side I should be able to get advice. I wonder, Miss Zyczynski, if you would spare time to come to Barclays with me this afternoon? I should like to get some agreement in general terms before I go back to Cambridge, and I want to insist that the bank makes all Sheila's affairs open to the police for their investigation.'

'Perhaps you should have someone more senior with you?'

He tilted his head to look at her directly. 'Your superintendent appears to have full confidence in you. That's good enough for me.'

'Thank you. I shall report everything to him, of course.'

'Of course. Now, will you have pudding, or cheese, or both?'

Z opted for coffee, wondering why he hadn't disclosed what was to happen to his daughter's shares in the company. As executor he should know by now.

12

Paul *Wormsley*. He smiled sardonically. The name had first appeared as a typographical error: some chit of a girl hitting the keyboard with a rogue finger. Worsley was the name he'd selected. *Wormsley* was how it came out in the initial paperwork, so they'd ordered it to be corrected. But it had amused him, so he'd stuck with it. Who would willingly *choose* a surname like that, reduce himself to subterranean level, allied to one of the lowest forms of garden life?

So here he was, a worm with its own birth certificate, passport, driving licence, life insurance: all the lying paraphernalia that upper officialdom provided to deceive its own lower orders. An ironic situation, and now with this added little quirk. He liked it.

While retaining his initials as a mnemonic, the pseudonym was the best part of his disguise, better than the hair dye, spectacles, coloured lenses and nose job. It made him feel safe — for most of the time. At others he'd wake in the early hours in a cold sweat, almost juddering, having been back in that other person, remembering Peader's huge, strangling hands, Micky's flick-knife, Monk's death-dealing eyes as he stared back from the dock, promising revenge.

They'd all gone down for a very long time. The charges of murder, and conspiracy to murder, had ensured that, on top of all the theft and fraud stuff. As for himself, he'd got off almost scot-free, sold them out, served his token term, washed his hands and run. And run and run and run, and must ever more keep running.

Witness Protection was all right for a time, until you got slack and the authorities forgot you; but the onus was on yourself, living the new life until the mask moulded the features underneath. Mentally, as well as physically.

That was his own life sentence. Piers Wilson was no more. There was just this fabricated half-person deprived of the familiar haunts, the easy women, the buccaneer life. He lived now as *they* allowed him to, at a level considered appropriate; *rusticated* — the literal version of his onetime headmaster's threat; tamely earning in a year what he could once have knocked off in a single operation.

So, he'd escaped a life sentence; yet it didn't mean he was free. When sometimes the present situation irked he needed to remind himself of the ultimate advantage: that now, according to official documentation, his

169

wasn't the hand that had dabbled in blood.

Driving to work this morning through layers of shifting mist, he was preoccupied as ever with this swinging between unease, resentment and a wry kind of relief. He could finally chase it with the thought that he'd put one over on a competent set of villains. Then he could glow a little, with pride at his own devious duplicity.

There was a pile-up just after access on to the M25. It held him trapped in the middle of a long tail-back. In his rear-view mirror he watched two cars immediately behind make awkward three-point turns and sneak out by the hard shoulder. Sourly he hoped they'd run straight into emergency services on their way to the crash.

Time was when he'd have been the first to do that. Not now, though. Had to keep a low profile, act suitably wormlike.

He looked in the mirror again and recognised the car now moving up on his tail. Martin Chisholm was getting out to light a fag and rubberneck on the snarl-up ahead. As he strolled by, Wormsley reached a hand through the open window and sketched a salute. Chisholm came across. ''Morning,' he said. 'Hope this isn't going to take all day.'

He was looking good, considering the hours he kept. Wormsley wondered if he knew

170

how his little boyfriend fretted in his absences, and whether it would bother him at all if he did.

'Looks as if they're clearing one lane,' Chisholm commented, staring ahead, nodded and returned to his car.

As they started off it struck Wormsley that the man was heading in the wrong direction for London. A few miles farther, and in his mirror he saw Chisholm's Saab indicating to turn off. On a sudden urge he flashed to do the same, made it in time, dawdled up the exit towards the next roundabout and let the other man overtake. Well, that's what powerful cars were about, weren't they? He would put money on Chisholm's Saab against his run-of-the-mill Peugeot any day. But speed limits being what they were, he'd every chance of keeping the man in sight.

He switched his car-phone to open speech and pressed the listed code1. 'Jill? Something's come up; may take an hour or two. Anything in the book that you can't manage on your own?'

Reassured that there wasn't, because the pert little miss thought she was better at the job than him in any case, he smirked, said, 'Right then. Be seeing you,' and cut the call.

Martin Chisholm had turned left and left again. In the 30mph zone of Chiswell Green he became aware of Wormsley nosing up behind. By profession primed to caution, he weighed the possibility that he was being deliberately followed.

The man could just be nosy. There was, though, a faint chance of something less innocent, though he didn't see how Wormsley's life and his own could have crossed at any point. He just hoped that Neil, in his contact with the agent for Ashbourne House, hadn't let any indiscretion slip out. He would need to enquire just when the man had shown an interest in Beattie Weyman's place, and where he'd first heard of it.

With minimal warning he took another left turn at speed, heading towards the RHS rose garden, and grinned in the mirror to see Wormsley go gunning past on the main road. Chisholm made a circuit and came back towards where he'd entered, pulling up close behind a large furniture van unloading on to the pavement.

After three minutes he saw Wormsley turn in and roar past in supposed pursuit. So, why? he asked himself. Merely a case of idle curiosity? Or was the man on to him? Either way, it could be dealt with.

He reversed from the furniture van's cover, then shot out again into the traffic stream. Let the fool wander through the Royal

Horticultural Society's rose gardens, under the misted skeletons of arches and pergolas, searching among the starkly wintering bushes with their crinkled leaves and flowerless stems. For himself, he had no business there, and no intention of lingering to be caught up with. He had a meeting set up in St Albans which he couldn't afford to miss. Wormsley was something he'd deal with at a later time.

Wormsley's Peugeot was parked a little way before the entrance to the show gardens. It was warm inside the car, and the frosted vista ahead uninviting. He waited, de-misting the windows, considering it most unlikely that his prey was ordering bushes for spring delivery. No, the man had arranged an assignation here. The unlikely venue meant underhand business.

It wasn't his first suspicion of Chisholm. He knew already that he was a phoney. He might run a decent car and know all the dealer-spiel, but he didn't sell from any retail agency in the West End. When he'd thought up that background detail he hadn't known there'd be someone living in the same building who knew the far side of the London car trade, new and secondhand.

That welcoming dinner party which Beattie threw had provided a deal of useful information. Watching Chisholm so closely

173

had stirred an elusive memory. He'd seen the man somewhere before; or else someone very similar indeed. Not in this country, though. Japan, he wondered? Dubai? Dublin? It hadn't been all that long ago, but the circumstances escaped him.

There was a possibility he worked undercover for one of the government agencies. Not that that should cause panic. By now his own tracks were competently covered. If the other started to dig he'd be firmly met with official stonewalling. Any file on him was no longer accessible.

He waited a full half-hour before braving the mist and frost to climb out and scour the area for the Saab. It was nowhere to be seen, and the traffic gates to the RHS's gardens were dismally padlocked, entrance accorded only to whatever hardy pedestrians cared to brave the monochrome wasteland. He wasn't fool enough to draw attention to himself in there.

But failing to discover Chisholm wasn't total disappointment. Clearly the man had caught on to being tailed, and taken evasive action. Which, in itself, looked professional and was proof of something to hide.

Old habits die hard, even for a worm conversion. He was intrigued, and the scent of potential profit was growing stronger in his nostrils. Profit while retaining anonymity: that was vital. The risk was too great otherwise.

It wasn't until he was halfway back to his little studio and photographic shop that two unrelated facts merged in his mind. The late Sheila Winter, fellow resident at Ashbourne House, had owned and managed a garden centre. Martin Chisholm, mystery man, had disappeared in the neighbourhood of a wholesale rose supplier.

Was it too great a leap of imagination to suppose a connection between the man and the murdered woman? Something sinister? Wormsley wasn't sure after all, that he wanted to follow up that question. Getting himself noticed today might not have been a smart thing to do.

Safer, perhaps, to assume that Chisholm was simply part of the investigation into the woman's death. Which made one wonder what she'd been up to, that required an undercover cop working on the case.

★   ★   ★

By mid-afternoon Neil Raynes, deserted first by Marty, then by the chick Rosemary, was beginning to regret he'd not gone in to work. Out here in the comparative wilds, he felt cut off from real life. He could think of nothing

175

to do but unearth his vintage Dawes bike from the stuff stacked at the back of the garage, overhaul it and go pedal-pushing to relieve himself of spleen.

Down by the converted stables he saw that the Winters' silver Alfa Romeo had been returned and was parked outside. The local television station had mentioned little more than that a woman had been discovered stabbed to death in the driving seat of a car at Henley-on-Thames. Her identity had been revealed by Sunday's police presence at the house. And now here her car was, looking perfectly normal.

He went close with ghoulish curiosity to peer in. There seemed to be no bloodstains on the front seats. The police must have returned it after forensic examination. Their speed, and the evidence of a garage valet service, amazed him. It wasn't as though anyone was in great haste to drive the thing again. Which was a pity. He'd give a lot to get behind the wheel and slide up in it at work; give the others in the porters' room an eyeful of high living.

He ran an exploratory hand under the front wheel-arch, encountered something small, and heard a soft tinkle as the remote-lock key fell to ground. That was a really ancient dodge! You'd think the pigs would have some

176

slicker contrivance up their sleeves. It was the sort of thing a garage might consider adequate precaution.

He picked the key up, turning it in his fingers, idly clicked it, and the car's lights flicked once. As he heard the door locks released he felt some similar response in himself. He looked around; was reassured that no one was watching.

He considered the stabbed body. He'd overheard Beattie say it was naked. There could be minute traces of the blood remaining. Blood was a substance that took a lot of removing. His face showed distaste, but he was compelled to open the driver's door and lean in. Nothing but the usual car smells. No bleach; nothing in the nature of decaying meat. They'd done a good job cleaning the interior. Nobody would have guessed.

This lump at the back of his throat was there again, and the familiar nausea threatening. It was the mental linking of car and blood. He doubted he'd ever be free of it. Years had gone by and it still made him want to throw up. It had been his father's Mercedes and his father's second wife. He'd fancied them both.

No, that wasn't fair. He'd gone for the car in a big way, before ever Miriam started on him; and because they couldn't do it under the old man's nose they'd devised ways of going off together. Miriam had liked him to drive; preferred him on top. He'd discovered too late how a woman can manipulate by appearing the fragile one. And in the end she'd paid for it. So had he. But at least he was still alive.

To hell with *nil nisi bonum*: she'd been a harpy. Not like the pathetic Winter woman, but both had tried to pull him for the same reason. And look where it had ended.

He turned a morose gaze back on the car. These days he would sometimes drive Marty, but he never took the Saab out alone. Sooner or later he'd have to get over the shakes. This Alfa couldn't be all that of a challenge: a woman's car.

He considered the dashboard and in his mind went through the procedure for starting up, slipping into gear. He slid, self-indulgently, into the driving seat and reached for the pedals. Not that he meant to commit himself.

The engine turned over like silk, purred seductively.

It was too easy. He drove it gently, almost silently, round to the front of the house and turned into the driveway. It felt all right, quite good really.

When he had almost reached Mill Lane, Z,

178

sitting at a window to make out her report on the morning spent with Fenner, glimpsed the car disappearing. So the bumper was fixed and the garage had returned it. She was amazed that Vanessa had so soon recovered to use it, and hoped she'd offered Beattie a lift into town. It would be a good way of repaying the old lady for her kindness.

Neil Raynes settled his shoulders back in the driving seat. These country roads were no place to try out the car's capability. The Eyeties built their wheels for speed, didn't they?

He made for the M25, keen to find out how fast he could put a ring round London. An hour and a half was the accepted run. He knew he could beat that.

13

Superintendent Yeadings frowned, listening to the taped interview with Barry Childe. The man should never have been charged. As he now claimed, the electrical equipment at his cottage just might have been intended for the indoor culture of legitimate exotics.

Salmon had been too hasty following up Beaumont's report. There had been no need to let the man know that the loft had been searched and yielded its secrets. After a few days spent cooling off, he might otherwise have continued with the project, contacting the illegal seed supplier, and the DI catching bigger fish.

Fish — *Salmon*! The connection was inevitable. An apt name for the man; it was something to do with his mouth. Unconsciously Yeadings dropped the corners of his own and performed slow jaw functions, glassy-eyed.

Beaumont, alongside, must have been suffering similar doubts, muttering almost inaudibly, 'Salmon, a prey to read herrings.'

Of all non-runners in Thames Valley Police, Kidlington had inflicted that wet fish on them. *Recommended for the task*, for heaven's sake — because unacceptable everywhere else!

'Is the DI still investigating the small-holding arson in Denham?' Z asked. So she too had the man on her mind.

Yeadings sighed, straightened his back. 'He is. Which indicates,' he told his two sergeants, 'that the upper brass expects we may find both incidents connected. And, while it can leave our DI precariously balanced with a foot on two galloping horses, his main weight must be on our present case, since murder takes precedence over malicious damage or fraud.'

What made him uneasy was the possibility that one of his own team might be sidelined on to the lesser case. It struck him that if personnel were stretched, this was an opportunity for his own Little-Jack-Horner thumb to be firmly dipped into the pie. And happily so, since Nan had rightly complained that excessive desk work played havoc with the shine on his workaday trousers.

He would drive out on the A40 and take a look at the charred remains of what had been, until the previous week, a pleasant cottage with outbuildings and a couple of acres put down to chrysanthemums and young spruces intended for the Christmas trade. Unless there was a direct connection with Sheila Winter, the only tenuous link would be that of horticulture.

Before he went there he would get DI Salmon to wise him up on the case. Meanwhile, Z should tell him everything she'd learned from Dr Fenner's visit to his daughter's solicitor.

'Not a lot,' she admitted. 'There was a will, but he didn't choose to disclose what it contained, except that he's sole executor. So I guess that's the end of the solicitor's interest. Fenner will probably deal with it himself.'

'His ex-wife may call her own brief in to see fair play. In which case you can probably get all you need from her. I'd be interested to know what's to happen to the business.'

'He told me he owned 40%, Sheila just 12%, and Barclays Bank the rest.'

'So can we assume she's left her share to her father? In which case he could dispose of the whole as he wished. If she divided it equally between her parents that would leave the bank with the lion's share and the family wishes could be out-voted. I think you should try to find out, through Beattie if necessary, about bequests, and the funeral arrangements.'

'Sheila left a letter with instructions. Her father is to arrange for cremation. A quiet occasion; no flowers; no eulogy; minimal C of E service.'

'No flowers?' Yeadings queried. 'And she expected her father to outlive her?'

'Apparently she had a premonition about dying young. It does seem strange about the flowers, since she seemed so fond of them.'

'Perhaps she'd been involved with too many elaborate funerals professionally. Beaumont, what's your immediate programme?'

'Sticking with Salmon and his *sole* suspect,' he punned atrociously. 'Looking for a link between Childe and the Denham arson. Chasing up the old lags he was inside with, particularly any with a taste for horticulture. Checking with the prison what gardening books he had out of the library, just in case there were specific instructions for growing his own drugs indoors.'

After the necessary quiet groan evoked by the pun, Yeadings almost smiled. Present allocations seemed to leave Greenvale Garden Centre for him to take a leisurely look at. He reminded himself that he was to take the family there for their Saturday lunch. 'Who is currently examining the CCTV tapes?' he inquired.

'DC Silver,' Beaumont offered. 'He fancied the dead woman being behind whatever Childe was setting up at home, so he's been

183

given a free hand on that theory.'

'But he's held up because no one has yet found the password to access Sheila's laptop computer,' Z complained. 'The experts are working on that now.'

'And Sheila Winter's personal life, have we any gossip on that? Her father implied she could have been interested in at least one man. 'Like myself, not celibate,' is more or less what he said.'

'Nobody has come forward so far, and she seems to have kept that side of her life pretty low key. It's a pity about the funeral ban on flowers. Notes pinned on the wreaths can tell quite a lot about the senders.'

The black phone on Yeadings's desk gave a double buzz. He lifted the receiver. 'Yes?' The two sergeants looked hopeful.

'Good. I'll come down and see him,' said Yeadings. He rose and came round the desk. 'Dr Fenner has called. I think this time I'll see him on my own. He hasn't a lot of hair, but he just might want to let it all down.'

He found the academic in the duty office. He had declined the offer of a seat and stood towering against a notice-board, his overcoat over one arm. 'This is an un-cosy place to talk,' Yeadings observed. 'Shall we go out and sit in your car?'

It still held the heat of his journey. Fenner

switched on the engine, adjusted the fan and opened his near window.

'There seems no point in my staying on here any longer,' he said, coming at once to the point. 'Since it will be a cremation, I'm sure the body can't be released for some days.'

'There are a number of questions we'd like settled first,' Yeadings agreed vaguely.

'But before leaving I thought I should find out if you have any idea . . . '

'We have discovered a number of facts, but have had no time to sift what may be relevant.'

'You'll need to know about her financial standing. I can't be more precise than to say I believe the business was starting to make a reasonable profit after heavy initial outlays. In the will she leaves her share of it to her mother who had paid for the new apartment at Ashbourne House. Maintenance there and all household expenses were to be covered by Sheila, but now they won't, of course.'

'There was an earlier property, in London, I believe.'

'Yes. It had been in both their names, but three years back Sheila covenanted her half to me when she needed capital to develop the centre. On the strength of that I took out a loan to buy a 40% share in the company,

185

without voting rights. Sheila retained 12% and her bank the rest. Your Miss Zyczynski will have informed you of this.'

'She did.'

'And now you need to know how her will disposes of it.'

Yeadings waited. Fenner gave a wintry smile. 'My daughter left a letter for me with her solicitor which expressed her strong desire that I should never be required to support my ex-wife either financially or in any other way. I was to 'remain totally unshackled.'

'For that reason only, she left her entire interest in Greenvale Garden Centre to her mother. Neither of us had been aware of this provision, Superintendent.

'To me it comes as a shock, because I had hoped to keep the centre going as a memorial to her. As it now stands I shall lose any control. What Vanessa chooses to do with her interest will decide the final outcome. She would never be capable of taking Sheila's place or using her voting power wisely. It is more than possible that, recognising this, the bank will prefer to dispose of the business to one of the bigger horticultural chains, and Vanessa will be adequately paid off.'

'Is Mrs Winter aware of the will's contents?'

'Not unless Sheila mentioned it to her, which I doubt. I shall leave the papers with my own solicitor in Cambridge and he will advise her of her position.'

'I understand.' Yeadings opened the passenger door and climbed out. 'Thank you for being so helpful, sir. If anything comes to mind regarding your daughter's more personal life perhaps you would get in touch again?'

'I knew nothing, I'm afraid. Except that — just after her last birthday, which was in August, I noticed her letter appeared more light-hearted, younger somehow. She wrote that it was time she had a little fun in her life and I would hear all about it at some later date. I thought then that perhaps she had met someone who had proved to her there was more to life than hard business sense.'

He paused, seeking the right words. 'I had even begun to hope for a wedding invitation.'

His smile was a wry one. 'My second marriage was unfortunate, but I believed her capable of better judgement than mine.'

'She gave no hint of the kind of man she could be involved with?'

'None. Indeed, I may well have misunderstood her intention altogether.'

Yeadings watched the car drive off with a twinge of pity. Could Sheila Winter ever have

187

imagined what she deprived her father of in severing his interest in her business? She had ensured Vanessa's financial independence, but at some cost to him. If the garden centre had been her baby, what could it have proved to him, her survivor?

He turned towards his own Rover, unlocked it and sat inside waiting for it to warm. His mind was still on the man who had just left. On a sudden inspiration he reached for his mobile phone and punched in Beaumont's number.

'Just a notion about Sheila Winter's laptop,' he said as the DS answered. 'Tell Silver to try FENNER for the password.'

It seemed possible that Sheila had resented being summarily deprived of her family name. This could have been a way of reinstating herself.

Then he pressed out the number for DI Salmon's mobile and made an arrangement to meet up at his office.

'I need to be put in the picture about the arson case at Denham,' he told him. 'So bring along all you've got on that so far.'

Salmon took his time in complying, and passed out the information with surly reluctance. Yeadings affected to be blandly unaffected, nodding at the sparse evidence and watching the audio tape winding left-to-right inside the half-open top drawer of his desk. 'That's the lot?' he asked mildly at the end of an inconclusive account of the damage sustained in the fire.

'It was clearly kids.' said the DI. 'No tools were taken, just a ghetto-blaster from under one of the potting-house stagings. The usual sort of vandalism.'

'But torched,' Yeadings insisted. 'That's something rather novel for the area. Denham's a quiet little place normally, wouldn't you say?'

'It was school half-term. Kids run wild when they're let loose.'

'Halloween,' Yeadings reminded him. 'D'you think it was trick-or-treating? Any mention of fire crackers in the Fire Chief's report? In my experience there's always some trace left.'

'Accelerant was used, and two two-gallon petrol cans found slung into the undergrowth.'

'From local garage forecourts?'

'The cans were old ones. And people are filling up the things at the pumps all the time. Nobody takes any notice.'

'They do in the case of underage customers.' Yeadings swung his office chair to face the window and let a silence build.

'So it seems you haven't anything to go on.

Why, then, should our masters bracket this arson with the Sheila Winter murder?'

Salmon set his mouth in a hard line and considered how he could defend his being upgraded to the more serious crime. 'It's possible someone has it in for the garden trade.'

The superintendent's black, caterpillar eyebrows shot up to their highest level. 'A nutter seeking revenge for a faulty conservatory or a bad outbreak of fungal black spot? I thought it was young lads you had in your sights. The fact of petrol being used inclines me more to suspect adult naughtiness, which the murder almost certainly was. So, assuming there's a connection, can you suggest a scenario? An organised protection racket, for example?'

Salmon looked ill at ease. 'Enquiries among the other small-holders rule that out. The damaged place wasn't the biggest, and none of the others had been threatened. The idea was laughed out of town.'

'You hadn't mentioned this before. I expect a report to contain positive and negative findings.' His voice had sharpened. 'Have you any other suggestions?'

Salmon was beginning to look defiant. 'Industrial sabotage?' he tried.

'Chrysanthemums and conifers,' Yeadings

190

reminded him. 'I really don't see those modest crops threatening any rivals of similar magnitude, do you? From what I recall, apart from half an acre of rose bushes, that's about all that's grown on that stretch of the A40. At this time of year the small-holdings make most of their money from imported vegetables, bulbs and cut flowers.'

He watched Salmon making up his mind to come clean. 'From the continent,' he prompted him innocently. 'The Netherlands, mostly.'

'Which is also our main supplier of illicit drugs,' Salmon at last admitted. That implication was a card he'd intended to hold close to his chest.

'Ah.'

'Well, there's this thing Childe was setting up. He says orchids, and oleanders and such. But for my money he's on to something a damn sight more profitable.'

'I wondered how soon you'd get round to him,' Yeadings said drily. 'Well, if that's the bee in your bonnet you'd better get after it at speed, because the most you have to hold him on at present is the dubious removal of Miss Winter's laptop computer.'

'We've let him go,' Salmon admitted tightly. 'On bail.'

He'd have done better to withdraw the

charge entirely, Yeadings considered; but Childe free to go his own way was some relief. He hoped the man was brash enough not to trim whatever ambitions he'd set his heart on. And perhaps when the laptop gave up its secrets they'd get to know some history of Sheila Winter's introduction to the ex-con.

14

Beattie left it until after ten o'clock before she went to rouse her upstairs neighbour.

'You shouldn't have bothered,' Vanessa complained, squinting at the breakfast tray. 'I think I'll lie in for a while. I had a really diabolical night, awake for hours and hours. My poor head simply pounds.'

Beattie addressed a space above the pounding head. 'Today you'll need to check on your fridge and cupboards; make out a shopping list. Else you'll go hungry.'

What a disagreeable old person, Vanessa thought, a delicate hand across her eyes.

A sort of washerwoman, standing there all lumpy, intent on organising her into distasteful activities. What on earth would she suggest next?

'Isn't there someone who could come and stay with you for a few days? — until you're feeling more ready to take over for yourself.'

'No, there isn't. I'm not so fortunate as you, with that sweet daughter of yours. Where is Rosemary? I thought she might have called in this morning.'

'Gone to work, I suppose. She can't take

193

any more time off to sort things out. And she's not my daughter. Just a young woman I've grown very fond of over the years.'

'*Not* yours?' Vanessa struggled feebly to sit up, then thought better of it. 'I'm sure everyone thinks you're related. But it's true, you're not in the least alike.'

She ran a distracted hand through her corn-silk hair. 'In which case, I wonder if she'd consider . . . '

'Consider what?' Beattie asked suspiciously. 'She has her own life to lead, you know.'

'Of course. But if she's on her own . . . as I am . . . And I could do such a lot for her . . . ' Vanessa struggled again to sit up against her pillows. 'Take her about; up to town. Show her things. Go to theatres; shopping. A young girl like that — and she's really quite pretty. But she could make so much more of herself. She should be mixing with more interesting people; not hiding away in the country.'

Beattie's jaw set. Give the wretched woman half a chance and she'd be aping the Edwardian chaperon, living off a debutante's brief season. If she'd tried to push that existence on to Sheila, no wonder she went in the opposite direction and opted for gardening. Really, Vanessa was impossible.

'You'll find Rosemary enjoys life as it is.

194

And she's plenty of friends at work.'

'That's what poor Sheila thought, but she was wrong. Choosing such an unsuitable occupation! If she was so keen on flowers, her father could have bought her a little shop somewhere pleasant, like Knightsbridge. Life would have been so much more fun for us both. But that *garden* place! And employing quite unpleasant people. That was asking for trouble.'

'Her dad was really proud of her,' said Beattie defensively. 'I'm sure you'll find she 'ad lots of admirers.'

Vanessa didn't seem to be listening. 'What's to become of me?' she wailed. 'I'm utterly alone now. I can't stay here. I simply won't.'

Beattie settled the tray on the bedside table. 'Breakfast's there if you want it. It's still there if you don't. Please yourself. But then you would anyway. I've got me ironing to get on with downstairs.' And she padded out.

Left on her own, Vanessa lifted the cover on the two crisply grilled rashers, halves of tomato and buttery scrambled egg. She shuddered delicately, pushed away the duvet and gingerly reached her feet to the floor.

Perhaps she might manage the tea. It looked pale enough, and there was a little bowl with thinly sliced lemon. All it needed was some life added. She thought there must still be a half of single malt in the drawer with her tights. Just a smidgen, to make the tea drinkable.

Hugging the bottle close she climbed back into bed, poured a cup and doctored it. It tasted strange: not her preferred brand of tea. She lifted the lid and unsteadily poured the liquid back into the pot, then refilled her cup with the last of the whisky.

Drinking it exhausted her. She lay back, the day yawning before her. She'd gone out by taxi yesterday to have her hair and manicure done. She must think of some other place to go. If only someone would whisk her away.

Rosemary could drive. It would be more sensible for the girl to move in, just for a while. Then little by little she would discover the advantages. She could rent out her own flat, and just think what a saving that would be. There must be a way she could be prevailed upon at least to try it. She didn't seem to have an important job. Maybe, if it was pointed out, she'd see the point of giving that up too.

The girl was too fond of that old woman downstairs. Stroking her fine eyebrows, Vanessa nodded at herself in the mirror doors of the wardrobe. She would explain how it could save Beattie's poor old feet on the stairs if someone was on the spot to do all that was necessary.

The thought itself seemed to lift the burden a little. She found the energy to shower and dress. When she had made up her face to complement the coral-flecked tweed trouser suit, she remembered the other person who should be concerned for her welfare.

Dr Fenner was in a seminar and had forgotten to switch off his mobile phone. The call cut across an oral presentation by a young student who always doubted his own ability. He hesitated, spluttered, lost the thread of his argument and stammered to a finish.

'Don't be put off,' Fenner ordered. 'It's nothing important.' He glanced at the number that had come up and promptly switched off. It wasn't familiar, but he recognised the area code. If Superintendent Yeadings wished to discuss his daughter's death he could find a more convenient moment.

An hour later, when he was free for lunch, Fenner remembered and returned the call. Vanessa answered, starting in at once on a catalogue of complaints. He cut her short.

'There's just one thing you should know, Vanessa. Sheila has named me as her executor, so you will shortly be hearing from my solicitor about your inheritance. Her entire interest in Greenvale Garden Centre is bequeathed to you. You will need to take advice on how best to deal with that. What you choose to do is no concern of mine, but there is no reason why you shouldn't arrange to have a regular income from it to keep you in comfort for the rest of your life.'

'What would I want with that place?' Her voice was querulous. 'What did she leave you?'

'Quite rightly, nothing. Beyond the business, she had little enough to leave. There are one or two small personal bequests to staff and friends, but beyond that everything comes to you.'

Vanessa replaced the receiver with his voice still ringing in her head: 'Nothing.' Gabriel had been left *nothing*! Despite that pointless correspondence which he'd kept up with Sheila over the years, here now was what she'd really thought of him! It was gratifying, and more than made up for any disappointment over her own, paltry legacy.

She paced between the drawing-room windows, arms crossed and hugging her breasts. Sheila had lumbered her with the garden business and this godforsaken country apartment. She would sell both and get back to London. She'd always fancied one of those modern penthouse flats in docklands. She'd have it done up in vibrant colours by a fashionable designer, throw out all the traditional stuff she had now and go minimal. Inside, it would be huge. Marvellous for parties. She could fill it with fascinating people: actors, directors, artists, writers. It would be a new life. Who knew what it might lead to? She felt liberated, euphoric with hope.

From one of the front windows she saw Sheila's silver car appear from the side of the house and depart by the long drive. She found her hands were shaking. Something was wrong about that. Sheila was away, wasn't she? That's what all the fuss had been about yesterday. If she'd gone already how could she be leaving now?

Vanessa felt her way towards the nearer sofa and fell against it, holding her head with both hands. This was one of her silly turns. Sometimes things got so muddled. For quite a while, days sometimes or longer, it didn't happen. Then, without warning, she just couldn't tell where she was, because her memory was all jumbled. It was hard to work out the order things had happened in. Or even *what* had happened. Sometimes time seemed to go backwards, or bits were left out.

Life became unreliable, mocking her.

At times she suspected that events she'd been most sure of had maybe never occurred. That was the worst part: being afraid that nothing which mattered had ever been real; only a sort of puffball fungus in her mind, or a half-remembered part of a play, but much more sinister than let's pretend. It was like being a puppet, with no script. Isolated in — in a void.

It wasn't just her hands shaking now. Her whole body was possessed by the tremor. She had to lie down, cover herself up, shut out the fear. Stop being, she told herself. If she couldn't force herself to fall asleep, maybe it would just happen on its own. As it had done, several times before.

★   ★   ★

She awoke at about three o'clock. It was still light, and after a few minutes she thought she could recall fragments of the morning. She was almost sure she'd been talking to Gabriel, but had no idea of what he'd said. Something vaguely pleasing, and that wasn't the feeling she usually got from thinking of him. Yet the idea floated up; a little island appearing out of a misted lake.

Mist. Yes, for days now there had been

mist. Around this godforsaken house it lay over the water meadows like sheets of fine, fine muslin. But outside this mist there was something she'd meant to do. See somebody? Who, then?

Rosemary! Yes — Rosemary, who was going to move in. But not here. Somewhere else. They had a new plan. She tried to focus on that but it escaped her. Where were they going? No familiar walls came to mind; no floors, or doors leading into rooms she'd lived in before: nothing.

Rosemary. Where was the girl when you wanted her?

Vanessa dragged herself up, went out, walked unsteadily the length of the gallery. She had raised a hand to ring the other flat's bell when the door opened in her face. Not the girl she was expecting, but the boy.

'Bloody hell!' said Neil. 'Sorry, but you startled me. Hello.'

He looked almost guilty, but managed a grin. 'I mended Ros's gas boiler yesterday. Just checking it's still OK.'

She stared at him. 'Can you drive?' The question came out of itself, unrelated to what she had just been thinking.

It startled him. He guessed she'd caught sight of the car as it passed under her windows. 'Well, yes.'

She looked odd. Odder than usual, actually; awkward, as if she'd forgotten how she meant to go on. Maybe he could swing her round a bit; get himself off the hook. 'It's a great car.'

His hopeful smile reached her, and for a moment she remembered what had pleased her before. Gabriel, left nothing. 'The garden centre,' she said. 'It's mine now.'

'Ah. You'd like to go and see it?' *Mafeking relieved!* With luck he'd get to drive the car again, and this time with her blessing.

She wasn't sure. She'd been expecting Rosemary, and this young man confused her. But if that was what he wanted, why not? He was a charming youngster, Graciously she gave him her hand.

'You'll need to put something warm on,' he said. 'I'll bring the car round to the front, shall I? You come down when you're ready.'

★   ★   ★

Briefly, as they drove, the oyster sky showed fragile strips of turquoise, but evening was closing in. The mists from morning still hung under clumped trees, faintly bluish like thinned milk, waiting to creep out and take over the open fields again. Even in the car there was the faintest, smoky taste of fog. As they turned into the drive to Greenvale, coloured lights of welcome suddenly sprang out, turning the outer dusk into dark.

'Getting geared up for Christmas,' the boy said. He wondered if Marty would still be away by then. The sooner he went, the better chance that they'd get Christmas together. It shouldn't matter. Christmas was just another day in the calendar, but they usually made something of whatever it was supposed to stand for. Childishly he liked the extra eating and drinking; wrapping and opening presents. So now he was all for the coloured lights and gilt angels, however tawdry and vulgar.

Passing through the glitzy entrance, Vanessa observed the queues at checkout points. People's trolleys were crammed with evergreens, pink or scarlet poinsettias, potted cyclamens and azaleas, plastic garlands, vases, tubs, small conifers, boxes of fancy crackers.

The whole huge glasshouse shimmered with red, green and blue lights. It reminded her of childhood visits to the pantomime. This was the Transformation Scene summoned in a flash of magnesium at a wave of the Fairy Queen's wand. (Santa's Grotto was already being constructed behind screens beside the lift which would provide 'Flight by Airship to Lapland': children £2; 1 adult accompanied by a child FREE.)

203

With every step into this wonderland Vanessa yielded more to the enchantment. And this was all hers: this bustling activity, the myriad stacks of goods for sale, these uniformed assistants, the customers with their cash and cheques and credit cards. Her empire — all perfectly functioning on its own, with Sheila gone.

A woman in a green overall, balanced on a step-ladder, was re-arranging gargantuan artificial flowers in a monster vase. Vanessa pulled at her skirt. 'This is mine,' she told her.

'Pardon, madam?'

Neil was trying to draw her away. Vanessa gesticulated to include the whole scene.

The woman began to climb down. 'What is it you want, madam? Let me find someone to serve you.'

And then, before the boy's appalled eyes, it began, Vanessa suddenly revitalised, marching about the aisles, ordering armloads of cut or artificial flowers, shoals — van loads — of useless, eye-catching stuff, until a little knot of assistants gathered round, gazing at her in puzzled disbelief.

'She's Mrs Winter,' Neil hissed in excuse. He hadn't reckoned with her behaving like a madwoman 'She's Sheila Winter's mother.'

They must all have known the news by

now. The police invasion and closure of the office, and Barry Childe's being held for questioning was made public in last night's Evening Echo. The staff would have been on tenterhooks all day, worrying what was to become of their jobs.

'Look, there's a coffee shop or something, isn't there?' he asked in desperation. 'Vanessa, shall we go there? Have a bit of a rest, eh?'

She didn't think much of the set-up in there. While she allowed herself to be served with coffee and a choc chip muffin, she was euphorically redesigning the décor, the uniforms, the staff, the china. At least she left the menu unaltered. Neil supposed, rightly enough, that she knew next to nothing about food preparation.

Three green-overalled plant salesmen were hanging about uneasily eyeing them as they ate. When he went to the cashier to pay he asked her to ring through and put a stay on the gargantuan order. 'Mrs Winter'll have to arrange for somewhere to store the goods first,' he explained. They seemed relieved. One raised a query about the invoices.

'Leave them for the present,' he said. 'She may want to adjust the quantities before delivery, but we'll take some cut flowers for the house if you'll put them on her account.'

'Miss Winter's usual order?'

205

'That seems a good idea. You know the address.'

They let him pay for the coffees and muffins. It seemed that staff and company directors didn't get anything for free.

Set off-balance by Vanessa's eccentric outburst, he found the journey back a horror. Much worse than that; it was a replay of reality. He hadn't allowed for the difference night might make, never having driven this car in the dark. The unfamiliar dashboard and siting of controls played on his initial nervousness, but facing the oncoming glare of headlights from traffic homing at speed in the treacherous country lanes made his guts seize up. He found himself responding with almost hysterical acceleration. The car bucked and shuddered; its tyres screamed on cornering.

He was back in another time, another car, with another woman alongside. That fatal time. It was going to happen over again. He thought he felt the impact and the chaos of spinning, heard again the splintering swear of metal. The taste of blood soured his mouth, and his nostrils were filled with the sickly sweetness of it. He knew he would crash again. And die.

Shaking uncontrollably, he swung the wheel, tore at speed into the grass verge, slewing the big car as he savagely braked, then sat there in the terrible following silence, his head sunk on his chest. He'd hit a ditch and the bank beyond it. The windscreen was blurred by the pressure of dense hawthorn branches. Vanessa's head lolled on his shoulder.

Dear God, not again. Had he killed this one too?

Then she laughed, a rook-like caw. 'Wheeeeh!' Drunk on speed, but she'd be no bloody use for helping get the fucking car back on the road.

Nothing for it, he guessed, but to phone the emergency services. There'd been a yellow AA badge on the front bumper. He started pulling things out of the glove compartment, which no-bloody-body ever used for gloves. Sheila had been a practical sort of person. Chances were he'd find the phone number somewhere in there.

There was a folder with everything he needed. Just the same, the first number he pressed out was for Marty's mobile phone.

★   ★   ★

They didn't have to wait more than fifteen minutes before the breakdown van arrived. A cheerful uniformed man in his forties slashed a way through the hedgerow to open up the bonnet. 'You've been lucky with the wind-screen and headlamps. Just a few deep scratches on the bodywork,' he announced. 'Engine's turning over sweet as a bell. We'll have you out of there in a coupla shakes. Would the lady like to take a seat in me van?'

With Neil standing by, the Alfa Romeo was attached and hauled back on to the road. 'Think you're up to carrying on now?' the AA patrol man enquired. 'Got a valid licence and all that?'

'Yep, and I'm twenty. And no, I've not been drinking.'

He was asked to sign the work sheet. 'You're not the owner of the car?' was the final question.

'It's mine,' Vanessa claimed, 'and I don't drive.'

The man returned the card to its folder. 'Right, Mrs Winter. I'm going out your way. Maybe the young man would like to follow me up.'

It was humiliating to return in convoy, but Vanessa appeared gratified by the attention. Neil dropped her off at the front door and unloaded the cellophane-wrapped flowers the silly old trout had insisted on crowding in the rear floorspace and boot. He parked the car in the open where he'd found it the previous day.

With his arms full of flowers he was

halfway up the front stairs when he heard the shrieks. Vanessa came stumbling out of the flat and hung on to the gallery rail, her face contorted with horror.

'What is it? For God's sake get a grip on yourself.' He dumped the flowers and tried to pull her wrists free, but they were locked fast on the wrought iron, as the shrill screams continued, pumped out between soughing breaths. 'I can't . . . ' she managed to get out.

'Stay here,' he commanded

'Don't leave me. For God'sake, help me.'

Her fingers fastened on his arms, biting into the biceps. His heart pounding, he looked round wildly for a means of escape. She'd lost it completely. He'd always thought she was borderline, and now . . . Shit! — she was dragging him down the stairs again and his feet had tangled with the dumped flowers. The whole damn lot went over, and they were both falling together, head-over-heels-over-shoulders, in an unholy grapple.

He heard his head bash on the lower newel post. It felt split open.

'Let go, woman!' That wasn't his own voice, but Marty's. Where had he materialised from?

He sat up, heaved with nausea and felt Vanessa pulled off him. She was gibbering now. 'There's a *dead body*. On my bed!'

209

15

Rosemary Zyczynski, driving home through the early dusk of Wednesday, had consoled herself that one advantage of being considered useless was that that berk Salmon hadn't kept her on for overtime. She slewed the Ford Escort round the rear corner of the house and pulled up opposite her garage. The silver Alfa Romeo, which had been returned yesterday, was no longer there. So someone had run it under cover. She wondered idly what would become of the car. Beattie had mentioned that Vanessa didn't care for driving, so doubtless she'd be putting it up for sale, possibly get something smaller and easier to manage.

Pity I can't afford it, she thought. Not that I'd dare own a car like that. There'd been mockery enough at the local nick over her upmarket new address.

She operated the electronic door-lift and drove in, switched off, collected her notebook from the glove compartment and made for the house. There were no lights on in Beattie's flat, so she'd managed to fit in the appointment with her hair-dresser. Good:

those little silver streaks above the ears didn't quite suit her

The house appeared quiet as she let herself in at the front door. Upstairs, taped to her own door panels, was a note. 'R, if you can spare time, would you look in on V? She's having a fit of the willies. B'

Z gritted her teeth: yet more angst, after a day of being belittled by the new DI. Well, here at any rate her existence might be appreciated. Not by Vanessa, though. For her, other people were a mere convenience, a tissue to wipe her hands on. Strange woman: if her total blanking out of others was the aftermath of shock, then it was unlike any in Z's experience. There had been no outward show of grief, but this was surely not from ingrained discipline. Vanessa was like a self-pitying child who punished the world for her misfortunes. Perhaps that made her slow to face reality.

The negative response to her daughter's sudden, violent end must be what psychologists dubbed the denial stage of trauma. Beattie had described Vanessa's present mood as 'the willies'. Z wished she'd known the woman better before tragedy struck. It was hard to judge whether this was a typical or transitory state. Whichever, it wasn't proving easy for those close to her.

She dumped her shoulder bag, filled the kettle, told herself not to be a hardhearted cow. (Did cows in fact have no finer feelings? Surely not, with such amiable faces and sad, brown eyes.)

While she waited for the tea to brew she looked through the post which had arrived after she'd left that morning. There was another instruction from an unknown mail order firm to write instantly and claim a stupendous mystery prize. She promptly binned it together with a couple of offers to lend money at advantageous rates.

More demanding of attention were a reminder to renew her TV licence, and a hastily scribbled note from Aunt Alice to complain that Uncle Ted was no better, and she was at the end of her tether with him.

Evil old man, Z mouthed silently. Alice was another case of someone being ground into the earth because she was stronger than those who made demands. She was sorry for her because thirty years ago when she'd married him she couldn't have guessed how he'd turn out. Respectable English ladies weren't so worldly-wise in those days, taking marriage on trust, with no — or minimal — advance experiment. So she'd drawn a bad'un, which wasn't really her fault. And maybe in their earlier days together he'd been tolerable.

All the same, however willfully blind, Alice should have had some inkling of what was going on under her own roof. Almost from the first week of being left with them, Rosemary, newly orphaned at ten, had had to put up with his petting. Taught to be respectful, and afraid of seeming rude to this husband of her dead mother's sister, she'd found herself drawn into scary collusion, only half understanding the awfulness of what he started doing to her, but knowing no way to get free of this imposed 'special secret' they shared. And Alice, busy with new child-based adjustments and her personal grief, hadn't found time to encourage confidences.

Z sighed. The three seizures Ted had suffered in recent years weren't anything she'd wish on her worst enemy, if she'd had one. It was difficult to tell just how much of his mind was still active. She wondered if he could remember what he'd done, and feel any remorse. Behind that empty gaze, did he flinch, knowing what she must think of him?

Poor Alice. She should get her Welfare visitor to arrange a short stay in hospital for the old man, to let her off the leash. Z decided to ring and suggest this later that evening; then perhaps put a cheque in the post so she could book herself in at a decent hotel.

Meanwhile there was what to do about Vanessa. It was all very well for DI Salmon to snarl at her that she wasn't working for social services. There were times when she thought that, apart from Beattie, she was the only one in the world still doing just that. She rinsed her used mug under the tap and went to call on her neighbour.

Vanessa's door was slightly ajar, so clearly she was expected. She knuckled the panels before walking in. From the far end of the apartment she heard a muffled clatter, then rushed, stealthy movements. Had she interrupted Vanessa at something private?

The drawing-room was empty. 'It's Rosemary, Mrs Winter,' she called as she moved farther in. A wedge of light spilled from the bedroom door across the ochre carpet.

'Vanessa?'

As she pushed open the door, there had been a sound like a flock of birds taking to the air. She caught a brief glimpse of the disordered room, as a huge shadow rose and blocked out the light. Something flung itself on her. She swivelled, and her hands, thrown up to protect her face, were a fraction too late. The blow felled her. Her brain seemed to judder inside her skull as she struck the door jamb in falling. Darkness swept over her. She thought only, *There was somebody . . .*

Gingerly Neil Raynes sat up to lean his back against the wall. Marty had his phone to one ear and gave a little flick of the other hand in acknowledgment. 'Two, yes. Both with head injuries. One unconscious. I haven't moved her. Twelve minutes? OK.'

Neil twisted to look for Vanessa. She was sitting bolt upright on a hall chair, chalk-white and with the same stricken look on her face. But conscious. So who else was injured?

'Don't think of moving,' Marty ordered him. 'You were out for almost a minute. I'm sending you to hospital too, for a checkup, just to be safe. Don't worry. A thick-skulled chap like you should be able to take a toss downstairs.'

'Who else? Vanessa said there was a body . . . '

Marty came and hunkered alongside, lowering his voice. 'It looks as though there's been a break-in upstairs. Stuff thrown all over the place. Young Rosemary must have walked in on it and got knocked out. But the bird's flown. He left her on the bed.'

'God, he didn't . . . ?'

'Just coshed, I think. Her clothes weren't interfered with. I'm going to leave you now, if you're feeling all right. I need to take a look around up there before the police and paramedics get here.'

'I'm fine,' said Neil, feeling nausea threaten in his throat. His eyes weren't focusing properly. Bloody hypochondriac! he accused himself, visited by a sudden fear of retinal injury.

It was Rosemary he should be worrying about. How long had she been out cold? Was it serious? He should have shoved Vanessa away and gone to look after the girl.

Then he realized that the hospital they'd be taken to was his own. He'd be portered in by his — what? — scarcely friends. *Colleagues* sounded a bit too fancy. Mark and Paddy; maybe old Grunter. At least now he'd a genuine reason for sick leave!

And what would they make of Rosemary? Both injured, it might look as though they'd been fighting each other. What a bloody mess.

That was the moment Vanessa chose to slither to the floor in a near faint. He crawled over and settled her in recovery position, undid the top button of her jacket and loosened the blouse underneath. She gave a little moan. 'You're going to be fine,' he told her. He'd heard that hollow comfort from so many nurses that mimicking them made him feel a phoney.

'Darling boy,' Vanessa murmured, then

opened her eyes and smiled into his. 'You're a good boy, Gordon, whatever they say.'

He heard the distant braying of the ambulance approaching, then Marty ran downstairs to let the paramedics in. They were a pair Neil knew, but he cut them short with, 'Not us. Upstairs.'

The man thundered up like a herd of buffaloes. The woman returned to the ambulance for a stretcher. Neil pulled himself to his feet and watched the blue light strobing through the open door.

It seemed to take an age before they had the girl's body downstairs, strapped flat under a red blanket. They draped another round his shoulders and helped him up the ambulance steps as if he were an old man. 'Mrs Winter?' he asked.

'She'll be all right. More comfy at home here than waiting in hospital corridors.'

'I'll follow in the car later,' Marty promised. 'Someone has to stay and let the police in.'

Having checked again on Vanessa and handed her over to the schoolteacher, Miss Barnes, who opportunely arrived home at that moment, the woman paramedic elected to drive. Inside the ambulance the man's great bulk, in its Day-Glo uniform, was bent over the stretcher, when Neil needed to watch

217

the unconscious girl's face for signs of life. She appeared to be wearing a neck brace.

'How bad is she?'

'She's out, man. Tha's all you need to know. Did you do this?'

It knocked the breath out of him. 'No!' he shouted. 'I wouldn't have hurt her for all the world!'

'Your girl, eh?' The big black face was sympathetic now. He planted a heavy hand on Neil's knee and gave it a friendly squeeze. 'BP's a bit low, but she'll do nicely. Looks like you'll soon be among friends, eh?'

★   ★   ★

Martin Chisholm helped Miss Barnes settle Vanessa on a sofa. 'I'll give her doctor a ring,' she said briskly. 'She says she's a private patient, so he'll probably be here in no time.'

'Is there anything you'd like me to do?'

'Maybe clear those crushed flowers off the stairs? We don't want the police skidding or tramping them into the carpets.'

Feeling dismissed like a preppie, he was relieved that the woman seemed adequate to the situation. Flowers weren't really his thing, but he'd transferred most of their carnage to the utility room's sink before a flashing blue light announced the police presence.

He blocked their entry at the outer door. 'It's a crime scene,' he said. 'You'll want it secured until CID arrive, won't you?'

Whatever they'd wanted, the uniforms resented the suggestion. 'You watch too much TV,' the older one said. 'We have to ensure the injured are properly cared for. Where's the medics?'

'Come and gone. I can tell you what I found on coming in.'

'Any eye witnesses to the actual attack?'

'Just the victim and the attacker,' he said drily. 'But after that there was a double trip on the stairs. One person has accompanied the unconscious woman to hospital, the other's just dazed, and resting in Flat 2. I doubt if you'll get much sense out of her at present, but she was the one who discovered the unconscious woman in her flat.'

The woman PC had her notebook out. 'Maybe you'd explain who 'she' was and whose flat 'hers' was. Can we have some names? Your first, sir, if you would.'

'Of course. I'm Martin Chisholm from Flat 5, upstairs rear. Flat 4, upstairs right, was the one broken into. It belongs . . . ' He broke off as a second car arrived at speed, spraying gravel.

The passenger door sprang open and a burly man in a waxed jacket and brown

219

corduroys squeezed out. He flapped a leather wallet at them from a distance. 'Detective Inspector Walter Salmon,' he announced himself. 'Who're you?'

The two uniforms appeared to shrink slightly at sight of him. A fourth policeman got out of the driving seat. He too was in plain clothes. 'And DS Beaumont,' he told them. 'Is the injured woman Mrs Winter?'

'No, but it happened in her flat. She was out at the time; came back and found Rosemary on her bed. She'd been knocked out.' Chisholm was equally terse.

'*Rosemary?*'

'Another resident, from Flat 3, upstairs left. She was keeping an eye on Mrs Winter. Are you dealing with her daughter's murder?'

'You mean it's Z who's been hurt?' Beaumont exclaimed, and simultaneously the DI barked out, 'I'm in charge of the murder case.'

'Who's Z?' Chisholm demanded. 'The injured girl is Rosemary Weyman.'

'Wrong surname,' Beaumont informed him. 'Her name's Zyczynski. Weyman is her ex-landlady's name.'

'You know her?' Chisholm pursued.

The two policemen exchanged hard glances.

'You mean she's one of yours? She called

herself a civil servant.'

The detective sergeant's wooden-puppet face stayed deadpan. 'Civil enough. Where's she now?'

Chisholm explained, and the DS started punching numbers into his mobile phone. 'Hold it!' Salmon barked. 'No outgoing info at this point.'

Beaumont's eyes held his. 'The Boss has to know. He'll deal with it.' He moved away into the driveway and began to speak. Furious at public defiance, his senior officer turned on Chisholm. 'I want the eye-witness.'

'I've already explained there wasn't one: just a confused elderly lady who walked in on the scene when the attacker had left. She's the mother of the woman found murdered at Henley-on-Thames. This second shock entitles her to a little consideration; wouldn't you say?' His acute hearing had picked up an approaching car, which he hoped would disgorge the wretched woman's doctor before the DI waded in.

It seemed he'd held the man off just long enough. Behind his back Miss Barnes was letting a tall man in by the front door. It seemed certain that Dr Barlow would forbid any contact until he had spoken with Mrs Winter and ascertained whether she was up to seeing the police.

'Right!' snarled Salmon, 'and I know what he'll want next. She'll be sedated; so the trail goes cold.' He made to push his way up the staircase. Beaumont reached out a hand to restrain him. 'The Boss says to wait for SOCO. The team's on its way.'

'So he's taking this over himself?' demanded the DI, steaming.

'No chance of that.' Mildly Beaumont regarded the other man. He knew Yeadings well enough after all these years to guess where he'd be right now: in a commandeered patrol car with emergency lights and siren going full blast. On his way to see Z in hospital.

16

Rosemary Zyczynski had come to in the ambulance as it made the last hundred yards to the A&E department, but not before she had vomited down the paramedic's white coat.

'I knew there wuz a reason we got waterproofs,' he said, grinning broadly at Neil. 'Pity I just threw it off.' He stripped off down to little more than a g-string and disposed of the mess in a plastic bin.

Z's waking gaze homed in on his ebony pectorals. She gave a low gurgle.

'Yeah, man,' he said. 'Thought that'd bring yuh round.' He reached for a clean tunic. 'Gotta disappoint yuh now.' He climbed in and buttoned up. 'So, honey, how yuh feelun? Nuh, sorry. What I mean is, what's yoh name?'

'Muzzy,' she said. 'But I know who I am.'

'Good. Your buddy here has just given birth to a set of fire-irons.' He grinned reassuringly. 'Looks like we've reached base now, so we have to unload. Mind if I come in with you?'

'Stay for coffee,' she invited feebly.

'Good gal, yuh'll do.'

The rear doors were swung open, the step lowered and the stretcher slid out on to a trolley. Neil, clutching his blanket, followed on foot as the paramedics rushed the patient through the entrance. He saw now she'd had a line put in and the driver had come round to hoist the fluid bag.

Neil knew it was bad. Rosemary had lost consciousness, then vomited. There could be concussion, so they'd watch her like hawks for at least twenty-four hours. He felt a fraud expecting to be treated here himself.

'Well, look what's turned up,' said a familiar voice. 'Nurse, take this one into a cubicle and clean him up. I'll come along when we've got the young lady fixed up. Have you two been fighting, lad?'

An invalid chair was pushed under him. He raised his feet submissively while they got the flanges dropped. Then he was whisked off, out of sight of whatever they were up to with Rosemary. He was too overwhelmed to protest.

His forehead was mopped up and disinfected. Tapes were being applied to stick the gash together when Marty put his head through the curtain. 'They told me I'd find you in here. How's it going?'

'How's Rosemary?' he overrode him.

'Sent upstairs. If you're well enough to

come back to work, you may get the chance to drool over her bed.'

'I'll live,' he said miserably. 'God, what a mess!'

'A bad day? Still, your hair's OK.'

'Very droll. Imagine landing up here. Back at work.' He sounded disgusted.

'I've brought in your medication and some essential gear. Trust you to fall among friends. You'll be asking them for your sick note, then handing it back again.'

'Can I see her?'

'Rosemary? I shouldn't think so. There's a queue at the moment, and neither of you should be getting excited.'

'That would only be me. I doubt she knows I exist, except as a handyman. I fixed her gas boiler yesterday.'

'You're talking too much, old man. I think you're for a bed upstairs when they can get one free. *Male* surgical ward, though; so don't expect too much.' He flipped a hand in his direction.

He saw no need to warn him that the girl might be police. If he dropped her suddenly, or started getting defensive, she would probably smell something a bit off. Anyway he knew nothing that mattered as yet.

★ ★ ★

'Just two minutes,' Sister told Yeadings. 'I don't have to tell you not to upset her.'

'This is purely a sympathy visit. No mention of work,' he promised. But he'd reckoned without Z. Her bandaged head turned towards him as he entered the private room. Her face was bloodless and her eyes enormous.

'They've fixed you up nicely here.'

'Sir, I've been trying to recall what happened.'

'Don't push yourself. It's bound to be vague at present.'

'It's coming, though. But it was all so fast. I never saw whoever it was. Heard noises. I think I'd disturbed him searching the place.'

'So you'll not be giving a description?'

'I was expecting Vanessa. It was her bedroom. But this was someone much larger, bigger than me. I just remember this huge shadow coming at me. I think now that the wardrobe doors must have been open. That whole wall is glass and what I saw was his reflection in it; not him at all. So when I ducked I got it wrong, and he slugged me.'

'With a table lamp. You're lucky that it broke, being china. I wouldn't have given much for your chances with a brass one. Though I guess you don't feel so lucky at present.'

She pulled a face. 'I don't understand what an intruder would want in *Vanessa's* room, unless he was a burglar. It's Sheila who was killed, and we've been through all her stuff.'

'Someone who didn't know one bedroom from the other? Or thought Sheila might have hidden something among her mother's things?'

'Yes, or someone who knew that Vanessa raided her daughter's cupboards for anything she fancied. I've once or twice seen her wearing Sheila's clothes. Even dresses. They fit all right on her, apart from looking too long. Maybe there were other things beyond clothes that she helped herself to. Someone could have noticed that she did that.'

'So everyone in the house is a suspect.'

'I guess so, because the outer doors are never left unlocked. Was there any sign of a break-in?' she suggested hopefully.

'No. Whoever attacked you came from indoors. So a resident, or else someone he or she let in. Beaumont is to look into everyone's whereabouts. Also into the question of spare keys.'

'Sir, who found me?'

'Mrs Winter. I've just had Beaumont on the phone with a rundown on events. Your young neighbour is in here as well. He tripped on the stairs, dealing with the distraught lady.'

'Neil? Oh, I'm sorry. Is he badly hurt? And how's Vanessa standing up to this second shock?'

'I haven't checked on the young man yet. As for Mrs Winter — I've no idea. Her doctor's looking after her.'

'At home? So Beattie's dragged in again, I suppose.'

'Beattie was out at the time. Everyone claimed to be. Which doesn't help. At present Mrs Winter's with another neighbour, a Miss Barnes, who took over on arriving home.

'Look Z, Sister's making signals at me through the porthole. I have to leave you, but Nan will drop in tomorrow sometime. She'll ring up first to ask what you'd like her to bring along. Get some rest now. Take all the time you need.'

★　★　★

'Right,' DI Salmon began grimly, demanding hush and reviewing the briefing assembly. 'We're one CID officer down. Which means that everyone must pull on his oars that little bit harder.'

Now that she'd gone missing, it seemed that Z had been of some value to the team.

Beaumont, sucking the end of his ballpoint pen at the back of the room, pondered the imagery. Pulling on oars brought Henley-on-Thames regatta to mind, but scarcely seemed to suggest a combined uniform and CID operation. A right assortment of crab-catchers they'd be.

So, Henley-on-Thames. The location hadn't yielded any clues. None of the staff or regulars at the White Swan had apparently seen the dead woman before. Or so they said. Her photograph, touted door-to-door in the town, had failed to raise a response. It looked as though the pub car park had merely served as a random dumping ground for whoever drove the body there; or was driven there by Winter when still alive. Which raised the question of how he got away afterwards. Taxi firms in the area hadn't yielded anything of promise. So had a second car driver been involved for getaway?

Henley folk presented a tight little community, only heavily swelled in the summer months. At this time of year outsiders would be remarked on. So the car was probably left at a time when the good townsfolk were all in bed. The days were gone when a beat constable walked the streets all night and spotted anything amiss.

The question of Animal Rights Activists had been raised because of the slashed mink coat. There were none known locally. That sort of vicious damage hailed more from urban leftists than these rural parts of Thames Valley. Round here nobody even got sentimental about foxes. That possibility must still be considered, though, because Sheila Winter's garden centre had a small section devoted to household pets. Although their accommodation seemed reasonably comfortable to him, God knows what the crazies would make of it.

And the expensive fur coat raised a second point. Why that and nothing else? Had she started out that Saturday evening fully dressed, dolled up for a dinner out or some kind of entertainment? If so, who with? Or *with whom?*, as the Boss would put it. And where were the rest of her clothes? Her mother had been useless when asked what she'd have been wearing.

The linen basket contained only what Sheila had worn at work. And she'd certainly come home to change, because the borrowed Vectra had been parked at the front of the house, outside the Major's windows when he went to draw the curtains before watching the six o'clock TV news. It had gone an hour later when Miss Barnes arrived back from a staff meeting at school. And nobody had the least idea where it had gone, until the body was discovered in it on Sunday morning.

Yesterday they'd received the first bit of gossip on the woman's private life. And it was offered by Z, for what it was worth. Salmon had fired a broadside at her for not speaking up before. It seemed that on the previous Tuesday she had walked in on her neighbour in *flag. delict.* And been too ladylike to stay and find out who it was humping her. The interesting thing was that it had been a moment of sudden passion, to judge from the scattered clothing in the hall. And Sheila Winter had dared to take her lover to bed, or rather to drawing-room sofa, in her own flat where anyone might have walked in on them.

Z had denied that last supposition. She claimed that there was little come and go between the residents. Despite Beattie's hopes of creating an extended family, they all liked their privacy and respected each others'. She'd just happened to bring up the Winters' post from the hall and found the latch hadn't been dropped on the flat's door. She'd knocked, and called as she went in, but there was a lot going on at the time and the participants hadn't heard her.

She'd claimed that to her one set of white buttocks was much the same as another. So she hadn't volunteered any name; only mentioned that the two men in Flat 5 had spent most of August sailing round the

Canary Islands and their suntan was probably all-over. So that seemed to knock out Chisholm and the boy Neil Raynes, who were possibly an exclusive item anyway. That left two other possibles from the residents: Paul Wormsley, Flat 6, and the retired major in Flat 1, both from the lower floor who would have needed to cross the hall to go up the stairs behind Z's back while she sorted the post. Naturally Salmon had expected her to have eyes in the back of her head — or to be as insensitively nosy as he was himself. Someone had certainly gone up, but she'd no idea who.

According to her story she hadn't gone straight to the Winters' apartment after sorting the post. She'd dumped her own letters in her kitchen and made a pot of tea, giving Sheila, or whoever, time to settle in. What she hadn't explained was where the older woman would have been at the time. Sheila was unlikely to have left her door unlocked for an expected lover when her mother might pop in at any moment. So presumably the older woman had gone out by taxi and wasn't expected back. Beaumont made a note to check on Mrs Winter's movements on the early evening of the Tuesday before her daughter's murder.

His slowly chugging train of thought was abruptly derailed.

'So did you?' Salmon snarled. His gaze was fixed on the DS and he'd clearly had to repeat his question, which notched up another degree or two to his temperature.

'As far as possible,' Beaumont ventured, totally at sea. And then, lamely, 'It's early days yet.'

Everyone's eyes were fixed on him. DC Silver attempted to bridge the gap. 'There are only three copies of the tapes so far, sir. We've circulated two among uniform branch since they're more familiar with staff at the centre.'

'Yes,' Beaumont said briskly, picking up on the cue, 'and I want one copy to go to the hospital for DS Zyczynski to view. Security there have facilities for examining CCTV film, and they'll allow her to use it.' He hoped there was some truth in that. Wasn't the Raynes boy employed at the hospital? He'd surely be able to wangle something of the sort, even from a ward bed.

Salmon let it go at that. Since releasing Barry Childe, only one success had resulted from widespread investigation employing swollen numbers drawing overtime. DC Silver had at last gained access to the laptop computer, surprisingly acknowledging help from Superintendent Yeadings, who was renowned as a technological dummy.

While he was still wading through Sheila's correspondence, both business and personal, he had found nothing to suggest that she had any connection with Childe's project out at the Marlow cottage. Unless, of course, code words were used for any illegal substances. Someone would need to check in a horticultural encyclopaedia that each species quoted was genuine. He couldn't remember offhand if any constables had a background of classical Latin. Maybe they'd need to call in an expert.

Civilian office staff at the local nick had been allocated to listing wholesalers and the more important account-holding customers. The personal stuff, which included originals of the dead woman's annual correspondence with her father, had yet to be sorted.

Salmon now decided to divert more on to DS Beaumont who struck him as far too relaxed in his attitude to the job. Silver could do the hacking and pass on what he found.

With questions of his own to find answers for, Beaumont was not enchanted. 'What else are we covering?' he demanded, suspicious that the DI hadn't allocated any of the labour to himself.

Salmon recalled Yeadings's instructions. 'I want everyone in that house thoroughly vetted,' Salmon ground out. 'Starting with the woman who had the conversion done. I want to know how she advertised for purchasers, the dates the contracts were taken up, and a full life history of all involved. Hobday, get on to Beattie Weyman's background. Fanshawe, you have the rest of the residents. Somewhere there's a connection with the dead woman that we haven't learnt of. Maybe a shake-out of Criminal records will give us a lead.

'And Beaumont, that Dr Fenner — I want an hour by hour account of what he was up to on the night of the murder, and who he contacted right from leaving Cambridge until he got back there after visiting his ex-wife. It would appear that the terms of his daughter's will were a surprise to him. If he's in low water financially he may have been relying on a quick fix from that. Now go and dig the dirt, and dig deep.'

Beaumont slunk off, following DC Silver to the office, little more than a broom cupboard, where he'd been occupied printing out reams from the laptop. He was riled at Salmon's jumping on him at the briefing. He'd had better lines to follow in his mind at the time. There was a disturbing sense of having nearly been on to something important. Now, distracted, he knew it had got away. He wasn't quite sure where his reasoning had been leading him, to a point of almost-revelation. Just a half idea — something beginning with 'but . . . '

It had gone. He sighed.

At least the DI had let up on his obsession with Barry Childe. Now the Salmon fishing was into more widespread waters. Not deep yet: but up to the DI's fishy neck.

'I'm to collect the CCTV videos,' he reminded Silver, who was immersed in the laptop's data.

The DC gave him a harassed glare. 'I've only one copy of every video here and I've no idea what's in them. I had this other thing dropped on me before I could get cracking.'

'That's because our new man likes the sound of your name. He hasn't managed to memorize more than half a dozen, so we lucky sods come in for the full load.'

'Where'll you be working? You need to book a screen.'

'Just hand me the goods. I'll do the rest.'

Silver indicated a black plastic sack under a corner of his desk. 'Let me know where you'll be, sarge. I need to be covered, in case the DI comes charging in.'

Beaumont smiled beatifically. 'You can tell him I'm in hospital. I fancy joining Z in there. There's no reason why she should take it easy while we bend our backs under the lash. I'm going to commandeer a bit of National Health Service property and hold her hand in the back row at the movies.'

17

Miss Barnes poured tea for Mrs Winter and smiled as she offered the madeira cake. The woman was taking this second blow very well. She seemed the indomitable kind, sitting there like a dowager at a formal reception, stiff-backed and attempting to be gracious. After such appalling things had happened such poise was almost unnatural; perhaps the false recovery after shock, and time would eventually break her down.

The schoolmistress took a furtive glance at her watch. Her visitor had been here for almost ten minutes now. If only the doctor would arrive. Then perhaps they could broach the subject of what had actually happened. Major Phillips had kindly offered to look out for him and direct him to which bell to ring.

She wished that Mr Chisholm had given her a fuller account of the incident. He had briefly explained that when she came home Mrs Winter had found young Rosemary unconscious in her apartment, had run out and then tumbled down the stairs. Neil Raynes had fortunately broken her fall but sustained injury to his head. Both young people had been taken away in an ambulance by paramedics. It was a curious catalogue of disasters.

Why Rosemary was in the wrong flat at all was uncertain, nor was it mentioned what had caused her to faint. Miss Barnes hoped there was no connection with the terrible murder of the woman's daughter. The Winters seemed to be pursued by gross misfortunes. It was an alarming introduction to life at this house, which had at first promised to be admirably peaceful.

The doorbell shrilled and she started in her chair. 'He's here,' she told Mrs Winter, rose and went to let him in.

The man who stood with the Major under the portico was tall and spare. 'Dr Fenner,' he introduced himself. 'I was told . . . '

'Yes, doctor. Do come in. Mrs Winter is through here.'

He followed her in and laid his briefcase on the side table under the Vauxhall mirror while he removed his driving gloves.

Mrs Winter's reaction was electric and incomprehensible. 'What are *you* doing here?' she demanded imperiously.

He turned to face her. Miss Barnes felt caught in the middle of two strong opposing forces. 'This is the doctor, dear,' she said placatingly. 'We were expecting him, you remember.'

'This,' Mrs Winter declared dramatically, 'is the man I was once so ill-advised as to marry. I don't wish to have anything to do with him.'

'Vanessa, you rang me,' he reminded her patiently. 'You sounded uncertain. I've come back specifically to discuss what I told you then on the phone.'

'The discussion is over,' she declared, like a quotation from some play.

Of course, Miss Barnes reminded herself, the woman had been some kind of actress. It was understandable that parts she had played were still locked in her mind. It was the same with literature: passages you'd admired and loved, even found formidable, surged up and escaped when similar situations recalled them. One was looked at askance when colleagues failed to recognize the source of what one quoted; those in the sciences particularly.

The man — not Mrs Winter's personal physician after all; from his title perhaps an academic like herself — did not appear dismayed. It was as though his patience increased and he addressed his ex-wife more slowly.

'Vanessa,' he said, 'believe me, I'm pleased

and relieved that Sheila has made provision for you. And I'm sure that following wise advice you will find it more than adequate for your reasonable needs.'

'Whose advice?' she demanded. 'Yours, I suppose. Not in a million years.'

'I mean professional advice. I'll admit I've never been outstandingly successful with money myself. Nor interested in it. But if you'll consult Sheila's accountant I think you'll find him reliable in protecting your interests. Have you taken thought yet what you'll do with your shares in the garden centre?'

Vanessa stared at him. She could counter his attacks until the cows came home, but demanding answers of her was unfair. He wanted to know what she would do with Sheila's business? Well, sell it, she supposed. On first sight it had quite impressed her, decked out with Christmas glitter. She had almost been carried away with the heady sense of ownership. But it was only tat after all; and all those eager assistants were just gardeners and shopgirls. They meant nothing to her. Yes, she'd sell it and use the money to — to what? Back a play? A shiver of excitement went through her. She'd be what the profession called an 'Angel'. She could hire a theatre, entertain exciting young dramatists, choose a new production. Star in it.

Dr Fenner watched her recede into some inner world, and sighed. He raised his eyebrows at Miss Barnes, shook his head and reached for his gloves and briefcase. It was useless trying to help. He might as well have stayed on in Cambridge, for all the effect his efforts had produced.

Miss Barnes showed him through the hall to the outer door, unsure quite how the score stood between the two of them, but aware that they were combatants and no less so because of his well-intentioned visit. 'Goodbye, Dr Fenner,' she said, and couldn't truthfully add *it was nice meeting you.*

He looked sombre. 'I shouldn't have come. She can't understand. It has yet to hit her.'

She supposed he meant her daughter's death as well as the situation she found herself in as a result. It was going to be difficult. Miss Barnes wished she hadn't been brought into it. But to whom could she hand over the poor woman now? She had less responsibility for her than an ex-husband had. Did he expect her to offer to do more than at present? It was unreasonable: she had a full-time job which took all her energy and patience. She couldn't, wouldn't, make promises which she'd never be able to fulfil.

Instead she said simply, 'I'm sorry,' and shut the door on him.

★   ★   ★

Pursued by an awareness of duty avoided, Dr Fenner pulled off the motorway and, as soon as a convenient space presented itself, ran the car on to the grass verge and pulled up. This was his second attempt to get back to normality and Cambridge, but, as ever after coping with Vanessa, he felt he'd been batting at thin air. It took a little while to get his thoughts reassembled.

Going back to confront her again was out of the question. If he was tactful, maybe he'd get what he needed from the kindly Miss Barnes. It meant first demanding her number from the directory service and, thankfully, he found it wasn't a withheld one.

On answering, she sounded a trifle distracted, which didn't surprise him. Anyone coping with is ex-wife could very soon . . .

'It's Fenner again, Miss Barnes. I apologise for disturbing you, but did Vanessa's doctor turn up?' he asked in concerned voice.

'Oh yes, Dr Fenner. He's just left. He's given her a prescription for her high blood pressure and a repeat of the sleeping pills she had before.'

243

'And there's no real damage from the tumble she took?'

'He said there would be a little bruising to the upper arms and knees, but nothing serious.'

'Good. You didn't mention his name, Miss Barnes. I wonder if you would give me his phone number too. I'd like to make sure she has every care possible.'

'Dr Barlow's number?' She hesitated. 'I don't know that I . . . I mean, I don't know it. Someone else got in touch with him for me. Maybe Mr Chisholm, or the police . . . '

The woman was lying, and not very good at it. Vanessa must be listening in and making signs of refusal. What had the wretched woman been telling her about him that suddenly made her so disobliging?

'No matter,' he said casually. 'I'm sure it's in the book. Thank you, Miss Barnes, for your kindness to her.'

'It's no more than anyone would do,' she disclaimed.

But more than many would care to, once they knew Vanessa, he thought grimly. It was bitter that Sheila should have had to spend her short life yoked to such a demanding harridan, but there had been no alternative after the divorce. All those years ago, in a court battle, any judge would have given

244

custody of an eight-year-old girl to the child's mother.

Even at that time Vanessa acknowledged no family. She had chosen to outgrow their modest existence when she took to the stage.

He wondered if the superintendent knew that she wasn't actually alone in the world. Someone would need to take her on now. It seemed sensible, advantageous even, to ring the man and let him know. Somewhere in an inner pocket was a card from Yeadings with a note of the police station he was at present working from.

Fenner switched on the car light and read off the number, rang through and was answered by Detective-Sergeant Beaumont.

★ ★ ★

Superintendent Yeadings sat slumped behind the wheel while the car warmed up. Walking back through the overheated hospital corridors the whim had seized him to rebel against his wifely-imposed diet; but not here. The café in Outpatients was half full with arthritic pensioners and youngsters with splints and bandages, or on crutches. Any of them, or the middle-aged, middle-class do-gooders who voluntarily staffed the place, might recognize him and try to strike up an inquisitive

245

conversation. Besides, he specifically needed real, black espresso and a darkly crisp doughnut sparkling with sugar, but soft inside and oozing rich seedless raspberry jam.

He relished them mentally, almost drooling, then sighed and stoically dismissed the dream.

His Rover was parked at the extremity of the ever-increasing acreage for which he was expected to fork out more than the price of the snack he'd denied himself. One comfort was that the car parking money went back to hospital services.

Over to his right, uphill, extensions were continuing. He watched a mechanical digger at work, a long-necked dinosaur scrabbling at the stony soil; and nearer, its upper floors catching the last of the evening light, rose a stylish red-brick block, new since he was here last time. Ahead, as he sat at the wheel, was a temporary fence and a monochrome view down the valley which disappeared into the ever denser mist as dusk came on. Along the fence's wires, and scabbing the rough wooden posts, frost was returning, sparkling like the sugar on his dreamed-up doughnut. And in stark close-up, harshly sentinel, stood teasel flower heads in stiff, black silhouette.

It struck him that the scene summed up his present situation, the lack of definition to this murder case — appropriately *Winter* case — and in the foreground the abrasive presence of the man he resented.

He had tried to avoid prejudice, admitting that anyone appointed in Angus Mott's place would be a letdown; but the new DI's bull-at-a-gate performance over Barry Childe had sounded alarms. To be fair to the man, by now he'd let second thoughts switch him on to other tracks, but at present — to mix the metaphors thoroughly — he was spinning on his axis and firing wildly from the hip.

Yeadings grunted. What wouldn't he give for Mott's subtle approach and steady touch? Small wonder that his own mind was demanding comfort food! However, with Angus gone, helping to police the post-war chaos in Kosovo, Serious Crimes must make do with what was on offer. The onus was on himself to make good any deficiency, steer Salmon off the rocks — God, he was punning as badly as Beaumont now! (Beaumont, who'd gone as spiky as a porcupine over the new appointment) — soothe said DS and ensure that Z didn't return to work before she was really fit.

With his prize team in disarray, he had to rally it while accepting the unwelcome outsider and his unsubtle approach. He reminded himself that within the system's limits everyone had his, or her, own way of taking up a challenge.

Somewhere under his overcoat the mobile phone was vibrating. He pulled it out. It showed Beaumont calling.

So, what now? When the DS had rung him directly before, it was to report that Z had been injured. Yeadings switched to Receive, prepared for more bad news.

'Sir,' the DS began, 'can we talk?'

'Now is convenient, or in twenty minutes in my office.'

'It'll keep till then.'

Not urgent, then; but clearly important. Yeadings slid into gear and reversed out of the parking space.

Beaumont arrived only two minutes behind him and he came in carrying a computer printout. The espresso machine was already hissing under pressure. 'There's no fresh milk,' Yeadings warned him, 'so you'll not be getting a cappuccino.'

'Black's fine,' the DS assured him. 'I've been talking to Silver.'

'He's dealing with the CCTV film, isn't he?'

'Was. Now I'm in overall charge of that. Among other odds and ends.' Beaumont sounded gritty. 'Silver's been churning out stuff from Sheila Winter's laptop, but hasn't had time to go through it. Instructions were to print everything out.'

'Sounds thorough,' Yeadings commented.

'But a massive job, and nobody allocated to do the reading. So I picked over a few bits of her correspondence and guess what I found?'

The superintendent passed a full mug. 'I'm waiting.'

'Copies of a letter thanking one Nat Baker, who had apparently known of Childe in prison and recommended him to Miss Winter as 'suitable for the purpose'.'

'That sounds interesting.'

'Except that I got straight on to Pankhurst Prison governor's office and in the last forty years they've never had any inmate of that name. Bakers galore, but no Nathaniel or anything like it. So maybe the two of them were stringing her along.'

'But why should anyone pretend to be an old lag if he wasn't?'

'Because she needed someone at the garden centre who wouldn't be above a spot of criminal malarkey, and what better recommendation than one from someone she already knew who claimed to be in the same line of business?'

Yeadings agreed that that had a certain kind of logic. 'It makes her enterprise look more than a trifle dodgy.'

'That's why I asked Silver to pull out every reference to Baker or Nat elsewhere in the files. It seems that was the only letter she ever wrote him.'

'Ever wrote on that laptop,' Yeadings corrected him. 'There may be something on the hard disk of the office computer. And it's not entirely impossible for her to have written by hand from home. Check the name against her personal address book. If she didn't write, maybe she saw him on a regular basis. See if anyone at the garden centre knows him or can come up with a description. But don't approach Childe on this. At least, not for the present.'

'Right, sir.' He sounded anything but chuffed. Clearly he was feeling overworked, and that his responsibility had been discharged by passing that much info on.

'So what are the other odds and ends you mentioned?'

'I have to chase up Fenner, for the day and evening of the murder. Also for any contacts he made when he came across from Cambridge to see you.'

Reasonable areas for investigation, Yeadings considered. Salmon had been thorough ordering that. But the work should have been more widely distributed. 'Fenner, yes. He was a major shareholder, of course. He could have been involved.'

'I've just had a call from him. It seems that Vanessa Winter has a sister, Kathleen Patterson. She seems to have been a bit of a black sheep according to the parent's strict way of thinking. She's four years younger, which now makes her fifty-three. She left home, or was turned out, at the age of seventeen, made pregnant by an unknown, 'had an irregular lifestyle' — that's Fenner's expression for prostitution — produced two more children and eventually married a butcher. None of her activities endeared her to her sister who, in her Cambridge years, was persuaded to pay her to stay away. Since then, Fenner claims not to know what's become of the fair Kathleen.'

'What's his motive in coming up with her now? Does he think it's relevant to the murder?'

'He seems to think Vanessa won't be happy all alone in the world. I guess he welcomes any alternative to himself to be held responsible for her. It's none of our business in any case. We're not social workers.'

Yeadings considered this. Perhaps Dr Fenner still had enough feelings for his ex-wife to pity her aloneness, yet kept a cool eye out for self-preservation. To judge by their attitudes earlier, there would be no chance of them getting together again.

'Another thing,' Beaumont complained. 'He's just been back to see her. Miss Barnes rang to tell us. She sounded a little put out. He wanted Vanessa's doctor's number so that he could discuss her condition. She thought it better not to supply it.'

'Vanessa's condition, or situation? He could be genuinely concerned for her.'

'Miss Barnes seemed to suspect his motives.'

'A cautious woman, more used to wily youngsters than adults, I imagine. Well, no harm in our contacting the medic. The doctor *is* a man? Right. I wonder if he was the daughter's GP too. He won't have had a great deal to do with either of them since they came here from London only a couple of months ago; but their records will have been sent on. He should certainly be put on the list for interviewing.'

He regarded Beaumont's stiffly glowering face and relented. 'I'll mention it to DI Salmon myself and suggest someone to take that on. Your coffee's gone cold by now. Slop it into the Swiss cheese plant, and I'll pour you another.'

18

Detective-constable Hugh Fanshawe wasn't getting far in checking on the residents of Ashbourne House. He found only the oldies at home when he called next morning.

Major Phillips, a widower, was champing at the bit, impatient to be whisked off by a civilian driver he addressed crisply as 'corporal'. He claimed he had barely known the dead woman and denied ever having visited any of the upstairs flats at any time.

'In fact,' he claimed, 'the only resident I ever catch sight of is my next-door neighbour, Miss Barnes. I am pleased to find that, after the one dinner at which we were all introduced, it is possible to live in decent seclusion. And now I really must be on my way.'

He had described himself as retired, which shouldn't prove difficult to confirm from army sources; and the business he was in such a hurry to be about was obvious. The rear of the car was stacked with golf clubs, rugs and a large wicker hamper. The Major himself wore an old-fashioned pepper-and-salt pair of plus-fours, and under a checked hacking jacket several woollen garments, the top one of which was mustard yellow. All his clothes appeared to be of good quality but well worn. Fanshawe, a martyr to family shopping sprees, rightly guessed that since the late wife's much earlier departure Major Phillips had seen no reason to extend his wardrobe.

As for golf, Fanshawe, a non-player whose only interest in sport was attending Wycombe Wanderers' home matches, accepted that the game might be a relaxation for some, but he was worldly-wise enough to know that it didn't rule out profitable dealing in, or on, the course of nineteen holes.

He bravely dared to demand a list of the parties Major Phillips was accustomed to play with, and stood hangdog but persistent until given the name of his club, any of whose par-level players the gentleman found acceptable for a scratch game.

Fanshawe made a note to consult his cousin Derek who occasionally played at the same club at a time and day of the week set aside for artisan members. Women also were segregated, with one afternoon's freedom on the greens. The DC, passionately opposed to any form of apartheid, scorned to drink his beer anywhere his company was likely to be held in question, but he wasn't above tapping for information others with less social conscience. Derek was a great gossip and would happily pass on any current info the bar staff might exchange for the price of a double.

Fanshawe looked through his notes. That much, or little, would have to satisfy the new DI. Padded out and printed double-spaced, it should look more impressive.

The next resident he tackled was Miss Beatrice Weyman, Z's ex-landlady who'd apparently inherited a fortune, bought the old, failed nursing-home and had it converted into flats. He glanced at his watch and was pleased to see that it showed ten forty-five, a favourable hour for elevenses. Beattie's reputation for hospitality had reached him via the canteen grapevine.

He caught her working over a floured board, kneading and slapping down dough as though she had some personal grudge against it. He watched her shape the loaves and rolls, set them out on greased baking sheets and commit them to the Aga which gushed out a further burst of heat on the already cosy kitchen. 'I'll jest rinse me 'ands,' she told him, 'then we'll 'ave a nice potta tea.'

She performed a fussy little job over setting out the tray, where he observed three cups, saucers and plates. When the kettle was switched on she spent a moment patting her bright, burnished-copper hair and inspecting herself in a little mirror over the draining-board. Apparently satisfied, she looked expectantly at the clock.

Almost simultaneously Fanshawe heard a diesel-fired motor in the drive beyond her kitchen window. A car door slammed and she went to open up, greeting the newcomer with a warning, 'We gotta special visitor 'ere today. Come in and meet 'im.'

A tall, stringy man with a weathered face and tufty brown hair entered wearing ancient jeans and a brightly checked shirt daubed with pale paint splashes. His large feet, in thick grey socks revealed that he had tidily disposed of his boots on the tiles outside.

'Hello there,' he said, grinning cheerfully, and stretched out a massive, work-hardened hand. 'I'm Frank Perrin. So what job's she pulled you in for, then?'

Beattie clucked in mock annoyance. 'This young man's a policeman, Frank. He's looking into that awful business with Miss Winter.'

'Oh, yes.' All the grinning wrinkles dropped off his face. It was left knobby like an old potato. A sad potato, Fanshawe thought.

'Terrible,' Perrin said grimly. 'Have you got anywhere yet, finding out who done it?'

While Beattie produced a plate of buttered scones with damson jam and a home-made lemon sponge, Fanshawe parried the man's questions and rolled out the usual neutral clichés: early days yet, pursuing several lines of inquiry, and so on.

It seemed that the man was a builder of sorts, and he'd been responsible for most of the conversion. Obviously too there was more than a client-tradesman relationship here. The old girl was sweet on the man, though he could be a few years her junior. And he was quite happy lapping up the benefits.

Fanshawe tried to hide the hunter's gleam in his eyes. His policeman's suspicions were instantly aroused. He wondered how much more money the old lady had left. Even if she'd spent a good part of her inheritance on the house purchase, she'd have received more back when she sold off the other six flats. There'd be a bank loan in it somewhere, but she must be worth a pretty penny all the same. And Frank Perrin was in a good position to know all the details. This little story was worth writing up while he was on the Sheila Winter job.

Could there be a connection? It struck him then that Perrin could have been the intruder Z had disturbed in the Winters' apartment. He was evidently a regular visitor here. And

Beattie had been out that afternoon, at the hairdresser's. He'd have had a clear run.

'You considered installing alarms here, I suppose?' Fanshawe asked innocently, as if Crime Prevention was his line of business. (At that thought he reminded himself that the new designation was 'Crime Reduction'. Not before time: an honest admission of how policing was dropping off!)

Perrin scratched at his head and the tufted hair stood up more wildly. 'Thought about it, didn't we? Decided we'd leave it to the residents to make up their own minds. Individual, like. There's only one of 'em went for it. That Mr Wormsley. He's got a thing about security and no mistake. Never saw so many extra locks and bolts and grilles on the windows. You'd think he was a jeweller.'

'So what is he?'

''E's got a photographer's shop over in Luton,' said Beattie mildly. 'Not that 'e does any of it in the 'ouse. I asked 'im if 'e'd take a snap of the party we all 'ad together that time, and 'e said 'e'd send a girl across to do it. Well, we didn't want outsiders in, so I said no.'

'Do you employ a locksmith?' Fanshawe asked Perrin casually.

'Nuh. I'm more than adequate. Did most

258

of the locks meself, with my man Dave helping.'

The DC nodded. Of course. And Perrin could have had as many keys cut as he wanted, so giving free access at any time to any of the residents' rooms. DI Salmon would go frantic with joy when he brought this back to the debriefing.

Frank Perrin would be their prime suspect for the man who'd knocked out poor Z. He had perfect opportunity; the means were to hand in the china table-lamp; his motive was to cover up the fact of his snooping. And his reason for that? Maybe the man was a jackdaw.

He watched Perrin help himself to another scone and load it with damson jam. 'What'll your wife say lunch-time, when you've no appetite?' he asked, trying to sound cheeky-friendly.

Perrin wiped his fingers on the napkin provided by Beattie. He munched with swollen hamster cheeks until he had swallowed and could reply. 'Nuh. I'm a sad old bachelor. What good lady could stand me tramping all my mess into her tidy little home?'

Fanshawe thought he could name one right now. He looked across at Beattie who had a butter-wouldn't-melt look on her amiable face. He hoped she wouldn't be taken in by the plausible rogue. But perhaps it was already too late.

He was starting to make excuses to go when another van drew up outside, behind Perrin's pick-up. 'Looks like Jon,' Beattie said. ''E'll be wanting you, Frank, but ask 'im in. I'm sure 'e could do with a slice of cake.'

Fanshawe, trained to take note automatically of all vehicles, observed that it was an oldish but well-kept white Ford Transit with a set of aluminium ladders on the roof. In profile and screened by the window, its licence plates were hidden. Perrin went across to the door and held a conversation over the threshold.

'One of his men?' Fanshawe inquired.

'No, but 'e uses him sometimes when there's a rush job on. 'E's another nice feller, is Jon.'

By leaning sideways in his chair the DC could read the name off the van's side: *Jonathan Baker*, and underneath *Plumber & Heating Engineer*.

So the man ran a private firm. Yes, he supposed Perrin would have used him at times. There could always be rush jobs when pipes burst or tanks sprung a leak. Nothing of great interest there. The man wasn't a locksmith.

Frank Perrin came back in and closed the door. 'He says thanks for the offer, but no thanks. He's running late as it is. He's got me that special conduit I was after.'

Fanshawe, comfortably replete, prepared to take his leave. 'There's nobody else here for me to see. Everyone's gone to work. Except the two in hospital.'

'Young Neil should be coming home today,' said Beattie. 'I spect 'e'll need an eye kept on 'im if 'is friend's going away.'

'Is he?'

But she wasn't going into details. Instead, 'Well, there's Mrs Winter you could look in on, if she's feeling up to it. Ackshally she might rather like that, if you make a little fuss of 'er, like.'

She directed him through to the hall and showed him the staircase. 'Jest go up and ring 'er bell. It's the one on the right.'

Vanessa Winter came to the door in a coral satin bathrobe and her hair in a towelling turban. According to the printout notes he'd received, she was fifty-seven and a divorcee. Catching her barefaced like this he would have thought her older, something like Beattie's age or even more. 'Oh,' she said casually, when he'd explained himself, 'I'm just dressing. You can come along.'

A little uncertainly he followed her as far as

the door to her bedroom. When she seated herself at the dressing-table, back towards him, he advanced a couple of paces. It was only her face she'd be putting on.

She touched a button and small bulbs sprang alight all round her mirror. Of course, she'd been an actress. She would have considered this detail essential for her make-up. Fanshawe was ready to be impressed.

Her manner was offhand towards him, but he was aware of something behind it. The way she scooped the cream and lifted her hand, elegantly poised, flicking back the wide sleeve, while she leaned forward to scan the reflection of her face, with him in the background, was deliberate. A bit of an exhibitionist, he noted.

Fanshawe stared back, feeling caught out, as if the reflection were a camera shot that could be used later for blackmail. She was toying with him. It was time he took the situation in hand.

'We've been hoping you might have remembered something more by now,' he opened.

'About finding Rosemary?' she asked. 'No, I told them what happened. We'd been out. That nice young man offered to drive me. We returned, came upstairs, and there she was on the bed, with my room all topsy-turvy. I thought at first she'd done it and then fallen asleep.'

About as likely as the Goldilocks story, he thought. 'No, I meant the other occasion, the Saturday night when your daughter drove off in the black Vectra.'

She frowned and seemed to have trouble remembering. 'I never saw her leave. I was watching television, I think. Don't ask me what. It's all such rubbish nowadays.'

'Have you any idea what she was wearing?'

'Nothing. None at all.' She sounded confused. 'I'm not her jailer, you know.'

'Couldn't you tell, from what was left in her wardrobe?' Fanshawe, checking on his wife Megan, could quickly tell when she'd gone out tarted up to the eyebrows.

Having massaged the cream well in, Vanessa began applying peachy powder with a fat, soft brush, making facial contortions to expose each plane of her flesh to the brilliant lighting. The monosyllable which escaped her grotesquely screwed mouth could have meant anything.

'I beg your pardon,' he said with elaborate politeness, to shame her. This woman could really get on your Bristols.

She turned on him irritably. 'How do you expect me to know what she has in the way of clothes. They're dreary enough, for the most part.'

This wasn't the impression he'd got from Z. He remembered well enough that she'd spoken of the older woman sometimes raiding her daughter's wardrobe, and how they wore the same size, although Sheila's dresses were longer because she was three or four inches taller.

Fanshawe stared at her disagreeable face in the mirror. 'If you *should* remember anything about that evening — what she ate or if she took away something to eat later; that sort of thing — we need to know. You do want to help us find out exactly what happened, don't you?'

She leaned back on her Italian-quilted stool and spoke to her own reflection, enunciating clearly so that they'd catch it right at the back of the stalls. 'She — just — drove — off. That's all.'

There was something else she murmured, which he didn't quite get. But it sounded like, 'Out of my life.'

He felt a little late sympathy for her grief. Despite her staginess, this was an ageing woman who had suddenly, and violently, lost her only daughter.

'I'll not bother you further for now,' he said quietly. 'I can see myself out.'

Back at the nick, he started in at once typing up his notes, putting in a carbon, since Beaumont had insisted the Boss should be notified at the same time as the DI, 'just in case.' Whether that was because Salmon was suspected of holding out until he'd something big worth reporting, or because Superintendent Yeadings wanted to dog his every move, Fanshawe didn't know. Anyway he'd do as instructed and drop a copy in on the Boss before he left the building.

He found he'd enough there without irrelevant padding, because he included every detail of the conversation with Beattie and her builder beau. It came to three pages, double-spaced, and, leaving the top copy at the DI's empty office, he decided to look in at the Incident Room for an update.

There he found computers humming and keyboards rattling as four young constables transcribed info on to disk. Two printers stuttered, churning out reams of paperwork for the bulging files which computers were supposed to have replaced. Hadn't there once been a move to save the endangered rain forests?

He watched unchallenged for a moment, but the office manager was too busy to welcome visitors and nodded towards the door. He went off to deliver the Super's copy, was diverted by meeting PC Jenny Daler in the corridor, and ended in the canteen buying her a Danish and orange juice.

He'd no serious intentions towards Jenny, being a monogamous sort of bloke, but she was the target of the moment, and it gave your canteen cred a boost to be seen with her tête-à-tête.

To ensure she didn't wander off he put his own tea on the same tray to bear it off to a distant corner. Unfortunately Pip Torrence's table stood in their path and he managed to stretch out a cramped leg as Fanshawe passed.

By the time Fanshawe had picked up the broken china and gone for replacements Jenny had been sponged down of any imaginary splashes and was seated beside the broadly grinning Pip. Fanshawe joined them, seething and silently vowing an early revenge.

He flattened the copy of his report on the melamine tabletop and used his handkerchief to try and remove traces of the disaster. The tea had been strong and the stain had spread all the way through. It was just about legible, but would never do for the Boss as it was. He would need to retype the whole three pages again.

'You owe me,' he muttered at Pip and ground a heel into the PC's toecap. Jenny was sweet about the upset, as expected, but already had made some arrangement with Pip to book a squash court when their relief went off duty.

You win some, Fanshawe reminded himself, and you lose ... He stopped in mid-thought. His eyes rested on the ruined report. On the middle page, which recorded the meeting with Frank Perrin, builder, something new had sprung out at him. A tea stain on one side and a smear of orange juice on the other framed part of the word Jonathan. The first two letters were obscured, as were the final three.

He sat staring at NAT. That was the name, unusual enough, that Beaumont had found in a letter in Sheila Winter's laptop. There had been no address, and they hadn't been able to trace him at the prison. 'Dozens of Bakers,' Beaumont had said gloomily, 'but no Nat or Nathaniel.' And actually he was Jonathan, all this time driving around with his name clearly written across his van; Jonathan Baker, Plumber & Heating Engineer!

Fanshawe swore at the soggy report. He'd almost met the man, no more than two hours back. Would have done so if Frank Perrin hadn't halted the plumber on the doorstep.

Was Perrin the builder in it with them — the old lags, Childe and Baker? If so, he'd warned Baker off, that 'the filth' was present in the kitchen.

It certainly suggested taking a closer look at Beattie Weyman's trusted visitor.

19

Martin Chisholm grinned as he threw the bag of clothes on Neil's hospital bed. 'Right then, you're free to go;' but the younger man knew him too well. The switch from deadpan as he came through the ward door had been too swift.

'So what's wrong?' he demanded.

Chisholm hesitated. 'Marching orders,' he said quietly, and held the other with a steely glance that meant *don't make a fuss, particularly here*.

Sullenly Neil ignored the pulled curtains, grabbed his clothes and went off to change in the bathroom. Chisholm granted him a minor sulk and decided to wait in the corridor. Neil eventually joined him, 'What about the nurses?'

'I've seen to them. A bottle of bubbly and carnations.'

'I'm not going without seeing Rosemary.'

'That's OK. I can spare twenty minutes. Anyway she'll be discharged at noon tomorrow. You can manage until then without a Svengali.'

'She's not . . . Hell, I'll just run up and tell her I've gone.'

'Take the lift.'

'I meant to in any case.' Very much on his dignity.

Touchy, Chisholm reflected, but then he always was as he adjusted to being on his own. This time it was too sudden, though, and it was catching him in a vulnerable state. That had been an unnecessary dig, implying that Rosemary was his stand-in Svengali. Maybe Neil wouldn't need one. He could activate himself satisfactorily when he gritted his teeth and gave it all he'd got. Nevertheless, Chisholm congratulated himself, it was just as well he'd seen the girl first and warned her. It would do no harm that she knew of Neil's condition. He trusted her discretion, not to let on to the boy how much he'd told her. She was a policewoman, after all; a sergeant in CID, as he'd confirmed from his own sources. No dozer. She'd understand what a difference having the transplant had made. A lifesaver, but at a price. You never knew when the boy might need a sympathetic ear from that direction.

Neil returned quickly. 'She's just going off for physio.' He glared at Chisholm. 'How did you know she was being discharged tomorrow before lunch?'

'Consulted the ins-and-outs list at reception,' Chisholm lied easily.

The boy accepted it at face value. 'Car

keys?' he demanded. 'I'll drive us back.'

As he casually handed them over, Chisholm just hoped the sulk wouldn't last long enough to land them in a ditch. But he recognized the gesture of independence, a defiant refusal to be bugged by the nightmare recurrence of panic that still sometimes attacked him behind the wheel. If Neil was starting to take himself in hand, all well and good. His face showed nothing. It was only in his driving, too fast and a little savage on the clutch, that he displayed the state of his nerves.

'When?' he demanded, pulling up at the rear of Ashbourne House. He had already observed that the indicator showed a full fuel tank.

Chisholm glanced at his watch. 'Forty minutes.' He had no intention of apologizing for the lack of notice. It had been unavoidable. 'I've left a note with Lombard.'

Neil nodded grimly. *To be handed to Neil Raynes in the event of my death or disappearance.* And the time scale for waiting would be the usual eight weeks. Everything would be covered up until then and he'd be able to draw on the joint account up to the limit of ten thousand pounds.

'You've time for coffee, then,' Neil ground

271

out. 'I'll get some going while you bring your bags down.'

'I'm packed. Everything's in the boot,' Chisholm said casually. 'Yes, coffee'd be fine. Thanks.'

★   ★   ★

Fanshawe, returned to catch the other residents at the end of their working day, had already spoken with Miss Barnes, who appeared torn between her conscience's need to offer more support to Mrs Winter and cowering at the thought of further involvement.

She had little to offer on the dead woman, having rarely seen her. There appeared to be a zonal, but not class, division between these upstairs and downstairs people. It was comic, really. They spoke of each other rather as some natives to either side of Watford referred to the other lot as 'northerners' or 'southerners'.

She admitted that, after the dinner party which Beattie had given for all the residents, curiosity had led her to call at the Greenvale Garden Centre. She had purchased a Bromeliad there, which was perhaps a mistake because now she had to leave the temperature of the flat at a higher, uneconomical level, and the humidifier full on during her absence at school.

Fanshawe looked round for an exotic animal, but there was no cage. Miss Barnes picked up on his confusion and pointed to a brilliant, poker-stiff stem topped by a brilliant, torch-like bloom and surrounded by glossy, strap-shaped leaves. 'Right,' he said, vowing he'd never give such a dictatorial thing house-room, even if he found it attractive.

Thanking Miss Barnes for her patience, and silently congratulating himself on his own, he followed up that visit with one to the reputedly security-mad Wormsley, noting how he was inspected through the fish-eye lens on his fire door before being allowed in. A quick look through Criminal Records had satisfied Fanshawe that nothing was known of the man to make him paranoid in the police presence, so it had to be assumed that he was simply weird that way. Or hoarded objects of value in his home? But he wasn't a pawnbroker; just a photographer, according to information from other residents. Nothing about his furnishings or lack of ornaments suggested he had a fortune tucked away.

Wormsley listened, head tilted, to the DC's request for information and seemed quite pleased to deny any personal link with the dead woman.

'Or a professional one?'

'Er, whose profession? She's a sort of glorified gardener, isn't she?'

'You've never done any photography or advertising matter for her?'

'No; we stick to portraiture. Mostly kiddies, family stuff. The occasional portfolio for wannabe models. Nothing commercial.'

'So you never saw her?'

'The Winters live upstairs and towards the front,' Wormsley pointed out, as though that guaranteed segregation. 'So I only ever saw her from the window, when she fetched or put away her car. I see them all from here. See?' Wormsley waved towards the outer wall and Fanshawe walked across to look out.

Beyond the double glazing and an ornate wrought iron grille he saw the row of lock-up garages about fifty yards to the right and partly obscured by a screen of leafless trees. Only one car was visible, parked outside. As he watched, Martin Chisholm issued from the rear door of the house, went across to the Saab, unlocked it and climbed in.

Damn, Fanshawe thought: now I'll have to make another visit tomorrow. I'm not hanging about for him to get back from an evening out.

Wormsley was watching him with a waggish smile as though he knew, and enjoyed, what the DC had been thinking.

Really the man was a first-class shit. For that reason Fanshawe decided to take his time and rumble up some totally unnecessary questions. Not that it upset the other in the least. He even seemed amused and offered to turn off the oven where his supper was cooking. 'I can finish it off in the microwave later,' he said. 'Anything I can do for the forces of law and order.'

When Fanshawe finally ran out of ideas, he rose to leave.

'A pity you missed Mr Chisholm,' Wormsley said slyly, at the door. 'Especially as he seems to have gone away. Packed quite a bit of gear in the boot earlier. I should think he'll be absent for some considerable time.'

Bloody man! He knew all the time and enjoyed stringing me along. Well, I'll see we get the last laugh, Fanshawe vowed. It hardly seemed worthwhile tackling Neil Raynes on his own, especially since he was just out of hospital and known to have been in touch with DS Zyczynski there.

Still, he might give a lead on where Chisholm had gone. If it wasn't far they could still contact him for any necessary information. DI Salmon wouldn't be happy to hear he'd got out of reach. And an unhappy

Salmon, Fanshawe guessed, could undoubt-edly be a right barracuda.

Neil Raynes was plunged in gloom and a deep armchair, with the television on loud, showing a programme on volcanoes. The earth heaved and belched, spitting fire in a way he felt suitably in harmony with. He killed the volume with his remote, but dropped back in the same chair and continued staring at the hypnotic convulsions and hellfire flaming as Fanshawe settled in.

His answers were mainly monosyllabic. Yes, to whether Chisholm had gone away. No, to whether the man had left an address. No, he couldn't be contacted by phone. No, he'd no idea how long this absence would be. Fanshawe stared at him po-faced and waited.

At this point Neil volunteered, almost pettishly, that there'd been no time for conversation when he was picked up from the hospital.

'He must have given you some idea of where he'd be going.'

Impatiently Neil tore his gaze from the flame-spouting screen. 'Something came up while I was in hospital. He doesn't have to tell me where his work takes him.'

'So he's not on holiday, then?'

The boy looked undecided, then adopted a pose of bored superiority. 'I suppose he'll have as good a time as the situation permits. Club class, travel perks and all that, of course.'

'Are you sure he's gone abroad?'

'Well, he took his passport.' That had slipped out: the first thing Neil had checked on. The European Community one had certainly gone. He didn't know about the others, kept in the safe he hadn't a key to.

'Ah.' Fanshawe considered how he could present this, back at the nick. Imply the man had set out before he himself had been allocated the job? But if Salmon was into nit-picking, he'd winkle out from someone exactly when Chisholm had picked the boy up today, and know that Fanshawe was on the job by then.

He sighed. 'Can you tell me how well he, or you, knew Miss Winter?'

'Sheila? We'd say *hi* when we happened to meet. Actually, something a bit more formal from Marty. He isn't into Americanisms. I don't think I ever said anything apart from that to her. She didn't seem all that interesting as a person.'

'Interesting enough to get herself murdered.'

'Yes. That's odd, isn't it?' The boy — Fanshawe supposed he really should call him 'young man' because he was supposed to be twenty or so — seemed honestly puzzled.

'Still, if there's a nutter about, looking for a victim, I suppose almost anyone will do.'

What an obituary for the poor woman, Fanshawe reflected: to be almost anyone, a nutter's fancy. Only it hadn't been like that. There was no sexual attack, no mutilation. The stabbing had been violent and the body disposed of away from the scene of the killing. That made it personal, not random, according to CID wisdom.

There was only one more question that suggested itself to him as he closed his notebook and slipped the elastic band over it. 'Have you ever been to Henley-on-Thames?'

Neil Raynes rose out of his seat. 'Yes, of course. Often. I used to row there for my school, and later for Thames Club. I suppose I know that part of the world as well as anywhere, really.'

So did that apparent innocence clear him? Or was it bravado? Taken all round, Fanshawe supposed Neil Raynes could be crossed off the list.

'I'd like to know immediately you hear from your friend, or he returns. Is that understood?'

Neil shrugged. 'I'm sure he couldn't help you anyway.'

Fanshawe considered himself dismissed. As

COLD HANDS

Clare Curzon

A dead body is found on a railway line — a straightforward suicide, or something more sinister? When the dead man is identified as a customs officer investigating counterfeit currency, it seems like more than just a coincidence. Superintendent Mike Yeadings is suspicious, so he sends his undercover team, including DI Mott and DS Zyczinski, to Fraylings Court and the heart of the operation

DEATH PRONE

Clare Curzon

Bachelor recluse Hadrian Bascombe has summoned his family to announce his imminent death. They learn that his fortune is to pass to a single beneficiary whom he will choose from among them that night. However, when the company leaves he has given no more than cryptic hints of his intentions. On their way home the two youngest guests meet with a serious accident. When further violence reduces the number of potential heirs, Superintendent Mike Yeadings of the Thames Valley Police follows an intuitive line, which ends in confrontation with an embittered killer.

THE FACE IN THE STONE

Clare Curzon

Ex-Warrant Officer Class 1 Edward Mather died in his Cyprus villa from asthma — or so it seemed: two months later a post mortem laid suspicion of murder at the feet of his widow. Mather was an adventurer, with an eye for making a fortune — yet where was it and what had he been involved in? As the police investigation took its time, it looked likely that the stranger from Athens would crack the mystery first — but then the widow took an interest and the case blew wide open.

THE BLUE-EYED BOY

Clare Curzon

Blue-eyed boy Joel Sefton, handsome and attractive, was mugged and dumped behind supermarket trash bins. Yet there were less admirable traits underlying his charisma, and many had good cause to hate him. It was a secret in the past of a WPC that proved vital in penetrating the blue-eyed boy's activities, and their labyrinthine effects.

he unlocked his car opposite the house's imposing portico, a taxi arrived and Z got out. He waited while she paid the cabbie off, then carried her bag upstairs for her. 'Thanks,' she said, following him in. She looked washed out and there was a fresh dressing on the side of her head.

'Bring me up to date,' she demanded.

'I didn't think you were due out till tomorrow.'

'What's the difference of a few hours? I acted awkward and they let me go. I've things to see to here.'

'Such as?'

'That's private.' She spoke sharply, then relented. 'I can relax better at home. Besides I want to keep an eye on happenings.'

He stared at her. 'The job? You sound as though you think the residents are involved.'

'Aren't they? — either directly or as a result. Do you want coffee or tea?'

'Tea, if that's all right.'

'Suits me too. Actually I could murder a bacon sarny.'

'You sit down. I can manage that.' He went through and surveyed the range of cupboards, pulled out the grill pan and fetched gammon rashers from the fridge.

She took a chair opposite the kitchen door

279

and they conversed through it. 'So who's DI Salmon got in the frame now for killing Sheila Winter? I heard he had to let Barry Childe go.'

'I'm hoping it's a plumber called Jonathan Baker. He turned out to be the 'Nat' in a letter Sheila wrote concerning Childe's employment.'

'I heard about the letter.' She registered Fanshawe's puzzlement. 'The Boss dropped in, doing the grapes and flowers thing. But how does this Jonathan plumber come to be calling himself *Nat*?'

Fanshawe explained that he'd almost met the man on Beattie's doorstep, and how spilling the tea and orange juice in the canteen had drawn his eyes to the three letters in the middle of his name, Jonathan.

'Having the right surname, it was a leap in the dark even then,' he said, 'but I don't go for coincidences. I told the DI and he got in touch with the prison again. *Jonathan* Baker was known to them all right. Not as an inmate, but he'd been a maintenance man there before he set up on his own in Thames Valley with a secondhand van and a plumber's mate — who was also, as it happens, a youngster who'd done a stretch in Aylesbury for attempted mugging.'

'So he could tie in with Childe and the

suspected cannabis culture.'

'It looks that way. By now he should have been brought in for questioning. Even if Sheila Winter wasn't involved in the project, he certainly suggested she provide charitable after-care for an old lag acquaintance.'

'She must have had a lot of confidence in his judgment. She was a pretty down-to-earth person: not the sort to be conned easily. So that was what came out of visiting at Beattie's. Who else did you speak to?'

He listed them, and she nodded as he gave an outline of the conversations.

'I've just come from seeing your young friend Neil Raynes,' he added. 'Did you know that his partner, or whatever, has disappeared into the blue? Raynes denies knowing where, why, or for how long, but Chisholm's passport's missing, so we have to assume he's out of the country, possibly out of Europe.'

'I did know actually,' Z admitted. 'That's mainly why I didn't want to stay on till tomorrow. Martin Chisholm looked in on me to ask if I'd keep a sisterly eye on Neil while he's away on business. I'm not sure whether he knows I'm in the job, but chances are that he's picked up on that.'

'Does he think his boyfriend'll misbehave, then?'

'No; and they aren't an item in the way you

281

imply. But Neil is under pressure: has a health problem, and doesn't always trouble to take his medication.'

'D'you mean he's a nutter? In which case . . .'

'It's confidential, but I'll trust you not to spread it, Hugh. A few years back he was involved in a bad RTA and his passenger was killed. She happened to be his stepmother, and since then his father can't stand the sight of him. That and a personal sense of guilt have really messed him up. Chisholm's a sort of post-adolescence guardian paid to provide an alternative home for him, provided that he keeps well away from his own.

'Although Neil survived the accident he was badly injured, almost didn't make it, and required some complicated surgery including a kidney transplant. I don't know if you're aware of what that means, especially to someone young who's never had to think twice about taking risks.'

'A permanent invalid,' Fanshawe grunted.

'Not exactly. But there's a hell of a lot of precautions and medication and forbidden stuff. For his body to continue accepting the transplant he faces a lifetime of restrictions; and the drugs required to prevent the immune system from rejecting the alien matter reduce his ability to cope with bacteria and viruses we consider normal. It requires the outlook of a geriatric in a young and vital mind. Most of the time he manages, but it's hard on him, and with his mainstay away — Chisholm, I mean — he'll need twice the determination to stay on course.'

'So Chisholm expects to walk calmly off and leave the responsibility to you!'

'They're my neighbours, Hugh. Which is the nearest I've got to family. Besides, I like him, for all that he's a bit unpredictable. It's a purely personal decision: nothing to do with my being a cop.'

'I just hope he doesn't land you in any trouble. It sounds dodgy to me.' He came through the doorway with a plate in one hand. 'D'you want tomato ketchup or mustard?'

'Mustard, please. I hope you've made one for yourself as well.'

'Betcha,' said Fanshawe. 'Never could resist the smell of grilling bacon. Nearly as bad as my Jewish brother-in-law over that.'

20

Neil Raynes waited until Fanshawe's Ford reached the curve in the drive, then slunk back along the side of the house, reentered by the back door and went straight through the utility room and laundry to gain the front hall. There was no one about, He checked the table for letters, but of course Marty would have dealt with them. He'd have answered anything urgent by e-mail. Neil never received any of his own.

He went lightly up the stairs, turned left on the gallery and waited a moment before ringing Rosemary's bell. When she opened up he stuck out his chin belligerently. 'You weren't to be let out until tomorrow,' he accused her.

She looked weary. A slight flush appeared, then left her face ashen again under the pink elastic bandage. 'I knew I'd feel better at home. So I discharged myself.'

Neil sniffed the air. 'At least you've eaten.' He walked past her and stood in the kitchen doorway. She saw him register the two used plates and beakers in the sink.

'Fraternizing with the enemy,' he observed

angrily. 'That was another policeman who just left. Did you know?'

'Yes, he wanted to ask some questions about the attack on me. He seemed reasonable enough. I was hungry, so we had a snack together.' There was no call to explain so much, and it made her sound defensive. Although she believed the sharpeyed Chisholm had guessed her real job, she wasn't sure about this young man. Probably he didn't suspect, which was as well, seeing he'd referred to Fanshawe as 'the enemy'. She needed him to trust her a little longer, now that she knew how vulnerable he was.

She waved towards the sitting-room and he followed her in. 'When do they expect you back at work?'

He dropped on to a chair. She chose the sofa under a window, outside the circle of light from a nearby table lamp. The whole room was dim. He wondered if her head was still painful. His was tender, but no more than that. Now that he was with Rosemary he didn't have anything to say. He considered her question.

'Quite soon, I suppose. I wasn't seriously hurt. I'm to attend Outpatients in five days, to remove the sutures.'

'Me too. Let me give you a lift.'

'I don't think you should drive yet.'

She looked at him gravely. It was laughable really. Here she was, ready to keep an eye on him, and he was bothered about *her* welfare. It might be a good idea to let him continue with that. Then they'd both have an excuse to do what they intended. 'We could share a taxi,' she compromised.

He didn't answer because her cell phone fluted. He passed it across to her from the table at his side. 'Zyczynski,' she said quietly into it. 'Oh, Max! I didn't recognize the number . . . From where? I see . . . Yes, I'm fine and I'm at home now . . . Yes, really . . . Well, yes, I suppose: more of an incident than an accident. But I wasn't specifically targeted. Just wrong place, wrong time, as often happens . . . Of course, I would. Come whenever you can . . . Right then; I'll not wait up for you. See you. Bye.'

She grimaced, turned off the phone and faced Neil. 'That was Max,' she said unnecessarily. 'He's just heard what happened to me. So I'm in trouble for not getting in touch.'

'He's coming tonight?'

She nodded, getting up from the sofa and brushing creases from her cord skirt.

'You'll be all right, then.' His voice held a curious mixture of relief and wistfulness.

'It's kind of you to check on me, Neil,' she

said. 'Don't forget to take care of yourself too.'

'Yeah,' he answered, hovering by the door. 'Marty's away at the moment, so I've no one to spoil but myself.'

Funny boy, she thought, watching him cross the gallery and start down the stairs. He made her feel — what exactly? Motherly, she supposed. And yet there was slightly more to it. She recalled how he'd joked about a taste for older women. Maybe there was some truth in that. If so, had she a responsive taste for younger men? He was attractive, she'd admit: her frog prince. It was the large, wide-spaced eyes that had made her think of him as that. Not that she'd be kissing him and risk a transformation.

She went back to turn off the lights in the sitting-room, abandoned the dishes in the sink, and began to undress. She was dog-tired from the small effort of getting back home. As she climbed into bed she felt warmed through, knowing that when she awoke Max would be lying there beside her.

Clever of the Boss to delay telling him until she was over the worst. She cuddled her pillow close and was almost instantly asleep.

★   ★   ★

It was after ten next morning when Beaumont turned up with yet more videos from the garden centre's CCTV. 'They're just an excuse. You don't need to bother with them,' he told Z, who was still drinking breakfast coffee at the kitchen table with Max Harris. The aquamarine bathrobe reflected a greenish tinge on her face, but her eyes looked less sunken.

'I never knew about the attack until Mr Yeadings rang through to the office,' Harris explained. 'I'm just back from Kandahar.'

'So you're on the news desk now?'

'God, no! But even a columnist has to keep up with history in the making; not that things have really changed out there. Tribal tensions are much as they ever were. Only there's more concern at the moment with poppy harvesting than strict observance of Muslim law. As it happens, I was born in Rawalpindi, which under our crazy nationality laws makes me a Paki. And I spent my early years dragged all over Asia.

'But what's new on the crime front? Have you any idea who did this to my Rosebud?'

'We're trying to tie it in with Sheila Winter's murder. It was the Winter flat she was attacked in. The intruder was searching for something. Flavour of the moment is Jonathan — otherwise 'Nat' — Baker. He seems to have been Sheila Winter's man-friend, and he's connected with the old lag, Childe.

'DI Salmon is grilling him now, with the Boss sitting in. This time (glory be!) we were able to locate our suspect through Yellow Pages. I had the pleasure of calling on him last night with an invitation for 9a.m.'

'What's he like?' Z asked. 'I understand that Beattie and Frank Perrin know him. Has he admitted being in the house?'

'Not so far. I took his first statement. He seemed to be quite open about things. He'd known Childe in the slammer, as he claimed; but while Childe was an inmate, Baker was on the maintenance staff. He'd been impressed by the serious way Childe was into horticulture, even studying for qualifications. He's still a registered visitor to the prison, but gave up working there two years back, when he started up on his own as a Corgi approved plumber and heating engineer. That's how Frank Perrin got to meet him, when he was short-staffed. He did work on this house in the early part of the conversion, but nothing since it's been lived in.

'His contact with Sheila Winter goes further back, to when she still lived in London, but he's holding out on how they came to meet. She employed him to install a special watering system for the outdoor planting at Greenvale and tropical forest conditions in the glass-houses. Although he denied entering the house recently, he volunteered that he delivered some piping conduit for Perrin. That was when Fanshawe was in Beattie's kitchen and failed to set eyes on him.'

'He must know Frank Perrin well enough to guess where he drops in for elevenses,' Z pointed out. 'Do you think Salmon's really going for him? What about the suspected cannabis set-up at Barry Childe's cottage? Could he be in on that?'

'He supplied him with all the gear. Baker keeps his paperwork in his home office and he showed me it. On first sight the invoices look kosher, including a small trade discount. Childe will be clearing the debt in instalments, since he's barely paying his way as yet. There's nothing to prove Baker was part of the project or even knew what his gear was to be used for.'

'You haven't said what he's like.'

'Scrubs up well, as they say. In fact he'd pass muster as any average decent citizen. Physically he's long and lanky. Made me think of Mister Punch; the nose and chin thing, with a wide mouth stretching up towards the ears. Quite a humorous face, not that Salmon will give him much to laugh over as yet.'

'I wonder what the Boss is making of him?'

'He'll not let on. He's giving DI Salmon a lot of rope.'

'I wish I could be working on it,' said Z wistfully. 'I'm stood off for a fortnight, would you believe? Can't you find some way I can help, unofficially?'

'You concentrate on getting better,' Max interrupted. 'I have to go back to town tonight, but as soon as I've off-loaded this Kandahar stuff I'll be taking you off for the happiest, healthiest holiday you've ever known. So order some brochures from the travel shop and tell me what you'd fancy.'

When Beaumont had left, Max briskly surveyed the contents of fridge and freezer, then made out a shopping list. 'Get just enough for two days,' Z insisted. 'I need to make use of young Neil Raynes. Shopping will keep him out of mischief.'

'Good,' Max agreed, wryly wondering if too much propinquity might encourage Neil to try the opposite. He grinned, kissed her gently and took off.

Beaumont had tucked some folded papers between the bread crock and the dresser wall. She had watched him do this while Max's attention was elsewhere, and guessed that whatever they contained was for her eyes only. She reached for them now and smoothed them out on the kitchen table. They covered alibis for the period during which she had been attacked.

According to this résumé the house had appeared quite empty, and no cars had been parked outside when Neil and Vanessa Winter arrived back in her Alfa Romeo. A bracketed note admitted that no check had been made at that point on whether the garages too were empty. Z nodded. Her own car had been in there, she remembered.

Martin Chisholm had arrived in time to sort out Vanessa and Martin on the staircase, but until 15.48 he'd been at the car showroom in London arranging trial runs for a newly delivered Saab. This was confirmed by two colleagues. The times they gave for his leaving meant he'd driven home at an average speed of forty-seven mph, which was good going for the start of rush-hour.

Miss Barnes had returned from school a few minutes later, and Major Phillips was dropped off by his 'corporal' some ten minutes after that, having come straight from the golf course clubhouse.

Beattie Weyman had been at the hairdresser's up until it shut at six o'clock. Frank Perrin claimed to have been checking on some foundations out at Berkhamsted, but the foreman and labourers had left by then and the site hut was locked; so this was without confirmation.

All that afternoon Paul Wormsley had been working on the firm's taxation figures, PAYE and VAT, at his photographic studio. His assistant vouched for this. She had been coping at the vital time with a fractious family of three under-tens — 'real ankle-biters' — and resented his failing to help. 'Keeping his head well down, in case he got drawn in,' she had claimed with some bitterness. The DC taking down her account had noted that Wormsley's office was partially overlooked by the studio and sufficiently well lit for her to see his upper body bent over his desk. She hadn't noticed at what time he left, but it must have been after herself at five. His lights were still on. He didn't arrive at Ashbourne House until the ambulance had left and the doctor was with Mrs Winter.

As well as Frank Perrin, Beaumont had added Jonathan 'Nat' Baker to the list of residents. The latter's daybook showed he had worked for two customers that afternoon. One was booked in for 2.20p.m. and the other 4p.m. He claimed that the first job had proved considerably more involved than expected and he'd phoned the second client to explain he might be up to an hour late. He said he'd arrived there at 5.07p.m. and left at 6.18. Since he charged for labour by the first hour and then by subsequent half-hours, he had to transfer these details to the bills, and their carbons confirmed the timing he claimed. Both call-outs were for adjustments to central heating in Eton Village; one, in fact, at New House in the College.

'Very posh,' Z murmured to herself. Let DI Salmon challenge that one. Nevertheless, as she saw from Beaumont's note below, the DI was not entirely satisfied with this claim, so had arranged to call the plumber in on the following morning. This would be the interview the Boss was sitting in on at present.

Long and lanky, Beaumont had described the man. Z tried to bring back to mind the brief instant of entering Vanessa's bedroom. Had her attacker appeared like that? Big, she'd thought at the time, but then fear would have increased her impression of him; and she'd had a flash of real terror as he hurled himself on her.

Concentration didn't help. No clearer picture came. Her attacker could have been any one of this lot, or a total stranger, as far as she could tell. And they all had reasonable alibis, except Frank Perrin.

She wished that this nausea at recall of the incident would let up. Her earlier bacon sandwich lay uneasy inside her. It was nothing to do with the injury to her head. Just sheer funk. Which was silly, because as she'd told Max, the attack hadn't been specifically targeted at her. Her involvement with the intruder was over. She'd simply walked in on him, so he'd have been as shocked as she was herself. And by now, seeing the upset he'd caused, probably scared out of his criminal wits.

Superintendent Yeadings stole a glance at his watch and consciously straightened in his seat. Ten thirteen a.m. and the interview was stalling. Beside him Salmon slouched with one arm across the table and the other along Yeadings's chair-back. The DI's piggy eyes appeared to be tracing a crack across the Interview Room ceiling. Held in the fingers of his right hand, a ball-point pen prodded the tabletop with a maddening rhythm of which only he seemed unaware. He'd been over all the material three times and now had apparently succumbed to a mental block.

Yeadings cleared his throat. 'I was wondering,' he said mildly. 'I've never heard of Nat as a shortened form of Jonathan before. It's there, of course, in the middle, and it's certainly used for Nathan, again part of your given name. But in this case it's unusual, having no similarity of sound. How did you come to adopt it?'

Some of the strain went out of Baker's taut features. At last it didn't feel that he was being hammered. This senior officer was bumbling, unfamiliar with techniques of interrogation.

Familiar enough with stories the old lags told, he knew that it was CID at street level who asked the pertinent questions. This other was a desk man. He breathed once more deeply. 'Well, the obvious shortening is Jon, but there's a lot of Johns and Johnnies about. 'Nat' differentiates.'

Yeadings pulled towards him the report Fanshawe had typed of his mid-morning visit to Ashbourne House. 'I notice here that neither Miss Weyman nor Frank Perrin uses the name Nat. Both referred to you as Jon.'

'My customers do, mostly. They see what's written on the van. And I use the initials JB when I receipt their bills.'

'Ah.' Yeadings nodded sagely, enlightened. 'So it's more personal friends who call you Nat?'

There was an uncomfortable silence. Salmon stared sideways at Yeadings and made a show of superhuman patience. Baker's shoes scuffed on the floorboards as he changed position under the superintendent's gaze.

'You haven't answered my question.'

'I didn't realize it was one. People who call me Nat? Yes, they're closer, I suppose.'

'Like Miss Winter, for example. Sheila Winter.'

There was another silence; then, 'Yes, I think she was one who used that name.'

'The only one perhaps?'

Baker closed his eyes. Yeadings counted silently in his head. At twenty he asked, 'Why would that be, Mr Baker?'

The man's eyes re-opened. He faced Yeadings squarely. His voice was unnaturally controlled. 'She had — there were associations with the word John. She preferred not to use it.'

'Tell me about this other John.'

'It's irrelevant.'

'Let me be the judge of that. We know very little about Miss Winter, apart from what her father has been able to tell us. This is possibly something he knew nothing about. It would help our inquiries if you explained this to us.'

Baker looked down at his clasped hands on the table, considering how to pick his way out with least damage. Eventually he made an offering gesture. Yeadings observed the work-blunted fingers; but the nails were well cared for.

'His name was actually Jan, or Jani. A Dutchman. I think she dealt with him, importing plants and bulbs, and he did her down over some order.'

'She confided this to you?'

'She was upset and I was working on the spray system at the time. I couldn't help overhearing.'

Yeadings watched him. The man must realize that his story didn't quite hang together. Beside him Salmon had been alerted to the implication of a Netherlands interest. To him it would obviously mean a drugs connection.

'So if I question office staff at Greenvale, they will confirm this, Mr Baker?' Yeadings had to get the question out before the DI burst in and irrevocably changed tack.

'I — I've no idea.'

'No, I think it's outside their zone of competence. Because it wasn't over a business matter that this Jani let her down, was it? She had loved him and he cheated on her.

'Hadn't you better tell us everything now? You see, your own relationship with Sheila Winter was a very personal one, wasn't it?

298

And that is why she had a special name for you that no one else would use. After this Jani Dutchman, you became lovers, didn't you, Mr Baker? And her death has turned your life around.'

21

'Interview terminated at 10.27,' Yeadings said firmly, as Salmon opened his mouth to jump in. 'It is noted that your attendance at the police station was voluntary. You are free to leave when you wish, Mr Baker, but I suggest we allow you to think things over and return in twenty minutes. Perhaps by then you will realize the need to be completely frank with us. A constable will bring you tea.'

He left Salmon to finish off and quitted the room, but he was only halfway down the corridor when the DI came charging after him. 'He was on the point of coming clean,' he protested. 'Now he'll think up some screwy alibi.'

Yeadings barely spared him a glance. 'The man's grieving. He thought nobody knew, and suddenly his most private feelings are exposed. Have some decency, man.'

The DI halted in his tracks, flushing with repressed anger.

Red Salmon, like it says on the tins, Yeadings thought (with silent regret for a pun as bad as any of Beaumont's). But just let him stay buttoned up or he might be claiming there was no place for decency in police work — and mean it, which Yeadings didn't want to hear.

'Let's continue at 11.15. You'll have time then to visit the canteen.'

Back in his office, Yeadings made two phone calls while the coffee machine burbled. Zyczynski was at home and swore she was resting. Max had arrived but was out shopping; when Beaumont dropped in he'd left a list of alibis for the time of her attack.

'How do they square up with alibis for the murder of Sheila Winter?' she asked.

'That'll be complicated,' he admitted, 'and we haven't tackled Nat Baker on that yet. In his case I have a feeling DI Salmon hopes for a *crime passionnel*.'

She made no comment. Familiar with that tone of voice she knew he wouldn't commit himself to an opinion, and he'd gone as near as dammit to criticising the new DI.

'So could it all be sewn up quite quickly?' she ventured and was answered with a chuckle.

'You're beginning to sound like the media, Z,' he told her. 'Just concentrate on getting well again, and leave the case to us.'

He said goodbye and made a brief call to Beaumont, who was arranging to have the plumber's van taken in for forensic examination.

Rosemary Zyczynski was left mumbling to herself, 'Don't worry your pretty little head about it, *bimbo*!' and fuming at lack of material to get working on.

Yeadings checked his watch at 11.15 exactly, then re-entered the Interview Room. Baker looked up, his long face stern. 'I'd like to tell you about my — my association with Miss Winter. Are you going to caution me?'

'Not at this point. I will interrupt you if it becomes necessary. Shall we wait for the detective inspector?'

Salmon was three minutes late. He entered looking sour and took the seat beside Yeadings. He started up without more ado. 'When did you last see Miss Winter, and where?'

'On the Monday, five days before she was killed. It was at the garden centre. I called in with some receipts for goods I'd supplied.'

'Bills already settled? Why couldn't they have gone by post?'

'They could have, but I wanted to see her. We'd both been caught up by work and there were things to settle. You see, Sheila and I were planning to be married. We had fixed a date in January, and arranged with the registrar. I'd booked a week's honeymoon at

La Cluse in Savoy. We intended to get some skiing in.' He stopped abruptly.

'January?' Salmon demanded suspiciously, 'and you a plumber? Isn't that your busiest time?'

'One of them; for burst pipes and pump breakdowns. Yes, but it would be more convenient for Sheila.'

'So her job was more important than yours?' The DI seemed determined to control the questioning this time. Yeadings smiled, nodding encouragement to Baker.

'She dealt with living things. After the Christmas rush would come the low season. Everything was already tidied for winter, and it was too early for heavy pruning. My work was to be covered by a friend. We could both afford to take a week off then.'

'How did her mother regard the idea?' Salmon demanded, curling his lip.

'She hadn't been told. Sheila meant to offer her a health club holiday with beauty treatment while we were away, then present a *fait accompli* on our return.'

'Wasn't that asking for trouble?'

'She would be upset whenever she was told, but that way it would avoid any unpleasantness at the most important time for us.'

'Why would it upset her?'

'I think that's obvious. She was accustomed to having Sheila at her beck and call. New arrangements would have to be made, so that Vanessa became more independent. Sheila thought she might agree to stay on at the flat, possibly with a paid companion. I have a country cottage outside Chesham, not far away, and Sheila planned to buy the fields to either side of it for cultivation.'

'Am I right in assuming you would be financially better off by marrying Miss Winter?' Salmon asked with the hint of a sneer.

'And are deprived of any such benefit by the fact of her death?' Yeadings intervened while the man paused, needled at the implication.

'We hadn't discussed money at any depth. Sheila had her own business; I have mine. I'm not a pauper, inspector.'

'Earlier, when we discussed her special name for you — her pet name, so to speak — you refused to say how or when you came to meet Miss Winter. Are you ready to tell us now?'

Salmon was looking smug. He must know the answer to that already, Yeadings thought.

Baker straightened his back and gave the DI a defiant stare. 'We met through a London dating agency. It was while she and her mother were still living in Putney. I selected that one because I didn't care to have my private life talked about locally.' He spoke quietly, with dignity.

'Your private *affairs*; I see. So was Miss Winter the first — er, *client* you were paired with, Mr Baker?'

'I met four ladies in all, but we weren't suited in the other three cases.'

'This is a personal matter, and I'm not sure it's relevant,' Yeadings put in.

'I think it is.' Salmon was adamant. 'It isn't clear whether Mr Baker was looking for a rich wife or a fun companion.'

Yeadings was about to intervene again but Baker beat him to it. 'I was lonely. I admit that, and at first I wanted a personable woman I could take out for meals and perhaps to the theatre. Someone who could talk about the sort of things I'm interested in. Two of the women I was introduced to were simply looking for a rich husband, and I wasn't up to standard. The third — ' his Punch-like features twisted with sardonic humour, 'had an insatiable appetite for alcohol and bedtime athletics.

'I almost gave up on the agency then, but Sheila had just come on their books, after her failed relationship with Jani Nederkamp. She was hurt, seemed even a little bitter, but I discovered she wasn't like that underneath. She needed someone ordinary, like me. It took a little while, but she came to think the same.' His voice broke. 'We meant to — to spend the rest of our lives together.'

'The night of her murder,' Salmon said purposefully, 'where were you?'

'Waiting for her at the Burnham Beeches Hotel. If she hadn't arrived by nine o'clock I would know she couldn't get away. That was our standing arrangement.'

'So when did she arrive?'

'She didn't. I waited an extra half-hour, cancelled the room, got some food at the bar and went home, expecting she'd ring me in the morning from Greenvale. That would be Sunday, usually her busiest day of the week there.'

'And it seemed she'd stood you up.'

'I didn't think that. I don't know what I did think; just a horrible feeling that something was wrong. Maybe her mother was ill, or had found out about us and was making trouble. Something like that.'

'How did you find out?'

'I went to Greenvale. She wasn't there. Nobody seemed to know anything. Then the police turned up. Word went around like wildfire. I couldn't believe she was — gone.'

'Did you speak to anyone about it?'

'How could I? No one — knew about us. I got in the car and drove around, trying to understand. It didn't make sense. There was nothing I could do. Everything was over.'

Yeadings watched the fists balled on the table between them. The man was at the end of his tether, but Salmon wasn't giving up on him.

'You've said you never visited Ashbourne House once the conversion was completed. I want you to think about that again. Do you want to alter your statement?'

'No. I called recently to deliver some copper piping to the builder, Frank Perrin, but I stayed outside. He wanted it for a new job elsewhere.'

The DI leaned forward, fixing Baker with his little, piggy eyes 'So you weren't making love to Sheila Winter in what they called the 'drawing-room' two weeks back?'

'I certainly wasn't.'

'Then who was? — because somebody was hard at it, and never noticed my sergeant watching from the doorway!' They'd had to let him go, with the warning that he shouldn't leave the area without informing the station. He appeared dazed, incredulous.

'So what do you make of that?' Yeadings asked the DI.

'He'll do nicely.' Salmon's jaw jutted as he

kept pace along the corridor.

'I thought you had somebody else in your sights.'

'That doesn't rule out our man here. You heard what Beaumont said at the briefing. There has to be more than one person involved in the killing: one to drive the body to Henley, and a second to get him away afterwards. We've drawn a blank on taxis over the whole area.'

'If he needed to get away. Why couldn't he have stayed there, at least overnight?'

'It's hardly likely. I'd rather go for a bike being left there for him in advance. It wouldn't take long for Barry Childe to get back to Marlow that way. But what's wrong with the pair of them in it together? Both were connected with the garden centre, getting plenty of opportunities to plan it when they met up through work. And Baker has no alibi for after 9.30p.m. at Burnham Beeches. He'd already set up a meeting with the woman. We've only his word for it that it wasn't meant to be later elsewhere.'

He had the bit between his teeth, Yeadings thought regretfully. 'Motive?' he queried mildly. 'Sheila Winter's dead, so Baker loses any hopes of gain from the alliance. Unless, of course, you think there's a more recent will than the one left with her solicitor.'

Salmon stopped in his tracks. 'That wouldn't surprise me. Or a secret life insurance. Why not? Baker's a twisted bastard, making her keep everything quiet, even from her old lady. There's no confirmation of anything he claims. Sheila Winter left no indication she was planning to marry. Final arrangements were left for him to fix.'

A further thought struck him. 'Suppose it was all in his head and she suddenly faced him out with it. He lost his temper and . . .'

' . . . and happened to have a kitchen knife handy to stab her with? You can't have it both ways. Either it was premeditated or done in a fit of passion. And, if you remember, Dr Fenner, her father, believed she had some secret to share with him soon. He'd been hoping she would announce she'd found someone to settle down with.'

Salmon scowled. Bouncing his ideas off the superintendent was like hitting your head against a brick wall. Why couldn't he stick to his desk and leave the thinking to him? What he needed right now was a stiff drink and a chance to work out just where he'd reached in the reasoning. He had to hold on to the idea of Childe and Baker in this together, as a partnership. Hadn't the plumber been the means of the ex-con getting this cushy job with the dead woman? The trouble was that

Baker seemed every bit as thick with Frank Perrin, and Perrin had no alibi for the night of the killing. There couldn't have been three of them in cahoots over it, could there? But then again, why not?

* * *

Neil Raynes would have gone up to see Rosemary again as soon as Max went off to do the shopping but for a rankling memory of what Marty had said: 'your new Svengali'. Was that what he really thought? — that Neil couldn't function fully on his own; must have a hypnotist to control his mind, a puppeteer to pull his strings?

A bloody lie. He could hype himself up to take charge of his life when he knew Marty wasn't there. It was only at other times that he let himself go, took risks, knowing Marty could cushion his falls. But now he was in the driving seat, making the changeover. If he wanted, he could go and see the girl. Or he could choose not to. Sometime he had to get himself out of this cycle of dependence. It just took some catalyst. Maybe she was it.

Marty was mad to say anything so hurtful. Or manipulative; meaning to produce some effect. To keep them apart? Well, fuck Marty then. He'd please himself.

He burnt up his resentment by punishing the carpets with the vacuum cleaner and sloshing disinfectant round the kitchen, but he'd barely reached a decision when he heard Max's car return. Now it was too late, unless he walked in on them together. That might peeve her, having him act gooseberry, though he could pretend he'd thought she was on her own and might need some help.

With luck she'd ask him to stay on. He might learn what it was about the man that appealed to her. He seemed so ordinary; not a superman body, and he wore specs which slipped down his nose, so that he was always pushing them back up with one index finger. A wimp. Visually a sort of adult Harry Potter, but without the magic powers. Man for man, he was a better proposition himself.

He made the trek downstairs, through to the hall and up to the gallery. There was no sound of voices. Had Max Harris just dumped the provisions and taken her straight to bed? He put his head against the door panel and then there came the muffled sound of crockery. The fridge door slammed. He rang the bell. It was Rosemary who came.

'Hi,' he said brightly. 'Anything I can do for you?'

'Sure;' she said easily, 'share a meal with us. Max is putting something together in the

311

kitchen. Come through and keep me company.'

He followed her in. 'With Marty away, I'm actually missing the job. Never thought I could.'

'Yes, I heard he'd gone, just when the police wanted to ask him some questions.'

Neil hooted. 'They don't think he could be the one who attacked you? They must be more cretinous than I thought. Who told you they wanted to see him?'

She didn't seem sure. 'I think Max overheard one of the neighbours. 'What the great will do the less will prattle of,' you know.'

He eased himself into an armchair. 'I never took you for a Shakespeare fan.'

'There's a lot about me you don't know,' she teased.

God, but she was easy to get on with. No silly girly giggles. She was someone you could talk to. Totally wasted on that wimp Harris. 'So wise me up,' he invited. 'It's a fascinating subject.'

'I'm not sure that it is.' She paused, uncertain. 'I lost both my parents when I was ten and got passed to my mother's older half-sister.'

It wasn't something she would easily tell a near stranger, but it seemed almost in parallel with the boy's history and she hoped it might loosen him up. She stole a glance at him and saw his face go wooden. No confidences coming, then.

'I quite liked being sent away to school, but the holidays were pretty grim, unless I was invited to stay with friends.'

'I guess you had plenty of those.'

'One or two that I've kept up with,' she admitted, 'but children can be quite cruel if they think you're anyway different from them, can't they?'

'Until you learn that what they think just doesn't matter.' He was sitting forward now, scowling into the carpet, bony hands tensely clasped between his knees. She knew that he was going to come through with it. Not that he'd be asking for sympathy. He just needed to unload some of the rancour, get her agreeing that what went wrong was others' fault and not his; or perhaps not entirely his, because under it all he seemed honest enough.

'As I told you before, I wasn't totally orphaned like you,' he said, 'but I might just as well have been. Because Mother died when I was born, my father never could decide if it was my fault or his. But eventually he emerged from his work long enough to . . . '

He was biting his lower lip. ' . . . to marry

again. She was a — scheming — little — shit actually, twenty-five years younger than him. Had all the necessary female attractions, and knew how to use them. On anybody to hand. It was the original marriage from Hell.

'She taught me to drive, among other things. Underage, of course. Anyway, that's how I came to kill her. In a car crash. Well, it finished me with the old man. Once I came out of hospital, patched up, and the police had had their say, I was less than dog crap. If I'd been older they'd have had me put away on a manslaughter charge. He could have stood that. We don't meet. He pays me an allowance through Marty.'

'But you're making your way. You're holding down a job, doing something useful.'

'Yeah, like society should be grateful to me.' He had changed back to the coarse voice he'd used when they first talked, weeks ago. It was his disguise when he felt vulnerable. Z remembered how different he'd sounded when he claimed to have a taste for older women: sophisticated. His voice sometimes took on an echo of Martin Chisholm's irony. The older man had been his tutor in fighting back against the world, but he was still walking wounded.

A resounding crash sounded from the kitchen, followed by low-voiced expletives.

Max put his head round the door, grinned and explained in one breath, 'That was lunch and your best casserole. Hi, Neil, how are you? Let's all go out for a ploughman's, shall we?'

22

It was early, and in the Plough Inn at Speen the final place-settings were still being laid. Although the dining rooms were fully booked, Max managed to persuade the management otherwise. They settled in the bar to wait, and ordered a round of drinks.

Z made her kir last while Max worked through his pint. Remembering Chisholm's warning, she wasn't sure if Neil should have alcohol in view of his health, but she couldn't show that she knew more about him than he'd cared to tell. It surely meant progress that he'd opened up and told her so much of the story behind his trauma, although not details of his own injuries in the car crash. Those, she hoped, could be gleaned from press or police reports. All she needed was the date and locality.

When the young man insisted on his turn to order drinks, she suggested they went to table before the rush started. As they carried their fresh drinks through, she tapped Max on the elbow and shook her head. 'Ah,' he said, picking up her glance towards Neil.

They seated themselves and discussed the

menu. 'Let me do the wine,' Neil suggested, and was voted down. But since the subject was raised, and as a compliment to the chef's reputation, Max flipped through the list and ordered a single bottle of Merlot. 'Wine can't hurt you if it's the best,' he murmured, 'and we are having a meal.'

They chose separately from the main courses and Neil followed it with cheese, while the other two opted for fruit. The conversation stayed on mundane matters until, over the coffee, Neil asked Max about his work and the flow began. Even with an ingrained prejudice against the columnist, he had to admit then that Rosemary's man must be something special.

'You should read him,' Rosemary said. 'He writes the way he talks: shrewd, witty and a tad wry. He takes a simple subject and puts a new slant on it. Makes people think.'

'My number one fan,' Max allowed modestly.

'I wouldn't have thought Afghanistan was so simple,' Neil objected, after some thought.

'Sometimes I'm allowed to be serious.'

'So how would you write about the things going on at Ashbourne House?'

'I'd rather not. But it's obviously been exercising your mind. Have you arrived at any theory?'

Neil frowned. 'Weird things have happened, but nothing fits together. I mean, Sheila Winter — who would want to kill her? She was so ordinary; rather boring really, going on all the time about her precious garden centre. And then her stagy old mother. Do you know, she sometimes calls me Gordon. Do I look like a Gordon? She probably confuses me with her gin bottle. But weirdest of all is that creep Wormsley.'

'Creep?' Rosemary queried. 'I know he's rather paranoid about security, but why that?'

'He creeps about, spying. He's always watching, and sort of laughing to himself about us. Marty told me the Worm followed his car for miles one day before he shook him off.'

'Coincidence,' she said comfortably. 'They both just happened to be heading in the same direction.'

'No, it was deliberate. Marty turned off suddenly, to make the Worm go past. Then a few minutes later Wormsley drove back and started searching down the way he'd gone. Marty had the Saab concealed, so in the end the Worm had to give up.'

'Quite a cunning little ploy,' Max commented. 'Your Marty sounds very wise to the ways of the world.'

The young man's brow puckered. 'He's

318

— he's good at things to do with cars,' he admitted, sounding defensive. Z, in her CID hat, wondered if Martin Chisholm had any particular need to keep his comings and goings from public scrutiny. For a split second Neil had looked as if he knew he'd let something slip. So had the inquisitive Wormsley caught on to something there?

Returning after lunch, they made a detour and called in at Greenvale to pick up a giant poinsettia which Max was to donate to Rosemary's flat. 'Have you ever been here before?' he asked Neil.

'Yeah.' His voice was droll. 'I drove Mrs Winter out here two days back. She wanted to see what she'd inherited. Ended up nearly clearing out the whole place. Well, not exactly buying. I suppose the stuff was hers to take.' He sounded uncertain. 'Nice car, though.' He darted a guilty glance at Rosemary. 'Even if I drove it into a ditch.'

She watched him. He seemed surprised at himself, as though confessing to such a minor accident had been something special — which perhaps it was, in view of his guilt over the earlier fatal crash. Being able to admit this mishap could be a breakthrough for him.

'Country lanes!' she said ruefully. 'You barely get into top gear and there's a flock of sheep all over the road or a harvester reversing from a gateway. Don't I just know it! Reminds me I'm a natural townee.'

That seemed to pass it off. It was partly the drink, she supposed, that had loosed the young man's tongue, but he seemed to be steady enough on his feet as he carried the potted poinsettia upstairs when Max dropped them off at the front door.

'Thanks a lot,' he told her, depositing the plant in her kitchen. 'Marvellous lunch. Maybe we can have a return match sometime.'

He made way for Max to come through and left them to it. He guessed what they'd be up to, the minute they were on their own again. He minded, as he turned away from the closed door; but reluctantly admitted, 'To the hero the spoils.'

'Gordon,' said a husky voice behind him. Vanessa Winter was leaning in her doorway, one hand tucked behind her waist. 'I want you to come in.'

He began to refuse, but she reached towards him and seemed about to teeter. Her free hand locked about his wrist. 'I want you to come in,' she repeated.

It wasn't her usual voice, much deeper-throated, and it struck a chord in him. She was acting out a role, but he didn't instantly recognize what play it came from. Her hidden hand came into sight and held a bottle of Cointreau, half full. 'Come with me,' she commanded.

It wasn't what she said but the precarious state she was in that made him follow. She led him into the drawing-room. 'A little liqueur after your lunch. You went out with those people next door,' she accused. Her face was blotched and her hand shook as she fumbled in the glass cabinet. 'You like to party, don't you?'

She pulled out a tumbler, almost let it slip from her fingers but managed to pour a few inches into it.

That was far too much, and he didn't like that sticky sweet stuff anyway. He found himself tongue-tied, helpless, and that too seemed vaguely familiar. He had been here before, or somewhere eerily like it.

He moved away, the glass in his hand, looking for somewhere to put it, but turned at a soft susurration. She was shedding her dress. It slid, whispering, to the floor, and she had nothing else on. An old woman. She raised her arms imperiously. They were thin and the skin hung limply off. 'You know what to do,' she told him.

Then he saw why it all seemed familiar. 'Mrs Robinson,' he muttered. She smiled at his recognition and slithered on to the sofa, the crimson silk of her dress grotesquely caught about one ankle.

He'd seen *The Graduate* on the stage over a year ago, with Marty, and the promise of a celebrity in the nude had drawn a full house. It was well done, but the flash of flesh had been only a snack. The feast offered now was obscene and prolonged. Orgiastic. He pushed his tumbler towards the table and blundered from the room. He heard the glass fall and shatter as he gained the door.

He ran full tilt down the front stairs and through to the rear, heart pumping, stomach churning. He stopped at the stairs to his own flat and hung on to the newel post to regain his balance. The whole passageway was lurching. Over by Wormsley's door someone had dumped a black sack of rubbish. Or maybe the man had been too idle to take it to the refuse bins.

Clinging on while vomit hit the back of his throat and he bit his lips to hold the bitter stream back, he saw the sack move, try to heave itself erect, slide back and collapse into the shape of a man.

Then it was impossible to stem it any more. His stomach contents, lumpily undigested, pumped out over his chin and chest, soaking his jacket, plopping to the polished wood blocks of the floor. He couldn't breathe for the stench of his bile.

Dizzy, he tore off his jacket and dropped it away, wiped his face with his shirtsleeve and swept the back of one hand across his eyes to clear the involuntary tears. 'God, no! No!' But he didn't know what it was he repulsed: the odious woman, the humiliation, fear of the half-dead thing on the floor by Wormsley's door. Or worse: the nightmare return of the life he'd recklessly taken years before — Miriam, his father's wife, resurrected in another body, and the film running through again and again, the same frames and the same self-loathing, so that he knew he would never be free of it.

He felt his way to the stairs and sat there, shaking. Just once he thought there came a low rattling sound from the sackshape of the man he knew was dying, but he couldn't respond for a moment, had to hold himself together to go across.

There was no memory of getting to his feet or moving, but suddenly he was there, staring down at the stickily smeared red skull and the twisted spectacles hanging from one bloodied ear. The centre parting of the floppy, dark hair was a crimson line alongside the crushed skull. The face under it was Wormsley's, but such as he'd never before seen it, never wanted to see it again, but always would in haunting nightmare.

He screamed for Marty. Then he knew that was no use and began staggering again into the front hall, up the stairs, shouting for Max.

'Don't let Rosemary see,' he begged when the man came.

'What? Where?'

Neil pointed downwards. 'By the back door. It's Wormsely. He's been shot or coshed or something.'

Despite his warning Z ran past him, close on Max's heels. When he turned to follow he dully registered Vanessa's closed door and that under her arm the girl had a zipper bag with red cross markings on it.

Max was kneeling by the curled-up body, speaking urgently into his cell phone. 'Neil, keep away,' Rosemary ordered. He started to apologize about being sick but no one was listening. The other two had moved the body, laying it out flat, and Max was working on his heart while Rosemary's face was pressed against the injured man's, with only a doubled handkerchief between.

There was nothing for him to do. Not even a trolley to wheel anyone away on. It left him ashamed.

They went on, counting and pressing and blowing until Max said, 'Is there any point?'

Rosemary looked at her watch and sat back on her heels. 'No,' she said firmly when he offered to get something to cover the body. 'We have to leave everything just as it is. I'd like you to take Neil back upstairs with you. I'll wait here until they come.'

She called Max back as he followed Neil through to the front hall. 'Don't let him wash. Or drink. Just keep him sitting absolutely still, touching nothing.'

He looked startled. 'You surely don't think Neil . . . '

'For his own safety, because Salmon may jump to conclusions. We have to tell him about Wormsley spying on Chisholm. He could think it was motive enough; and Neil having been drinking. Let's hope there are tests which can eliminate him and save us time. But, until we find the weapon . . . '

'Rosebud, you frighten me. Your tortuous mind . . . ' He shook his head and went after the young man.

Nauseated by the stench of vomit in the enclosed space, Z stood motionless, her eyes scanning the walls and floor of the passage-way. At that instant the timer clicked off and all lights went out. In the darkness she was left wondering who had last turned them on, and at which of the three switches in the linked system.

As her eyes adjusted to the glimmer of evening sky from the tall window she was able to pick out shapes: the dark huddle of the body against the luminous gloss of the door to Wormsley's flat, still fast locked against his imagined enemies. His elaborate precautions hadn't saved him. Perhaps the complicated security system had even delayed his escape from the killer. It looked as though he had just come home; but he never reached sanctuary.

Across by the stairs, a smaller dark shape was Neil's discarded jacket. Had he thrown it down, going to attack the other man? She thought not. That jacket was the source of the sour smell. Neil too hadn't made it home in time.

From her front windows the others watched the ambulance arrive first and the paramedics being let in. They stayed no more than five minutes before driving off to another emergency. It seemed a long time before the police turned up, but actually only seven minutes. Then there were two patrol cars with flashing lights, each with a pair of uniformed constables, and on their tail the detective sergeant Neil remembered from before. Finally came a second unmarked car driven by the senior officer called Salmon. His loud, rough voice reached them through the closed windows. 'This is getting to be a habit with Z.'

'She's one of them,' Neil said hoarsely, piecing things together at last. 'Max, why didn't anyone tell me?'

23

Alone in the semi-dark Zyczynski was more concerned with the living than the newly dead. Wormsley had always been something of an enigma, but Neil was different. She was beginning to understand what lay under the flippant surface. He had known drama enough in his young life and it had left him vulnerable.

Tonight how much had he seen, or done, to upset him so? How had he spent the time between leaving her apartment and raising the alarm? Had he rushed for help only because he knew he'd left personal traces at the scene of the killing? Would he otherwise have let himself in to his own apartment and laid low, abandoning the body to grow cold and be discovered later by someone else?

And with Chisholm away, who would that have been? — probably Beattie, coming out next morning to let Frank Perrin in for his coffee and cake. The shock would have been awful for her: a second of her selected companions murdered within a week.

Oh, why didn't somebody come, bringing a

torch, and save her from all these futile speculations?

When the first blue revolving lights showed through the window she undid the door with a handkerchief held between fingers and lock. They were paramedics. She let them in, explaining, 'You'll need flashlights. I don't want the switches here touched until SOCO arrives.'

They took one look and knew they weren't needed. 'We should wait for a doctor to confirm death really,' said the male paramedic, 'but there's another call we should answer. Do you want us to stay with you, or . . . '

'You go. I'm fine,' she told them.

There followed another wait while she became over-conscious of being half-dressed. She assumed Max had his hands full with Neil Raynes or he might have thought to fling a bathrobe down for her. She felt her way through the swing doors to the front hall and called. His head appeared over the gallery railing, and she told him what she needed.

'Right,' he said and the required cover-up landed beside her. 'You OK otherwise?'

'Yes; get back to Neil. I think the cavalry have just arrived and they're pawing the ground outside.'

He waved and disappeared. She hoped

he'd think to get some clothes on himself before she had to bring visitors up.

DI Salmon fumed at being kept outside, but Beaumont was there to witness if he breached the secure crime scene. First in were the SOCO's team in their white coveralls. After a quick survey they brought in the angle lights, cables and generator, then set about photographing from detail to general. The fingerprint men started dusting the light switches, the door handles and the bunch of keys lying on the wood-block floor and still attached by a silver chain to Wormsley's belt.

'What's that gadget on the door?' Salmon demanded, peering over the shoulder of one stooping expert. 'Electronic entry system,' the man told him. Cards are out, these days. Thumbprints are the in-ID. Next generation works on an analysis of the eye's iris, but we haven't seen that in use locally yet.'

Salmon scowled. 'You mean that, to gain entry, we've gotta stick the body's thumb . . . '

'Correct. Can you give me bit of space, sir? Your shadow's in my light.'

'Shall we go upstairs?' Z suggested. The DI squinted up towards Chisholm's door and didn't fancy the spillage on the lower steps.

'Through this way.' She indicated the swing door that led towards the front of the house.

'Who was sick?' he demanded, following her. He expected her to admit to it.

'Young Neil Raynes. He's waiting up in my apartment. I've not had a chance to question him yet.'

'I'll do that.' He called back over his shoulder to the experts, 'Let me know at once when the doctor arrives. We might get something more out of him than confirmation of death.'

'Professor Littlejohn will want to see the body *in situ*,' she warned him.

'Not necessary. He hasn't been notified.'

Z forbore to argue the point. The Boss would have seen to that. Both men would be turning up shortly, whatever might have been exercising them elsewhere.

Everything looked seemly in her apartment. There was a strong scent of brewing coffee, but no sign of cups yet. Z introduced the two men who rose to meet them.

'So what made you attack him?' Salmon started off. Shake the scrotes, was his motto. It wasn't that he necessarily expected this one to be the killer.

Neil had had time to get his mind together and he recognized a bully. 'He wouldn't have been worth it,' he said shortly. 'I came down from here and there he was, on the floor. It shook me for a moment and my lunch came

331

up. I thought he made an odd sort of noise, but I was covered in mess and had to throw my jacket off. When I went across I couldn't find a pulse. He wasn't breathing. What I heard must have been his lungs emptying.'

'So you're a pathology expert?' The DI's tone was scathing.

'I'm a hospital porter. I've heard similar things before.'

'You didn't apply resuscitation?'

'I'm trained to yell for help before I try anything myself.'

'So while help was coming, what did you do to the apparent dead body?'

'Nothing.'

'Nothing,' the DI repeated, as if it were a crime.

'I looked at my watch,' Neil suddenly remembered. 'That's what the crash team do when they give up working on a patient. It was 16.12.'

'Make a note of that,' Salmon snarled at Z. He turned back to the young man. 'Did you see anyone else, hear anyone leaving? Was there a car parked outside?'

'Nothing and no one. As soon as Rosemary and Max arrived I came back up here.'

'And you'd been in here before?'

Neil seemed to think for a moment, then said, 'We'd been out to lunch together. I just came up to carry some stuff in that Max had bought. He'd gone to park his car round by the old stables. Then I left, straight after.'

Salmon switched his attention to Max. 'So you'd have been outside the rear entrance at the time Wormsley was coming in. Was there anyone with him?'

'I didn't see him or any other person. Mine was the only car, and I parked at the far side of the garages. I walked back to the front of the building where Ro . . . where Z had left the outer door on the latch for me.'

Salmon's cell phone played two bars of the Skye Boat Song. He snatched it out from an inner pocket and grunted, 'Yes?'

Beaumont informed him that Professor Littlejohn had arrived and that the car pulling up outside was Superintendent Yeadings's Rover.

The DI made an exasperated sound. 'Beaumont, find some way to get into Wormsley's garage and feel whether the car's engine is warm. Make a note and give the time. Tell the guv'nor I'm on my way down.'

It was getting crowded in the confined space by the entrance to Flat 5. The pathologist, familiar with the ways of the SOCO, asked civilly if they had reached a stage he could interrupt.

'Go ahead,' said Gowan. 'You've pipped

the duty surgeon at the post.'

'Splendid,' Littlejohn said, as if promised a treat. 'You can ring through and cancel him. I'll perform the double duty. Let's see now. Yes, definitely expired, and the time is precisely 17.02.'

There was a little easing around the back door as Beaumont left and Yeadings came in, to be joined by Salmon popping out like the Demon King through the utility room's swing door. The superintendent nodded. 'Another death, I understand. Carry on, DI Salmon. Do we know how many people are at present inside the house? I suggest you post a constable at the front door and have this area taped off at once.'

★ ★ ★

It was another three hours before activity petered out to leave a single uniformed man on duty and all residents briefly interviewed. Chisholm's absence — particularly in view of his having been 'spied on' by the dead man — had struck Salmon as distinctly suspicious, the more so since Neil claimed not to have an address where he might be reached.

'You mean you have no idea at all?' the DI insisted, his voice rising to a cartoon squeak.

'Have you had some lovers' spat or something?'

Z groaned under her breath at the man's crassness. Max could barely believe his ears, and observed Yeadings turn his back to examine a framed abstract print on Rosemary's sitting-room wall. Neil retreated into a dignified silence.

The next apartment being that of the first murder victim's mother, Salmon was with difficulty persuaded against instant interrogation. 'The lady is elderly,' Yeadings pointed out. 'I'll just look in to see everything's as it should be with her, and you can have a word with her tomorrow.'

With that Salmon had to be content, but in interviewing the other residents with Beaumont in tow, he banned Z as an interested party. It was left to her to visit them all after he had left, and smooth the ruffled feathers.

She wasn't surprised to find Major Phillips in Miss Barnes's flat, dispensing comfort and Chivas Regal. By now they had gathered what Z's official function was and declared themselves reassured to have her living on the premises. 'Not that I've managed to prevent any of this mayhem,' she told Max afterwards. 'In fact I guess I'm lucky not to have been one of three fatalities. It looks so far as though Paul Wormsley was struck down with a blunt instrument, just as I was three days back.'

They found Beattie a trifle tearful. 'I'm not frightened,' she said, declining Z's offer of a bed for the night. 'I'm just awf'ly disappointed. This was meant to be sech a peaceful, friendly place, and look a' it now!'

Frank Perrin, who dropped in after a phone call from Zyczynski, restored her good humour, and finally saw her to bed with a beaker of hot chocolate; but before he left he did a man-sized job with a bucket of scalding water and disinfectant, so that Neil, walked back home by Max, found no embarrassing reminders of his abject failure.

'Will you be all right alone?' Max asked.

'Never better,' the young man ground out bitterly.

'Tomorrow I have to get back to London. I wish it wasn't necessary, but there's no let out. It'll be pretty chaotic here, police everywhere. If you can extend your sick leave you could make it easier for the others.'

'Rosemary'll be working?'

'She's determined, once you've both been to get your stitches out. I'll drive you there. You can share a cab back.'

'I'd forgotten that. Anyway, Beattie's got her man-friend to look after her.'

'There's still Mrs Winter to keep an eye on.'

'That — *woman*! I'd rather shit pins.'

'I'll take that as a no, then?'

'Rosemary agreed we'd go to ER together, but once I'm there, I'll stay on. Will you tell her? Explain there's less blood and guts to cope with in hospital.'

★　★　★

Superintendent Yeadings sat in on the DI's briefing next morning. The three crimes were scrawled in chalk across the blackboard. *Sheila Winter, Murder by Stabbing; DS Zyczynski, Attack with a Blunt Instrument (ceramic table lamp); Paul Wormsley, Murder by Blunt Instrument (not found).*

'We don't know,' Salmon admitted, 'if these were crimes committed by the same person or persons. We'll look at the first murder first.'

He looked rattled. By nature a one-suspect man, he found them now crawling out of every available bit of woodwork. He faced up to it, though; had the crime scene photos pinned on the wall and wrote the full list up there for all to see. The first three names were Barry Childe, Jonathan (Nat) Baker, Frank Perrin.

'Any of those singly, or as a pair or a

threesome,' Salmon said truculently, as if expecting an explosion of protest.

Everyone sat silent. A hand went up. 'Sir, wasn't there a Dutch connection with one of them?'

'Jan Nederkamp,' Salmon said. 'A fax from Amsterdam police has provided him with a watertight alibi. He was in Stuttgart at a business meeting arranging to supply forced hyacinths for Christmas to German retailer. So if we can believe they still remember Christmas out there, he gets crossed off the list. In any case he is thought to have broken off his relationship with Sheila Winter last July, when he became engaged to a Belgian banker's daughter. They were married in September. According to a statement he made to a police brigadier, the break-up was by mutual consent and neither party had reason to feel resentment towards the other.'

He moved back to the blackboard to add the next name: Gabriel Fenner, D.Sc.

'Dr Fenner — (not a medical man, for those of you not familiar with academics) — is Winter's ex-husband, who held some shares in Sheila's garden centre. He is a don at Cambridge University and his subject's Archaeology.

'He claims to have had a good relationship with his daughter although he hadn't seen her since she was eighteen years old. They each wrote once a year. He was on bad terms with his ex-wife with whom the dead woman shared a home. Since the murder he has shown fresh interest in his daughter's affairs and holds a copy of her will, to which he is the sole executor.

'Despite this apparent sign of trust, it's noted that she left her 12% of the business to her mother who had never shown any interest in it as a working project. As a result of this, the future of the business depends on whether Mrs Winter allies herself to her ex-husband's 40% or the bank's 48%.

'This appears to be causing Dr Fenner some considerable upset. He is not a rich man and he expects Mrs Winter to sell out to the bank, who will dispose of the business as a whole. So upset in fact is Dr Fenner that he has been in touch with Mrs Winter's GP with a view to applying to have her sectioned under the Mental Health Act, with which you should all be familiar.'

He stared round accusingly. 'If she is declared incompetent a proxy would be appointed, over whom Dr Fenner might expect to have some influence as executor of the will. Until now we have found no one to recognize Dr Fenner's photograph either in the Henley area, the garden centre or the locality of Ashbourne House.'

He paused, and in the silence someone from the back muttered, 'He's hardly likely to kill his own daughter. Why not the ex-wife?'

A curious expression passed over Salmon's face. It seemed a mixture of relief and suppressed triumph. 'The fur coat,' he said with great significance, 'was interesting because the slits in it did not correspond with the injuries to the body. The fact that she wasn't wearing it when stabbed seemed to indicate sexual circumstances. I believe now it was a double bluff, meant to distract attention from someone unlikely to see her in that state.

'Dr Fenner claims to have spent the night of November 9/10 alone in his rooms in Cambridge. We have no proof that he didn't.'

With a sigh Salmon turned back to the blackboard and added two further names: they were Martin Chisholm and Neil Raynes. 'The couple upstairs,' he reminded the assembly. There came a snigger from somewhere.

'We continue to examine their movements closely,' he said. 'Chisholm disappeared immediately after the attack on DS Zyczynski, and could have been the intruder searching Mrs Winter's rooms. An alibi given by his assistant at the car showrooms is worth no more than his wish to retain his job. We are working backwards to reveal any connection between Chisholm and either of the Winters before they met up at Ashbourne House.

'His young friend Neil Raynes, the hospital porter, has a history of delinquency according to his father, and is mainly dependent on Chisholm whose home he shares. Shortly before the lethal attack on Paul Wormsley, Raynes had admitted to DS Zyczynski that his friend had been 'spied on' and followed in his car by Wormsley. We need to know what Wormsley discovered and whether that was of such importance that he had to be silenced. A search of his rooms today may bring something to light on that. The apartment has elaborate security and it's unlikely anyone could have got in to remove evidence.'

It was stultifying, Yeadings admitted. Here they were, almost into the second week of the investigation and they could eliminate nobody. He stroked his chin and held up a finger at Salmon to raise a point. In with a penny, he thought mischievously, in with a pound.

'Maybe we should add Wormsley to the others. If he had killed Miss Winter, somebody might have wished to take revenge.'

He watched Salmon's jaw sag before it snapped shut again. Now, that was almost malicious of me, Yeadings chided himself. The man is befogged enough without adding to his miseries.

24

A full day of relaxation with his family had given Yeadings the opportunity to sort his ideas and consider a line to pursue. 'How do you fancy a half-day in London?' he asked Nan casually at breakfast next day.

'Not if it means hanging about Scotland Yard while you swap memories with the Old Guard.'

'I wouldn't dream of going there. I thought perhaps Knightsbridge, a little window-shopping at Harrods and Harvey Nicks. Might even go in and spend a small amount of cash. Then lunch somewhere interesting.'

'You can't spend a small amount of cash in Knightsbridge,' declared practical Nan. 'In that area you go the whole hog or nothing. And it's nobody's birthday that I know of. I hope this isn't the sign of a guilty conscience.'

'I'm innocent as the day. Ring Maisie and ask her to childmind Luke. Then put on some glad rags and we'll drop Sally off at school on the way.'

'On a Monday?' she queried, half won over. 'At such short notice?'

'Yes. Wicked! Wear the new cream suit.

Here's an offer. I'll do the school run while you organize the event.'

Nan whipped off her apron. 'Consider me seduced.'

She knew there was an ulterior agenda but the offer was irresistible. She observed the large fibre suitcase being loaded in the car's boot but said nothing. When Mike returned she was ready and waiting. The entire operation went according to promise until, after coffee and a mooch around Harrod's, Mike retrieved the suitcase and steered her towards Harvey Nichols where it appeared he was expected. Her feelings were mixed as they entered the furs department and the suitcase was opened. Within, swathed in acid-free tissue sheets, was a black mink coat. A memory stirred in her head and she put out a hand to turn back the front edge. As suspected, there was a smear of blood on the lining.

Nan accepted a chair and was prepared to wait, relieved at least that she hadn't to face the embarrassing offer of dead animal pieces to hang on her shoulders. It wasn't that she objected to fur farming. The cyclical preying of one species on another was a fact of life. She accepted the nature-red-in-tooth-and-claw thing. What she recoiled from was inciting the rabid anti-humanity of those

— mainly women — who judged otherwise. Years before, Mike had brought her back a snug sable hat from a stint of work in Poland, and she hoped one day to feel free to wear it again.

Past history was what Mike was delving into here at this moment. An elderly man was introduced and clearly commanded a deal of respect from the present head of department. 'Our Mr Knowles', expressly brought back from retirement, examined the coat minutely, recoiling in horror at the stains and slashes to the skins. 'Yes, definitely one of ours. You saw the label, of course, and here in the lining are the lady's initials embroidered in gold thread by our workroom. This was customary, a complimentary service carried out before the article was delivered.

'You will understand that this was in the days before plastic cards, when payment was normally by cheque and it took three days at least to clear through the banks. The little service we offered was to cover that lapse in time.'

'A wise precaution with valuable items,' Yeadings agreed.

'And one that pleased the ladies. Now the initials in this case — yes, here they are, tucked discreetly into the Paisley pattern — would appear to be A.F. Does that help you at all, Superintendent?'

'Thank you, Mr Knowles. I am hoping now that you may be able to trace who actually signed that cheque.'

The old man's smile produced tortoise wrinkles. 'Since you warned us earlier of the period in which the purchase probably took place, I have had the relevant ledgers retrieved. Mr Stanley, forward please.'

Nan watched Mike pore over the book, running the pages through his fingers. When they stopped, he looked up with a broad grin. 'Have you any objection if I photograph this page?'

Mr Knowles looked doubtful.

'There will be no harmful publicity,' Yeadings assured him. 'I should merely use it to remind the purchaser, in case he has forgotten.'

'Very well, Superintendent.'

A need to remind someone that he, or she, bought an expensive item like a full-length black mink coat, female skins? Nan asked herself. Hardly likely; though to the Harvey Nichols staff such a casual memory appeared quite possible. She hummed quietly to herself. True: the rich were different.

Mike returned the coat in its suitcase to the car parked under cover, having been assured that the damage to the skins could be skilfully

346

repaired. He doubted there would be any call for that.

'Now,' he said, 'lunch, and I know the perfect place.'

'Not quite yet,' said Nan. 'Food isn't sufficient compensation for having been brought along on a job. Let's have a good look around first. There's a nice little pendant I saw in Harvey Nick's as we were passing through.'

She was only teasing and he knew it. But they went back all the same and Yeadings produced his plastic. 'Lunch now?' he asked meekly.

'Fine by me, love, but I'm getting a taste for being spoilt; so it'll have to be Italian. It's the only way to be sure they'll stock Punt e Mes.'

With the sapphire pendant tastefully boxed and consigned to her handbag, she was content to be sent home by train after lunch, while Mike pursued inquiries elsewhere.

They took him to Putney, to the GP with whom the Winters had registered when they lived there. Crossing the Thames, he smiled fondly on the dull pewter gleam of the water broken by a dazzling sheet of white as the sun broke through behind him. A light wind feathered the water in patches, and over by the boathouses four young men were toting a shell, ready to drop it in the river.

He remembered Neil Raynes reported as having once rowed at Henley for his school and Thames Club; Neil, who nowadays had a health problem. Well, the nature of it was a mystery no longer. Yeadings had traced press coverage of the fatal crash in which he'd been involved. The young man's injuries had been serious enough for a sympathetic judge not to have sentenced him to a stretch. Neil had attended the court hearing on a charge of manslaughter still in a wheeelchair and desperately in need of a kidney transplant. The medication he would need to continue for the rest of his life was to prevent his immune system rejecting the alien organ. It seemed that even such misfortune hadn't ruled out paternal rejection; but Raynes senior had made financial provisions for his son, channelled through Martin Chisholm who would act as his minder. That was a sentence a youngster might well rebel against, and it spoke well for the man that Neil appeared to remain on good terms with his flatmate.

★ ★ ★

Again Yeadings was prompt on his appointment and, while reluctant to breach patients' confidentiality, Dr Fielding eventually confided the name of a Harley Street consultant he had recommended before the ladies moved away. 'Correspondence on this matter was included in the case notes sent on to the new GP in Mardham, a Dr Stephen Barlow,' he explained, 'but whether he would act on my suggestion was entirely up to him.'

On the journey home Yeadings remembered to switch his mobile phone back on. There were three messages for him, or simply one with two repeats. The ACC (Crime) required his immediate attendance at Kidlington HQ. The first call had been timed at 09.05.

On arrival, the eating of Humble Pie was obligatory, but Mr Medlar was sufficiently worried to cut the performance short. He chewed his lips as Yeadings briefly accounted for the apparent gap in his official existence. The information gathered on the black mink coat and the Winters' health while in Putney, Medlar found less than riveting.

'It's the other murder that must take priority,' Medlar snapped at the recital's end.

'Wormsley's?'

'*Worsley*'s,' the ACC thundered. 'God, the insufferable man and his insistence on retaining that typist's error. It was bound to draw attention. Whoever heard a real name like that? I would have disallowed it here.'

Yeadings sat quiet and let his mind's clockwork tick towards an assumption. Not a real name? So a pseudonym: Wormsley was a man with a closed past and a synthetic present. Only he hadn't a present any more, now he was defunct. Small wonder the ACC was dancing on hot embers. Someone local had badly boobed. The skilfully embroidered new persona was wasted. 'Witness Protection?' he guessed aloud.

'It's obvious that his new identity was blown! West Midlands is seething. Who's going to trust the system again if a report of this gets out?'

'That's their worry,' Yeadings pointed out. 'Ours is to follow up the professionals who've penetrated our patch. If indeed his death is due to earlier involvements. I have to know the whole story, sir.'

'Is there any chance he was killed for some scam he's been running since he became Wormsley? He was a photographer, I believe; ran a small studio for portraits and such, with a single girl assistant.'

'He wasn't exactly popular among the other residents where he lived, but I know of no reason why anyone would want him dead. On the other hand, he was coshed, not gunned down or knifed, and inside the house

350

where he had an apartment. That doesn't strike me as a professional's job. I suppose West Midlands arranged for his new identity themselves. That would be where the leak occurred, sir. If there was one.'

'I want you in charge of this case personally. Let Samson keep on with the Winter case.'

'Er, Salmon, sir; not Samson. And what if the two killings *are* connected? It's possible that the attack on my Sergeant Zyczynski is a link between the two. Like Wormsley she was struck with a blunt instrument, though obviously not the same one. And it happened when she disturbed an intruder in the murdered woman's flat.'

'But there's no reason to connect the Winter woman with the crime Wormsley received a reduced sentence for.' The ACC sounded increasingly exasperated.

Yeadings assumed his most dependable plod expression. 'Before we can decide whether the whole series of attacks was local, I need to know the extent of the operation this Wormsley was protected from.'

'I was afraid of that.' Medlar was giving in. 'I have a For-Your-Eyes-Only report here. Just go through it while I have tea sent in. Don't take notes, and keep it under your hat, Yeadings. We don't need to aggravate an already bad situation.'

Left alone, Yeadings read, sipped Earl Grey and munched chocolate digestive biscuits. The story wasn't an impressive one, but a great deal of money had been involved. It was a brilliant scam while it lasted, and rested on the fact that in Japan cars were right-hand drive and used the left half of the road as in the British Isles and indeed most of South East Asia and the Commonwealth. Valuable cars were stolen in the main Japanese cities where, crime being minimal by Western standards, there were fewer precautions taken or investigations rigorously pursued. Instead of being unloaded under some scrutiny at Southampton, Dover or Liverpool, the stolen cars were shipped via Dubai to the Irish Republic where crime and investigative levels were almost as low as in Japan. There they were either sold off or re-crated for the UK. Several routes were used, but mainly direct from Dun Laoghaire or driven into Northern Ireland and sent on from Belfast.

'Wormsley' — real name Piers Wilson — was one of four principals, the others being toughies, two from Ireland and one from Brum. Peader O'Rourke, Micky Hennigan, Mark Sloan and Piers Wilson had been cashing in nicely on the scam until Micky got greedy and started running his private venture of drug-running alongside. And the IRA hadn't cared for the competition. A whisper got to the Gardai and the next consignment was ambushed. They were lucky to escape being caught, fleeing for their lives to Limerick, then separating to cross to the mainland and meet up again in Birmingham.

Micky blamed Piers for the leak, purely on the grounds that he was an Englishman. Piers threw the accusation back on Peader who went for him with his bare hands. At the end of an all-in barney there was Micky Hennigan on the floor with his own knife between his ribs and the other three covered in his blood.

That was when Piers Wilson went for the safest way out and turned State's evidence. The other two were found guilty of murder and he took a short term for theft and fraud in an open prison. When he came out there was a new life waiting for him.

But not a long one, Yeadings reflected. The question here was — did he get himself killed as Piers Wilson or Paul Wormsley?

The last straw for the ACC seemed to be the retaining of the original typing error — Wilson happy to take on that daft name. A quirky mentality. The chances were that that was one thing about him that hadn't changed. If, as Wormsley, he'd continued with his twisted sense of humour, whose expense had it been at? Had his quirkiness in this new life driven someone to the limits of endurance? Could that have been Chisholm because the man had found out something he could use to ruin him? Z had mentioned when she first met him that Chisholm looked like a highly successful conman. There was nothing to prove he had left Ashbourne House on the day before Wormsley's murder. They'd only Neil Raynes's word to go on.

Whatever the truth on that, Chisholm hadn't been the one to kill Sheila Wilson. Yeadings had someone quite different to get on that charge. He glanced at his wristwatch, guessed Z might be back home by now, and left the motorway by exit 4 for Chesham.

Twelve minutes later he was heading up the drive to Ashbourne House.

There were several cars parked by the entrance to the house and a little crowd of people staring up at the verandah. As he watched there was a flurry of figures up there, then one of them racing across the long windows with another in close pursuit.

Too late, he accused himself, and watched the collision, then the body fall, slowly turning, on to the stone steps below.

25

Gabriel Fenner had arrived at the house at about 5.10 that afternoon, looking pale and strained according to Miss Barnes, who had watched him park opposite her windows and sit deep in thought for some five minutes before he left the car, approached the front door, then went back to check he had actually locked the car's doors. He seemed for once uncertain, perhaps ill.

His was an older model, she explained pedantically hours later, so it had only central locking, not remote. But he had already secured it, automatically, as one does.

He had let himself into the house, having presumably retained his daughter's bunch of keys. Since neither Sheila's handbag nor its contents had ever surfaced after the murder, Yeadings was left to wonder how he had come into possession of the key-ring.

It was assumed that he had gone upstairs, rung his ex-wife's doorbell and gained access. Some five minutes later Rosemary Zyczynski had arrived, had driven to the rear and garaged her car. As she approached the front door Miss Barnes darted out to let her in.

'I'm a little uneasy,' she confessed. 'Mrs Winter's ex-husband is with her. He's not been here long, but he looked so strange, really odd somehow. Perhaps it's foolish of me to worry, but so many awful things have already happened . . . Do you think, as a friend of hers, you might just look in and see she's all right?'

Two other cars were now coming up the drive, Major Phillips's yellow Triumph and a Mondeo which Z recognized as belonging to DI Salmon. The major took charge of Miss Barnes, leading her away for tea and scones. Z felt obliged to wait until her senior officer should decide how warranted Miss Barnes's fears might be.

When Salmon and Beaumont joined her she explained the situation. The DI looked grim. 'We may need you later,' he said. 'Meanwhile, stay down here.' He stomped across the hall, making for the staircase.

'Mea culpa,' Beaumont breathed. 'He overheard my end of a call from the Boss. He guessed what he'd gone after in London and he's determined to get it in first.'

'Get what in?'

'The arrest. We've been following Fenner since a patrolman reported in that he was heading out this way.'

'Sergeant Beaumont!' roared Salmon from

the gallery. 'I need you here! Now!'

So what had the Boss driven to London for? Z asked herself. And why was everyone several steps ahead of her? There must be some vital clue that she had missed.

From below she heard voices at Mrs Winter's door. The two detectives had walked right through and left it open. The voices continued, the woman's a high-pitched complaint, Salmon's a rumble, Fenner's bitingly harsh. Z ignored instructions and began to follow them up.

Now Fenner's voice had risen in protest, almost desperate. There was a clamour as they all joined in. His final cry of, 'No! No, you can't! Vanessa!' was cut off by Beaumont's monotonous recital. 'Gabriel Fenner I am arresting you for the murder of Sheila Winter. You have the right to remain silent . . . '

How — Z marvelled — had they reached that conclusion? Had she been so completely taken in by the man's apparent controlled grief that she'd failed to see some indication of his guilt? Surely whatever it was that took Yeadings to London, it couldn't have swung things around so, at this point in a fruitless investigation.

She was on the threshold now and followed them in. Vanessa Winter stood against the opposite wall, mouth agape, the fingers of one hand tearing at her tousled hair, hysterically incapable of speech. Z went across to take care of her. That was surely what Salmon had expected of her.

But the woman was a wild thing, crouching, defending herself with a bottle that she drew from behind her and brandished like a weapon. She turned from Fenner to Z as she approached. 'Vanessa, it's all right,' Z told her.

'Mind out!' Fenner shouted. 'For God's sake. Can't you see she's insane?' He flung himself towards her, arms outflung.

Then the whole scene seemed to explode. While the others stood petrified, Vanessa sprang at the nearest window and threw it wide. Then she was away, Fenner the first to recover and be after her.

Beaumont and Salmon made for the opening and became wedged for a second before they were through. Z heard Vanessa's banshee wail as she ran towards the verandah's end. The men rushed headlong after her.

Lights from indoors shone out on the wrought iron screen. The tall mirror set in it glowed like an open doorway promising escape. Then the hideous image sprang out at her, framed in it — Sheila, risen from the dead, leaping at her with — only a pace or so behind — Gabriel swooping like an avenging angel.

Cut off on both sides as the detectives came panting up, she twisted away, fell against the verandah rail, shrieked at the hunting pack, hung rigid a brief instant, then flung herself over.

Her scream went on until the awful sound of her body reaching ground.

26

It was after eight o'clock before things quietened completely and all but two of the cars had dispersed, leaving a single uniformed constable to guard the taped off area from which the body had been removed. Lights would shine on from some of the windows until nearly dawn as residents picked over the possibilities and found their several ways of dealing with the new horror.

Surrounded by discarded coffee cups in her apartment, Rosemary Zyczynski was in consultation with the superintendent and her fellow DS. As bemused as any of them, at least she clung to the consolation that she'd been right about Fenner. There was no question of charging him once Yeadings had intervened. Not that the unfortunate man was in very good condition after DI Salmon's considerable weight had flattened him to the verandah's floor among Sheila's tubs of evergreens, and Beaumont twisted his arms back to cuff his wrists.

'Not Fenner,' Yeadings had insisted, panting upstairs to take overall charge and forestall serious charges of illegal arrest with actual bodily harm.

'She wasn't running from him, but from justice,' he now explained. 'I'd say from her conscience too, if I was convinced she had one. That must have disappeared some time back, along with her sense of reality. Fenner was right to hope for her being sectioned. He'd pity enough not to want her facing a charge of homicide.'

'So he'd guessed?' Z asked.

'He'd worked it out, partly from his knowledge of the way she was, and what she wore.'

'She was wearing one of Sheila's dresses.' The details of that crumpled body were still fixed in Z's mind. 'I knew she'd been raiding her daughter's wardrobe since Sheila was killed, but I remembered it too from another time. That was the dress I saw dropped on the floor when I mistook it for Sheila making love in the drawing-room as I came in.

'But Sheila wasn't the sort to cheat on the man she intended to marry. And I believed Jonathan Baker when he swore he'd never been inside the house since the conversion was completed.

'I realize now it was Vanessa I saw, but I still can't guess at the man.'

'That's interesting.' Yeadings said, 'but what I was referring to was the mink coat.

361

Her husband bought it for Vanessa almost twenty-five years ago, when she was making a name for herself as April Fenner. Those are the initials embroidered in the lining. She hung on to the coat even after it was politically incorrect to be seen in furs. Its monetary value had shrunk but she treasured its connections; the memories of past glories. She must have been panicked out of her mind when she let it be used to cover the body.'

'By whom?' Beaumont demanded.

'I'll tell you what I think. We knew Sheila came back here after work on the night she was murdered. Her 'Nat' was waiting for her out at the hotel in Burnham Beeches. She was elated, full of excitement about her coming wedding. Something slipped out and Vanessa pounced on it. She saw it as a threat of desertion. And the girl was going on to a happiness that she could never attain herself. As Fenner guessed, there was a burst of ungovernable anger.

'Sheila had snatched a sandwich because dinner at the hotel would be late. She started to eat it in the bathroom while she ran a shower. Vanessa took a kitchen knife and followed Sheila in. That's where she caught her, naked and unprepared. And that's where the experts will be looking for bloodstains tomorrow. A bathroom's an easy place to sluice clean, but there are always some minute traces that get overlooked.'

'But who helped her? She couldn't drive. We're agreed, aren't we? — that there was a second person involved in disposing of the body.'

'Who would she turn to but the mystery lover Z now says she caught *in flagrante delicto*? Let's consider who that might be.'

'Chisholm, Raynes or Wormsley,' Beaumont listed them. 'We can disregard Major Phillips, who's in full pursuit of Miss Barnes.'

'So, with Wormsley deceased and Chisholm absent, we'd best go and talk to young Mr Raynes, who has been lying suspiciously low during all this recent kerfuffle,' Yeadings observed.

Z got up slowly off the sofa and stretched her stiff legs. She walked through to the kitchen. They heard her open a cupboard door, then beat with a saucepan base on the water pipe supplying the sink unit. They waited in a curious silence until a minute or two later there came an answering, muffled tapping.

'He'll be coming round,' she announced, and went to leave the apartment door ajar.

'Prison-style communication,' said Beaumont admiringly.

There was a short wait, then a tentative rap

on the outer door and the young man came in, unshaven and in a crumpled shirt. 'What's this?' he demanded, eyeing the others with hostility.

'Like it looks,' Beaumont said shortly. 'A court of inquiry. We want to know if you were Vanessa Winter's lover.'

They watched the boy's face redden, grow purple at the shock of the implication. He was past speech. 'Neil,' Z said gently, 'he doesn't understand.'

'She was dis — gust — ing,' he ground out at last.

'Neil, she's dead.'

It shocked him. 'How? When?'

'Sit down,' Yeadings ordered him. 'It's been a shock for everyone. She went over the verandah railing some hours ago. Didn't you hear all the coming and going?'

Raynes shook his head. 'I've been asleep.' He looked sheepish. 'I'd missed out on some of my medication so I took a double dose to catch up. I went out like a light. Then I heard Rosemary hammering. What's happened?'

They all looked towards Yeadings. How would he put it?

'Dr Fenner was here,' he began. 'He suspected that his ex-wife had killed his daughter. He says he came to try and make her go away while he arranged for her to be sectioned under the Mental Health Act.'

'So that she couldn't be tried?'

'That was his idea. But several other people arrived more or less at once and she panicked. She tried to run away, fled along the verandah, and then . . . It's not quite sure what she thought, but there's a full length mirror there at the end where this apartment's verandah begins . . . '

'She was wearing a dress of Sheila's,' Z said haltingly. 'Except for height and age they were quite alike; same cornsilk hair, cut the same way. I think she saw her reflection and thought it was Sheila.'

'Her ghost, wanting revenge.'

'Something like that,' Yeadings agreed. 'We'll never know for sure, but she couldn't face it. She jumped.'

'Better that way. She was mad, you know.' Neil's voice held a mixture of shame and relief. 'I'd have had to go away. She was voracious. It was awful. If you'd seen her . . . '

'She tried to seduce you?'

He nodded. 'Twice.'

'But you didn't . . . '

'God, no!' It was heartfelt. Nobody could doubt him.

'Do you suppose,' Beaumont suggested, 'that she tried anything of the sort with your friend Mr Chisholm?'

The answer was a barking laugh. 'Even she would have known better. He could have anyone he wanted, and he's — particular, disciplined. If he was the last man left on the planet and she was the only woman . . . Never! I tell you, I know him.'

It sounded heartfelt enough, but how well does any young man know an older one, Yeadings wondered.

'Which leaves Wormsley,' Beaumont concluded, wholly convinced by the young man's denial.

'Ah yes, *Wormsley*. Since he too is safely dead, let me tell you about him,' Yeadings offered. 'As you may know I was called out to Kidlington this afternoon, for a word with the ACC (Crime).

'It appears that Wormsley's real name was Piers Wilson.' And he explained to them how the Japanese car scam had worked and that the villains had fallen out over its outcome. 'So he may or may not have been involved in that murder, and he'd escaped from it almost unscathed. What he couldn't afford was to blot his lily-white new identity by association with another killing.

'I'm assuming it was Wormsley whom Vanessa rang to beg for help when she'd stabbed her daughter. When he got here he found he was up to the neck in it. He'd no

366

connection with the daughter, whatever his secret relations with Vanessa might be. He opted for dumping the body nude, assuming suspicion must fall on a lover. But he had to wrap it in something and helped himself out of Vanessa's wardrobe to a fur coat she'd never worn for a couple of decades. We don't know how he got back from Henley. If Vanessa called a cab from a local firm that wouldn't have been investigated from the Henley end. But I doubt she had the courage to go there herself. It's more likely Wormsley got his assistant from the studio to drive out and fetch him. He had some reason to trust her discretion, because she provided him with his later alibi when we investigated the break-in. It would have been his quirky little touch to take the half-eaten sandwich along for display with the hip flask. All props for the dramatic scene.'

'That was Wormsley too?' Neil asked, incredulous.

'It's more than possible,' Yeadings told them. 'Later we shall be opening up his apartment. A locksmith will de-activate the electronic system and our experts will conduct a search. Then we'll know a lot more about the man.'

'Searching for what?' the young man pressed.

'For whatever we find,' he said simply.

Z shook her head. 'It's all gone so wrong. Poor Beattie had meant things to be very different: her dream of creating a set of friends brought together at random. A meeting of unlike minds.'

'A substitute family.' Yeadings nodded. 'And then there's Sheila Winter's dream too, tragically ruined.'

'Not entirely,' Z reminded him. 'Her shares in the garden centre will go to Fenner now, won't they? He'll have majority control and make the bank appoint financial and operational managers. So something will have survived.'

'Back to normality,' Neil murmured.

'What's normal?' Yeadings asked sombrely.

There was an unhelpful silence.

'God, I sound like Pontius Pilate going on about Truth.' He rounded impatiently on Neil. 'Isn't it time you came clean about your friend Chisholm? Just between the four of us. *Sub rosa,* so to speak. Exactly what is he up to?'

Neil hesitated, then gestured with open hands. 'It's quite legal. But risky. He makes trips abroad to rescue children taken away in a tug-of-love. It's usually English mothers who've won custody rights, after mixed marriages break down. Clients find him by word of mouth, or sometimes on the internet, in encoded messages. He has an office in St Albans — Chisholm and Watkins, Factors. There's big money in it sometimes. Other times he barely breaks even.'

'Legalized kidnap?' Z marvelled.

'That sort of thing.'

Yeadings made no comment, rising to take his leave. 'Listen folks, it's getting late and I for one am ready for bed. So I'll say goodnight and go see if I still have a family.'

★   ★   ★

Beaumont was preparing his final report on the case. Perhaps it was contact with Max that made it come out with a flavour of the press: 'On Tuesday November 19th, nine days after the discovery of Sheila Winter's fur-wrapped body in the car park at Henley-on-Thames, a SOCO team entered Flat 5 at Ashbourne House, which was the registered property of Paul Wormsley, deceased, originally known as Piers Wilson . . . '

Superintendent Yeadings had been present. He explained that his DI had been diverted to investigating a case of arson at a market garden in Denham, which had no connection with these inquiries. It had also occurred to him to send Beaumont along as punishment since he had, after all, laid hands on the unfortunate Dr Gabriel Fenner. However, in the event, he relented.

Because of the extravagant security precautions and Wormsley's newly chosen career as a photographer — or at least the owner of a studio where the work was mainly carried out by two young assistants — the searchers expected to find pornographic pictures. If any of the team had refined tastes in this line they were disappointed. Those efforts they turned up were amateurish, of poor artistic merit, badly lit and unposed.

'Exposures,' was Beaumont's unavoidable pun.

Among assorted prints was a wallet containing negatives and ten pictures of Vanessa Winter in various stages of undress and intoxication. 'I don't think we have to doubt any more who it was you saw with her,' Yeadings told Z. 'I suspect these were taken in order to have some hold over the poor woman.'

'Do you think he showed them to her?'

'I'm sure we'll find she has a set of her own.'

'Could that be what he was searching for in her bedroom when I disturbed him? He must have seen how unreliable Vanessa was getting.

She might have left them around when the cleaners were here, or shown them to someone who would talk. He couldn't afford publicity of that sort.'

'And Vanessa wouldn't have stood for blackmail. She had to be the heroine every time, not the pathetic fool,' Yeadings considered. 'In her precarious mental state that could have been aggravation enough. So can we assume she lay in wait for Wormsley coming home, then struck him with some heavy object as he went to open his door? She'd resorted to violence once before and got away with it. It's said to be easier the second time around. Her clothes would have been splashed with blood. We'll see what comes to light in her apartment.'

From a distance Yeadings watched the SOCO team at work. Vanessa's fingerprints on Wormsley's key-ring had appeared to confirm his theory. She couldn't find the photos and negatives on his unconscious body, and she couldn't get to them in his flat because of his secondary electronic entry system. Whether the single blow was meant to kill or stupefy was left to supposition, but in that way Vanessa Winter committed her second murder. If she hadn't jumped when she did that last evening, she'd have ended locked up for the rest of her life.

The final piece of jigsaw that condemned her was discovered in a black plastic bag in her waste bin: a foot-high bronze statuette of a figure Yeadings recognized as The Dancing Faun. It had previously stood on a walnut side table in her drawing-room.

There had been no attempt to wash off the blood, nor from the dress it was wrapped in. Again the photocopied finger-prints taken from her corpse were used to identify the smears on the figure's base.

'So all's well that . . . ' Z began on a cynical note. She was interrupted by the Boss's mobile phone that twittered from an inner pocket. She moved discreetly away while he took the message. When he came back towards them his face was creased in a broad smile. 'That was Angus, all the way from Kosovo,' he said happily.

'Is he coming back?'

'For a short leave. The message kept breaking up but I thought he said something about — '

'About what?' she demanded, impatient to see Mott's return and the uncouth DI Salmon displaced.

'Could it possibly be — a *wedding*?' he said uncertainly. 'I think Paula must eventually have given in.'

We do hope that you have enjoyed reading this large print book.

Did you know that all of our titles are available for purchase?

We publish a wide range of high quality large print books including:
Romances, Mysteries, Classics
General Fiction
Non Fiction and Westerns

Special interest titles available in large print are:
The Little Oxford Dictionary
Music Book
Song Book
Hymn Book
Service Book

Also available from us courtesy of Oxford University Press:
Young Readers' Dictionary
(large print edition)
Young Readers' Thesaurus
(large print edition)

For further information or a free brochure, please contact us at:
Ulverscroft Large Print Books Ltd.,
The Green, Bradgate Road, Anstey,
Leicester, LE7 7FU, England.
Tel: (00 44) 0116 236 4325
Fax: (00 44) 0116 234 0205

BODY OF A WOMAN

Clare Curzon

Called to investigate the death of a young woman found dumped in woodland, Superintendent Mike Yeadings and his Thames Valley CID team find the body in exotic evening dress, her face covered by a feathered, bird-featured mask. Yeadings realises he had once briefly encountered her, in quite normal circumstances. This was Leila, the dutiful if undervalued wife of Professor Aidan Knightley; owner of a little gift shop in a quiet Buckinghamshire town; devoted to her two teenage step-children; on good terms with her neighbours. The circumstances of her death seem totally alien to all who knew her.